We die with the dying:
See, they depart, and we go with them.
We are born with the dead:
See, they return, and bring us with them.

T. S. Eliot, 'Little Gidding'

Sarah Winman grew up in Essex and now lives in London. She attended the Webber Douglas Academy of Dramatic Art, and went on to act in theatre, film and television. She has written two novels, *When God Was a Rabbit* and *A Year of Marvellous Ways*.

Praise for *A Year of Marvellous Ways*:

'A truly enchanting book' *Irish Times*

'One to read slowly so you can savour every beautiful sentence' *Good Housekeeping*, Book of the Month

'Folkloric, poetic, gorgeous. All I needed was a campfire and a bottle of moonshine' Emylia Hall, author of *The Book of Summers*

'Winman has a poet's eye for nature and writes a beautiful line' *Daily Mail*

'She is particularly good at bringing the sensations of landscape to bear – its smell, sound and look – and in Marvellous has created a character of warmth and eccentricity' *Metro*

'The book vividly demonstrates how vividly we need family around us, whether homegrown or grafted, to live our fullest lives . . . By the end of this novel, we too belong in the world of Marvellous Ways' *Sunday Express*, S Magazine

'A lyrical story: funny, real, kind and brimming with life' *Sainsbury's* Magazine

'A beautiful book' *Heat*

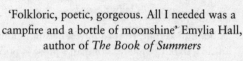
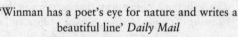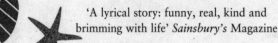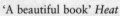

'A gripping waiting game' *Observer*

'Beautifully written' *Sun on Sunday*,
Fabulous Magazine

'A breathtaking reading experience . . . a beautiful
book that is unafraid to reveal the ugliness
of the world' *Toronto Star*

'The stories are touching and the twist of magical
realism lends them a joyful, fairytale element'
Daily Record

'A book to savour, to read in wonderful, rich little
bits like dark chocolate. Winman's prose is poetry,
with a rhythm, a heartbeat, that carries you through
like music' Emma Hooper, author of *Etta and Otto
and Russell and James*

'Moving . . . offbeat and memorable'
Woman & Home

'A lavish and clever read which will stand the
test of time' *Irish Examiner*

'The sense of magic infused through the novel casts a
spell over the reader that makes you not want to put
the book down until you've turned the final page'
Hannah Beckerman, author of *The Dead Wife's
Handbook*

SARAH WINMAN

A Year of Marvellous Ways

TINDER
PRESS

First published in Great Britain in 2015 by Tinder Press
An imprint of HEADLINE PUBLISHING GROUP

First published in paperback in 2015 by Tinder Press
An imprint of HEADLINE PUBLISHING GROUP

5

Cataloguing in Publication Data is available from the British Library

ISBN 978 0 7553 9093 9

Typeset in Sabon by Avon DataSet Ltd,
Bidford-on-Avon, Warwickshire

Printed and bound by Clays Ltd, St Ives plc

HEADLINE PUBLISHING GROUP
An Hachette UK Company
Carmelite House
50 Victoria Embankment
London EC4Y 0DZ

www.tinderpress.co.uk
www.headline.co.uk
www.hachette.co.uk

For Patsy

I

1

SO HERE SHE WAS, OLD NOW, STANDING BY THE ROADSIDE waiting.

Ever since she had entered her ninetieth year Marvellous Ways spent a good part of her day waiting, and not for death, as you might assume, given her age. She wasn't sure what she was waiting for because the image was incomplete. It was a sense, that's all, something that had come to her on the tail feather of a dream – one of Paper Jack's dreams, God rest his soul – and it had flown over the landscape of sleep just before light and she hadn't been able to grasp that tail feather and pull it back before it disappeared over the horizon and disintegrated in the heat of a rising sun. But she had known its message: Wait, for it's coming.

She adjusted the elastic on her large glasses and fitted them close to her face. The thick lenses magnified her eyes tenfold and showed them to be as blue and as fickle as the sea. She looked up and down the stretch of road once grandly known as the High Road, which was now used as a cut-through by heavy farm vehicles on their way to Truro. The familiar granite cottages – ten in all – built a century ago to house men for the farms and gardens of large estates, were boarded up and derelict, visited only by ghostly skeins of gorse and bramble that had blown in like rumour from afar.

They called it a village, but St Ophere was, technically, a hamlet, since the church that had given its name to the cluster of dwellings was situated in the tidal creek below where old Marvellous lived. There wasn't a schoolhouse either, for that was situated two miles west in the coastal hamlet of Washaway, a place that had lived up to its name earlier that year when the great drifts of snow had turned effortlessly into floods. But what the village did have, however, was a bakehouse.

Back-along, visitors to the area had often called the village 'Bakehouse' instead of its saintly name because Mrs Hard, the owner, had painted BAKEHOUSE in pink lettering across the grey slate roof: an elegant contrast to the once-white stone walls.

Every morning, when the oven was hotten ready, Mrs Hard used to ring her bell and her customers stirred, and unbeknownst to her, so did every drowned sailor from The Lizard to The Scillies as that bell had been scavenged from a salvaged wreck. The village women would take down their uncooked pies and pasties and loaves and load them into the burning embers. Mrs Hard use to call her oven 'Little Hell', and if you got the position of your pie wrong and took someone else's, that's where you would end up. Well, that's what she told the children when they came to collect their mothers' cooked offerings. It was the cause of many a disturbed night, as children burned up under their oft-darned sheets fearing what was to come if they ever chose wrong.

It had been a destination village on account of its bread. Now, in 1947, it was nothing more than a desolate reminder of the cruel passing of time.

The breeze stirred and lifted the old woman's hair. She looked up to the sky. It was lilac-grey and low, rain-packed, but Marvellous doubted that rain would fall. Blow away, she whispered. She crossed the road and stood in front of the bakehouse. She placed her lamp on the step and pressed her palms firmly against the weather-beaten door. Mrs Hard? she whispered softly.

It was Mrs Hard who had once told Marvellous that she was so good at waiting her life would be filled with good things.

Patience, that's what your father should have called you, she said. *Patience*.

But I'm not patient, said Marvellous. I'm *diligent*.

And Mrs Hard had looked down on the barefooted child with fancy words and ragged clothes, and thought how ungodly it was to rear a child in the woods, running wild and free like a Cornish Black pig. The girl needed a mother.

You need a mother, said Mrs Hard.

I had a mother, said Marvellous.

No. You had a *something*, said Mrs Hard. But I could be your mother.

And she waited for an answer but no answer came from the child's horrified mouth. Mrs Hard shook her head and said, Just you remember, though, it is patience that is a virtue and patience that is godly.

Mrs Hard liked the word 'godly'. She liked God, too. When her husband moved out in 1857, lured by the promise of wealth

5

from South African mines, Jesus and the well-loved reverend moved in. The transition was seamless, as was the first gold mine her husband went to, and the poor man was shunted from pit to pit across the Rand until he died scratching in that foreign dark for a glimpse of that golden key: the one that would fit a lock to a better life.

'*Breathe on me, Breath of God, Fill me with life anew*'.

That's what Mrs Hard had written above the bakehouse door when she heard of her husband's death. Later on, someone – and old Marvellous smiled as she could still make out the faint ochre words that had stained her hands – had changed 'breath' to 'bread', but Mrs Hard never knew because she rarely looked up.

Salvation, for me, will come from the dirt, she once told Marvellous.

Like a potato? said the young child.

The weather vane creaked overhead. October dusk fell quickly on the hamlet as crows upon the overnight dead. Must be nearly November, thought Marvellous. Lights flickered in the distant villages, a solemn reminder of the passing of this one. She took out a box of matches and lit her oil lamp. She stood in the middle of the road and raised the lamp to the hills beyond. I'm still here, the gesture said.

A shaft of yellow light fell upon the hedgerow where a granite cross grew out of a bank of flattened primroses. Marvellous had always believed the cross to be an after-thought, hastily erected after the First War, as she could call it now. '1914–1918', it read, with the names of long-gone faces underneath. But there was one name, she knew, that was not on the list. The name of Simeon Rundle had been excluded from the list.

Back in 1914 when the tide of war had rolled upon the

unsuspecting coast, village life had come to a sudden halt. There were no more fairs, no more dances, no more regattas because the men left and life froze in perpetual wait. A village without men dies, said Marvellous, and the village slowly did. The well-loved reverend was sent to a new parish in the City of London and shortly afterwards Mrs Hard received news that he had been killed in a Zeppelin air raid. She lay down on the shores of Little Jordan, as she referred to the creek, and willed her life to end. It obeyed straight away, such was the force of her will, and the bakehouse oven went out and God beat a retreat. Those left behind prayed constantly for peace but prayers came back with Return to Sender stamped all over them. Only the roll call of the dead grew.

But then one mild morning in May, Peace did appear, for that was the name given to a child born six months before the fighting stopped. Overdue, the child was, refusing to enter until the guns ceased, until the madness ceased, as if no amount of pushing or urging could force Peace into a broken world. And even then, when she came, it was reluctantly. As if she knew. Feet first and a head not budging, all mixed up, she was, feet and hands and legs and a cord. Like a calf.

A head weighed down by the burden of a name, said Marvellous as she whispered and twisted and pulled that child free.

Peace. It's just not as simple as that. And of course it wasn't.

Old ways of life don't return when the lives themselves have never returned. Only Simeon Rundle returned, came back to his new sister Peace, carrying a whole heap of horror with him. One morning, the villagers found him down by the creek, up to his neck in river mud and his own shit, waving a white handkerchief at a large hermit crab.

With his swollen tongue flapping out of his mouth like a slipper, he shouted, I thurrender, I thurrender, I thurrender, before raising his father's shotgun and blasting his heart *clean* from his chest. Or so the story goes.

The villagers gasped – two fainted – as it splattered against the church door like an ornate red knocker. The new lay preacher rushed out proclaiming it was the Devil's own work. Unfortunately, such a careless declaration flew swiftly on rumour's eager wings, and it wasn't long before the village of St Ophere acquired a taint that even the welcome addition of electric light in 1936 couldn't completely eradicate.

There was nothing actually wrong with the place. It was rightness that was at a tilt. Tides seemed higher, mists gathered there thicker and vegetation grew faster, as if nature was doing its best to correct the error, or if not to correct it then at least to hide it. But the suspicion of ill luck remained, and that's why the people slowly left: a steady stream of absences like bingo balls pulled from a hat. Migrating to distant villages whose lights still flickered in a low autumn sky.

Marvellous took a last look up and down the High Road, satisfied that whatever she was waiting for hadn't passed her by. The wind had picked up and the clouds were blowing through. She held the lamp high and crossed the road to the memorial and the standpipe, and made her way through the meadow where she had once kept a cow. The temperature was falling and the grass wet underfoot, and she thought the morning would reveal the first crust of frost. She could see the wood ahead, her ankles braced for the gentle incline and the careful march through the sycamores, the hazels and the sweet chestnuts down towards her creek. The tide was out. She could smell the saltmud, her favourite smell, the smell, she believed, of her blood. She would rake up a pan full of cockles and steam them on a fire that would burn a tiny hole in the night. Her mouth began to water. She stumbled and fell next to a blackthorn bush and made use of the mishap by picking two pocketfuls of sloes. She saw the light from her caravan up ahead. Felt, strangely, lonely. Never get old, she whispered to herself.

Late. An owl hooted and the dark eyes of night gazed unblinking towards the horizon. Marvellous couldn't sleep. She stayed awake sitting by the riverbank keeping the moon company, a pile of shucked cockleshells at her feet. She huddled in the warmth of firelight, her yellow oilskin raincoat bright and pungent and hot to touch. The stars looked faint and distant but it may have been her eyes. She once used binoculars, now she used a telescope; soon night would capture day for ever. She felt comforted by the blurred outline of her old crabber rocking gently on the tide; the familiar creak of rope against wood was a good sound in the undulating nocturnal silence.

She had lived in the creek almost her whole life long and had been happy there – almost – her whole life long. Islanded in the middle was the small church that had once been a chapel but was now a ruin. For as long as she could remember the tide had carved around the church until the church had broken away from the people or maybe the people had broken away from the church? It was so long ago now that old Marvellous couldn't remember what had happened first. But the tide had carved its path until church and headstones and faith had all gone adrift. Sunday services used to be held when the tide was at its lowest point, sometimes at daybreak, sometimes at dusk, and once, she remembered, in the dead of night, a lanterned trail of believers sang their way up the riverbed like pilgrims seeking Galilee.

> Yes, we'll gather at the river,
> The beautiful, the beautiful river;
> Gather with the saints at the river
> That flows by the throne of God.

She swigged from a bottle of sloe gin. Saint's nectar, it was, flowing by the throne of God. Amen. Light from the altar candle slinked out of the church, dusting the tops of gravestones that the tide had mercifully spared. It was its own star, thought Marvellous. She lit that candle every night and had done so for years. A lighthouse keeper, that was what she really was. That's what had drawn Whatshisname to her shore during the war years. That, and the music, of course.

Whatshisname. The *American*. She had watched him go into the church as a shadow, and when he had emerged he was still a shadow with deep hues of mauve emanating from his dark skin, and from his mouth the glowing tip of a cigarette pulsed like the heart of a night insect. He walked across the dry riverbed lured by a familiar song, and as he pulled himself up the bank, he saw the wireless, sitting in a battered pram parked beneath the trees.

He said, Louis Armstrong.

And she said, Marvellous Ways, nice to meet you at last.

And he laughed and she had never heard laughter like that, not in all her days, and his eyes flashed as bright as torch-light. He sat with her, and the table rocked and the river rippled as bombers flew over and the air raid sirens sounded and bombs fell over the Great Port, over Truro too, and barrage balloons cast deep shadows across the sky, and Louis Armstrong sang of lips and arms and hearts as anti-aircraft guns pounded against the indigo dark, and two strangers sat quietly under a tree that had seen it all before.

He talked about his grandfather back home in South Carolina in the Low Country, talked about the fishing trips they took along the oozy marshes, how the smell of mud and salt were the smells of home, and Marvellous said, I know what you mean. And he told her of the trestle bridges that glowed pink at dusk and cedars that grew out of the lush wetlands and the heavy scent of tea olive and jasmine, which reminded him of his late mother. He said he missed eating catfish, and Marvellous said, So do I, even though she had only ever eaten dogfish. Together they toasted Life and clinked their mugs and pretended they were somewhere far far away.

He came often after that. Brought her doughnuts from the American doughnut factory in Union Square, and they ate them with strong black tea even though he preferred coffee, and they listened to the radio Rhythm Club and tapped out rhythms with their jitterbug feet. Sometimes he brought tins of Spam, corned beef, too; he never let her go hungry. And once he brought her a poster of a film she had seen a couple of years before. He was thoughtful like that.

But then days before the planned invasion of France, he asked her for a charm.

A charm? she said.

A lucky charm. To bring me back safely, he said.

She looked into his eyes and said, But that's not what I do. I've never made charms.

Oh, but that's what people said you did.

That's what they've always said, and she held his hand instead and the only charm she had was hers and it radiated out.

June 1944 was The Last Goodbye. Those American boys were shipping out. He strutted over whistling, all gabardine trousers and Hawaiian shirt, gosh he looked so smart. He gave her all he had left – chocolate, cigarettes, stockings – and they sat down under the tree and drank tea and listened to Armstrong and Teagarden, Bechet, too, and someone else who would never be as famous. She watched the young man play rhythm upon his knees, watched his mouth turn clarinet. In that moment, either side of him, she saw two futures vying for space. In one he lay still on Omaha Beach. In the other he sat still, head in a book, trying to make something of himself in a country coloured by hate. When he stood up to leave she said, Go left, and he said, What's that? She said, I don't know what it means but you will when the time comes. You must go left.

So long, Marvellous, he waved.

So long, Henry Manfred Gladstone II, she waved. *Henry Manfred Gladstone II*. So *that* was his name.

It's been a pleasure, he said.

The night grew wild with movement. The concrete barges began to depart and thousands of men embarked from piers and beaches, and there was such a kerfuffle, and yet by morning all was quiet. The generators were quiet. The smell of diesel subsiding. The Americans had left and had left behind tales of romance and unborn children, and so much joy, and it was the women who cried because they always did.

So long, Henry Manfred Gladstone II, she whispered. It's been a pleasure.

2

AS MARVELLOUS HAD PREDICTED, A THICK CRUST OF hoarfrost had settled across the river valley by morning. A curlew called out incessantly from the creek until a plume of smoke rose from the gypsy caravan. A moment later, Marvellous opened the wagon doors and carefully climbed down the glistening steps. At the solid crunch of earth, she stretched her arms up towards the trees, down towards her toes, up towards the trees again. For someone so small she took up a lot of space.

She followed the sloping path down to the riverbank where the pit-fire from the night before smouldered timidly. She sat down heavily on the mooring stone and studied her mood as she did the daily flow of the river. She was troubled; had slept badly. A dream had pulled her from sleep – a blind dream again – one of words not images. Open the boathouse, dream had said. I will not, said Marvellous vehemently, but dreams don't argue.

She stood up and waited for the highest point of the tide, the moment when the movement of the river ceased. She slipped out of her yellow oilskin and well-worn boots and shivered as the frosty mud found space between her toes. She unpinned her hair and the limp curls of white fell beyond her shoulders towards a waist once slimmer, once held. One button now, two buttons. Her fingers weren't nimble and the action took a moment. Her heavy felt trousers slid to the earth. She pulled her wool sweater over her head and her breasts tumbled free and goose pimples rose in the crisp morning air. She lifted the shell box over her head and placed it carefully upon the ancient stone. She slipped from her bloomers. It used to be only the tops of her thighs that touched, now everything touched, but it would feel different in a minute, in the river it would feel different and she knew this because she knew so much because she had been old for such a long time.

She took off her glasses and stepped carefully to the bank, felt for the edge with her toes. The smell of high water was thick. She raised her arms above her head and the breeze caught in her armpits, at the juncture of her legs.

Now.

She bent her legs and dived into the creek, surfacing two yards from shore. She swam downriver with mullet and watched a cunning heron fly low and unseen and make an easy killing in the brittle light. Front crawl took effort so she opted for breast stroke. She liked the feel of chill water between her legs as they parted.

As she drew level with the boathouse, her stomach tightened as her eyes rested on the stone and clapboard dwelling. It looked majestic and serene, frosted as it was that morning, and it looked like the symbol of love and commitment that it had previously been when her father had built it all those years before. Once white, it was now green with moss, long-jettisoned to the vast maw of her past. Twenty-five years ago she had bolted the door and had imprisoned all that had resided inside just as she had done with her heart. The salt-caked windows pleaded with her as she passed. Open us up, they whispered. Nonsense, she said, and she dived under the water and held herself down with eelgrass. She stayed there as long as she could, surfacing breathlessly back upstream in the shadow of the mooring stone. She struggled up the riverbank and wrapped herself tightly in her oilskin. She turned back towards the boathouse. You can't speak, she said. No, I can't, it said. That's all right then, she said, and she stomped back up to her caravan in a mood as heavy as mud.

That afternoon, the engine purred as the crabber rode the ebbing tide towards the narrow sandbar that kept the uninvited world at bay. On the sandbar was the wreck of *Deliverance*, her old friend Cundy's fishing boat. At low tide the boat tilted portside revealing the wound from which it never recovered. At high tide the stern sat so low in the water that most people thought the boat's name was actually *Deliver*.

Through the sandbar, the vast stretch of Carrick Roads could be seen ahead, glistening as shafts of sunlight cut across the heaving grey waterway. A gunshot echoed beyond the meadows. Marvellous stopped and listened; heard a faint dog bark, too. A flock of gulls took off into the low white sun, patterning the valley with fleeting, half-glimpsed shadows. She raised her telescope and studied their flight, looking for unusual signs, but again there were none. She caught a tern surrendering to the current, joyfully drifting backwards on the fast out-going water.

She lowered the telescope and slipped off her glasses, quite sure now that whatever she was waiting for was not coming by water. There were signs with water – *obvious* signs – like the unforgettable night when two thousand starfish had crept in on the tide.

It had been a lifetime ago. A night when loneliness had taken her too early to bed. She had lain awake unable to sleep, willing her life to change as young women do, when all of a sudden she felt the creeping movement of company outside. She got up and when she saw the shimmering pattern of orange stars, she thought the world was upside down and the heavens finally within reach. And in a way it was, and in a way they were, because the following day Paper Jack marched through the shallows and cut a path through fifteen years of thorny silence.

He came with bluebells behind his ears and ramson stalks in his mouth and was trailed by lovelorn bees who knew the scent of a good man. He stopped outside her caravan and with arms out wide he shouted what the children used to shout:

> Marvellous Ways! Marvellous Ways!
> Is she well or is she crazed?
> She'll cast a spell and make you well,
> She'll cast a spell you'll go to hell.

Marvellous stepped out from the caravan that day and with as much indifference as she could muster, said, You again!

And he said, Me, again!

So what do you want? Wellness or hellness?

And he quietly said, *You*-ness.

And she said, Ain't no Eunice living here.

And he said, God damn it, woman, you've still got a mouth! Now come down from those steps and let me hold you.

And they held on to each other until Time Past crept between them and made them shy, and Paper Jack pulled away and smiled at her, and his smile broke like a spring morning and melted the long winter of her heart.

'Course he wasn't called Paper Jack then, the name Paper Jack came much later, as names often do. He was called just Jack or Singer Jack then, and he was quiet and watchful and eyed everything and everyone like the weather. He once called Marvellous *a band of high pressure* during an argument, and once when his brother, Jimmy, wasn't around he called her a *frosty start to the day*. Jack liked Marvellous from the moment he saw her on Jimmy's arm. Jack liked Marvellous more than any girl he had ever set eyes on. And once, when he was drunk, and she was alone, Jack said he would wait for her because she was worth waiting for, like *the first sighting of pilchards in the early morn of a summer day*.

That First Return was in 1900. Marvellous was forty-two years old and Jack, thirty-six. Both had been worn down by life and were an inch shorter than the last time they had met. Marvellous built a fire outside and cooked the crab she had hauled the previous day. They drank in each other's presence with ale and rum, and became so shy that even the leaves began to blush.

You got yourself a man? asked Jack.

No one permanent, said Marvellous. And Jack felt half glad, half jealous.

He said, A woman like you needs a man –

– is that so? –

– because a woman like you needs a child, he said.

Too late for that, said Marvellous quietly, and she began to clear away the stinking shell. Four hundred and seventeen children she had delivered by then and not one her own.

She stopped and said, I wanted your child, Jack. I wanted to love and care for your child, and she knelt down and rinsed her hands in a bucket of river water.

He sat in silence and watched her guiltily, listening to a nightingale in the leafy oak branches above. When Marvellous had finished, he stood up and pulled her towards his chest. They rocked from side to side as the nightingale sang in the leafy oak branches above, and they kissed and she wished they hadn't because she could taste his sadness on his breath. Could taste his other life and his other women too, and that's why she knew he wouldn't stay.

I'm not staying, he whispered.

I know, said Marvellous.

I'm going to make good and then I'll come back and fetch you.

I'll wait, said Marvellous, because she was so good at waiting.

You've only ever been the girl for me.

I'm not a girl, Jack, and time's running out.

You've never looked more beautiful.

Where have these words been hiding?

Taken me years to find you.

I never went far.

The silence was punctuated by bird calls.

She ran her hands over his face. Where have you been all this time?

Australia.

I thought I could see another sun on your skin.

I ended up south at the copper mines. Place called Moonta – Little Cornwall they called it because there were pasties there and Methodists too.

Food for thought, said Marvellous. Food for the soul.

And there were blackfellas, too, and they knew the land and they knew the sea. And I'd go down to the bay and watch them spear fish with harpoons made from stingray barbs. And this blackfella – Bob, he was called – well, he called me a whitefella. Can you imagine it? I'd never thought about being a whitefella before, not until that moment when I stood on that strange shore looking at the biggest bluest sky I'd ever seen, watching a blackfella spear fish for his tea.

Marvellous smiled. She took his hands and kissed them.

And he wanted to tell her that was the start of his homesickness: that overwhelming sky and those skinny-looking blackfellas. He wanted to tell her that nothing felt right and he missed his home because how could he make a home in a land that whispered angry words? In a land where flies outnumbered men, in a land where heat rose from the red-parched earth as fiercely as a kiln? How could he make a home in a land that didn't have *her*? And he cried on that beach and pretended he had the burning midday sun in his eyes, because when Bob looked over at him he laughed and said, What's with the fakkin tiss, mate?

What is it? asked Marvellous.

Jack fell silent. He pulled out a heavy gold fob watch and placed it between her hands. See, I came back rich, he said.

You came back a Gentleman.

I did. And could you love a Gentleman?

I'd prefer a sailor with no money.

Jack laughed. How did you know?

Because I know you, Jack Francis. And I can smell your life on your hands.

Marvellous refilled his mug from the flagon.

There was another accident underground and I lost my nerve, Marve. Couldn't go back down there again. Kept thinking of Jimmy. You ever think of him?

Now and then. But I think of you more.

Do you love me more?

Yes. Because I have more love to give.

He reached for his ale. I still have guilt, he said.

Time swallowed mine.

Lucky.

No. Just very very tired, said Marvellous.

I won't go underground again, said Jack. Just the sea for me now. I'll take my chances with the waves.

Swim with me, said Marvellous.

I can't swim. Don't know a sailor who can.

We'll stay shallow and I'll hold you.

I'm a lot to hold.

I'm a good anchor.

They stood by the mooring stone in the lamplight. They undressed each other and they looked all over each other's bodies and their eyes became hands and their longing caused the river to ripple and when they could look no more she walked him into the cold water, and he was so giddy he had difficulty keeping his feet on the ground.

As he dressed, she packed his bag with sloe gin and pickled limpets and saffron buns. Packets of dried sweet chestnut and comfrey leaves, too, to ease the rattling breathlessness he tried to hide.

That night, before he left, she asked him to sleep with her. Came right out and said it. Said they'd wasted enough time already and she was dying for it, quite frankly. Warmed by the booze, he followed her into the boathouse and in the golden candlelight the heat of the day gave way to the sweat of night. She pulled her shirt over her head and he touched her breasts, and kissed her breasts and reached under her skirt and his hands met no other fabric except her goose-bumped flesh. He unbuttoned his trousers, and she once again unbuttoned his heart. They were no longer shy.

They clung to each other and loved as if it was their last chance at love and where he entered he never left. And that was the night they began to share dreams because that's what happens when you both know the weight of another's soul.

Jack waited for her to sleep before he disappeared into the rise of dawn. He knew how to do that without making a sound because he filled his lungs like balloons and held his breath so tight they lifted him off the ground. And as he glided swiftly through the trees, her voice broke through the dreamscape and her voice said, I'll be here when you get back. Be quick, my love. I'll wait.

But he wasn't quick. But she did wait. For twenty years did she wait. And when he returned there would be no bright starfish laying down a golden path to her door. Just the unmistakable sound of rumour.

3

FIREWORKS PULLED MARVELLOUS OUT OF A DREAMLESS sleep. She had thought it to be war yet had found it to be peace when she staggered down from her wagon and caught the tail end of the spectacle: the sodden fizz as white and green and red embers disappeared behind the trees, plunging the creek into a soft milky silence, leaving only stars, and plenty of them.

She stood alone on the shore, confused and dishevelled, pressed upon by the vast inky Cornish sky. She didn't know if it was because her hand looked so old against the dense cluster of stars or because she didn't know who or what she was waving to in that perfect night sky, but her eyes began to water.

She stumbled down into her boat, part woman part child and neither knew what to do with the other. She lit a lamp and pulled a blanket across her lap and pushed away from the bank. The boat and her mind drifted. And again there was yet silence.

No sound now of aeroplanes, or electric generators, or sirens or bombs. No *caw* of gulls, no *drip drip* of sodden branches. A padded silence that lapped like flotsam at the shore of all she was.

The boat gently rose, gently rocked. Feet away, now, from *Deliverance*, and the sight of its breached hull saddened her because some days she thought that was exactly what her mind was becoming, a breached hull. She could feel a leak just above her eyes, had felt moments sucked out by the tide and she wondered if her mind would eventually become empty like the boat. And she thought that empty at this point in her life would be a very lonely place to be, because there was no one left to remind her of all she had done and what she had once been, which was young.

What if, on those quiet afternoons when she liked to sit and think back over her life, what if she couldn't recall Jack or Jimmy, or the lighthouse keeper who first taught her about love? What if she couldn't recall the rush of sun across the moors or the sound of hymns that rose from the mines as Christmas approached? What if she couldn't recall the haul of oysters that blistered her hands or the sight of square-rigged ships racing across the horizon to meet a sun when back home was still a moon? What if the sight of her father became the sight of a stranger and an owl was no longer an owl and its purpose was blank? What if a clock tower struck eleven and it was simply a sound? What if it all went? And night fell and she didn't know it was night? Or a sandpiper called or a mullet rose at surface break or a gannet dived and she mislaid their names like coins behind the backs of chairs? What if she held a shell to her ear and there were no words to describe the sound? A limpet, that's all she'd be. Good for nothing except hanging on.

She secured her craft to the hull and let the boats nudge one another like the old friends they were. She found a piece of gingerbread in her pocket and the scent was different against the ponderous stench of weed and mud. She felt it warm her stomach immediately, felt it dry the cold damp of worry. She ran her hand across the mossy starboard slats of *Deliverance*, and as the breeze quietened and the rocking ceased, she leant forwards and began to tell the story of the boat back to the broken boat.

Light was nibbling at the foot of the sky when she finished the story. The breeze had picked up and a smoky haze dawned stealthily from the earth. The river stirred, began to empty. Marvellous rested her ear against the damp wood and heard something that she hadn't heard before. Had she been listening to a human chest she would have called it a heartbeat. But because it was a boat, she didn't have a word for it.

The lighthouse bell began to toll announcing the incoming mist, and great swathes of the stuff crept towards Marvellous and caught in the trees like Spanish moss, laying salt on the leaves of the rhododendrons, on the fronds of palms. She felt scared. Old and scared. She pulled the blanket up higher and huddled down on to the bottom boards. *Open the boathouse*, dream had said. She looked back towards the sad white shack and thought of her life as a winged insect trapped in its amber past. Dawn broke with a whisper. Her mouth let out a sigh.

When the mist had eased and the sun committed she moored at the stone and staggered up to her caravan before the day attempted to change her mind. Hanging outside like a wind chime was a bunch of keys of various sizes: keys to boats, to cottages, to locks unknown, a key to understanding, too: a tiny key that hung from a ragged aquamarine braid, but why she had ever called it that she couldn't remember. She leant in close and looked for the unmistakable shape of the boathouse key, the one she'd last held twenty-five years ago. There it was! as recognisable as an old-time face. She prised it away from the bunch and marched back down to the moss-stained door with it held triumphantly aloft.

The key fitted perfectly. She took the padlock off and shoved the door open with all her might. She heard a moan and that last year with Paper Jack rushed towards her and she fell to the ground, and it wouldn't let her go until she felt it again, remembered it once again. All mixed up, it was, sadness and joy and a whole heap of pain.

She struggled free and gathered her breath and never took her eyes away from that boathouse door. Swinging to and fro, it was. Never took her eyes away because there was no breeze any more, all was still. A pendulum to Lost Time, it was, swinging to and fro in a nothing breeze.

Inside, the stench of long-gone years and briny damp unsettled her nose. Fine webs from a spindle spider connected floor to ceiling and wall to floor, and green mould spores gossiped and kissed and multiplied before her eyes. And all around was a sound like seeping gas or breaking wind or a great big sigh, a release of stale air from that tomb of two. She opened the balcony doors and the sea air rushed in, and the light startled through the gap and fell upon the wall and the clammy, unused bed. And on the wall above the bed, the starfish: as orange as it ever was. She unhooked it and cradled it in her hands and the woman she had been joined her on that bed and comforted her. Twenty-five years she had been without that man. Once even a day without him had been unbearable.

Twenty-five years! she said out loud. Do you hear that, you silly man?

She heard his wheeze. She heard his voice say, We were young. At least we had that.

Young! scoffed Marvellous. We were never young!

You've never looked better, she heard Jack say.

You're full of nonsense.

That's why you love me.

That I do.

You been looking after yourself, Marvellous?

When I can remember to. What about you?

Cough's gone. Got my strength back. Did you get my dreams?

'Course I did. Bit unclear, though.

I'll do better next time.

That would be a help. What's it all about, Jack? What am I waiting for?

You know it doesn't work like that, Marve.

Are you going to stay? Is that why I opened this place up?

Not right now. But I'm coming back.

That old song.

Be kind, my love.

Well, I've changed. And I might not wait, you know. I'm a lot older and a whole lot wiser.

Oh, you'll wait! she heard him say. You can't get enough of me. I drive you wild.

You drive me mad. Always have.

Mad and wild. You'll wait.

I might not! she shouted. Silly old fool! she shouted and she tutted loudly. She couldn't hear him after that. Heard only the stir of the river, the stir of the trees, the stir – strangely – of her fear. An owl screeched. She looked out and watched it swoop down and tuck into a breakfast mouse.

She put the starfish in her pocket and pulled the boathouse door to and went in search of soap and a brush and a pail of water. She would give the boathouse new life and a clean one at that. She would set the hearth alight and burn logs day and night and chase the damp until steam crept from the cracks, till only salt crystals glistened drily upon the window-ledges.

Hours later, she lay in bed exhausted; her hands red and raw and her arms too weak to unpeel her glasses. She listened to the distinct sound of a curlew, sonorous against the plangent mournful call of the fog bell: that fixed point in her shifting, swirling, unclear world. She felt cold. Even the roundels of slate she had warmed on the stove were proving useless against the damp chill. She moved a slate to her chest and eventually the weight and warmth led her to sleep.

And then, just as her lids closed, a dream lined up to take flight across her sleep, a dream that would deposit two images, at last, to the door of her mind: the image of a linnet, tentative and free, flying across the Thames with a chest full of song. The image of a young man looking towards a horizon that promised nothing.

The fog bell mourned.

II

4

SO HERE HE WAS, ON THE UPPER DECK OF THE SS *AUTOCARRIER*, spewing his guts out, missing the moment when the white cliffs of Dover loomed out of the grey October afternoon.

The sea had been relatively calm for most of the crossing, a slow undulating swell at most, but that was all it had taken to propel the remnants of his breakfast – that satisfying dish of *oeuf sur le plat* and *jambon cuit* – on to the foredeck as soon as the ferry had cast off from Boulogne.

The ship's horn tore through his head and Drake groaned as another wave of watery puke hit the air and splashed his brogues. He rarely thought about his father but at times like this he did. Wondered if the old man had ever suffered as he suffered: bent double and legless, gripping the rail with all his might, fearing something he could never quite put words to.

As the cliffs drew near, people began to gather on deck:

elegant couples excitedly chatting and pointing. Was that really Vera Lynn singing in his head or some woman behind? He turned round and she quickly looked away. Probably should have wiped his mouth first. He let the rails take his weight as he staggered up to face England. He wanted to salute, duty done. 1940 he had left. Now here he was, seven years later, with a fierce taste of bile in his mouth. That felt about right.

On the quay at Folkestone, a car swung precariously overhead as it was lifted from the ferry. People hurried along chatting about their holidays and the impending Royal Wedding, no talk of war any more. Funny how life had moved on. He pushed ahead of the amblers and boarded the train for Victoria for a night back in London before heading south-west. Just one night, he thought, it couldn't hurt, could it? Just one night in the old neighbourhood to see what damage had been done.

He entered a quiet compartment, occupied by three men and a woman. He lifted his suitcase on to the overhead rack and took off his hat and raincoat, careful not to disturb anyone. He sat down and sucked on a strong peppermint as the train jolted into motion. He felt his stomach ease, the flush of colour return to his face. He leant his cheek against the cool glass as the sea began to retreat from view, as the train trundled across the pier towards the junction, as his eyes closed to the rumble of wheels travelling across the sweet safe unmoving earth.

By the time the guard came round to check on tickets he felt as if he had slept for hours. He looked at his watch: thirty-five minutes that's all. He took out the ticket from his inside pocket and handed it over. When the guard left, he shifted back into his seat and was about to doze again when the woman opposite bent down and picked up something by his foot. Yours, she said, handing over an envelope. He thanked her and noticed immediately the familiar writing, the smudge of French soil, the address pointing to Cornwall. Nearly three years he had waited to deliver the thing. Always there at the back of his mind, thumping like a bell hammer, the tinny sound of guilt. All this way to lose it on a Kentish train. Genius, Drake. You're a fucking genius. His hands were shaking as he slipped the letter back into his inside pocket. He kept his hand against the letter and felt the racing beat of his heart. He closed his eyes and thought about things that made him feel good: always came back to a pint of beer, a full plate of food, women's legs – not necessarily in that order. He opened his eyes and the countryside passed by in a quick succession of blurred browns and greens, and he tried to focus on a tree here and a barn there but nothing was in focus 'cause his mind was back to that day in Normandy, a week or so after the landings of '44.

It should have been easy, the march into Caen, but it wasn't. They'd found themselves in Bocage country, and the front line was a battlefield of hedges and ditches and constant heavy mortar fire, terrifying dashes between islands of cover, German snipers everywhere. That's what had made the men jumpy.

Battalions had become groups of ragged, scared individuals, disillusioned and exhausted. Men had begun to inflict wounds on themselves just to get the fuck out.

The six of them had still been friends then, hard to believe now. Maybe it was the last battle that had undone them, peeled them like oranges, made them bitter. Maybe what came later had germinated then? Hatred doesn't need much watering or care. Just a nudge.

They had been waiting in the ruins of a newly abandoned farmhouse and the scattered belongings of a family remained. Christ! Here's mine! said Johnno, holding up a photograph of an aged overweight woman. The men jeered and whistled but Drake ignored them and looked away. Beyond the broken window he found the yellow of summer everywhere: in the sun, in the corn, in the small flowers that bloomed across field and meadow.

There was little for them to do in the waiting except smoke and sleep and he was heavy and dull with both, so he took himself off for a walk before the next push forwards. It wasn't long before he came across a field hospital at the edge of an orchard. Flies were abundant, joyful amidst the splintered limbs and pooling blood.

Don't just gawp, make yourself useful, said a nurse, rushing past. Him over there, she said, pointing. He followed her direction and came to a soldier lying on a stretcher, all but his face covered by a blanket. Drake sat down on the grass and pulled out a cigarette. The soldier's face was peaceful, resigned. It was quite beautiful really, and he wondered if he was actually dead, but then the soldier opened his eyes and spoke. Got one for me? he said. Drake lit a cigarette for him. Can't move my hands, said the soldier, so Drake placed the cigarette between the man's lips. He took deep drags and never coughed and said, Tastes good, thank you.

You'll be getting out of here soon, said Drake.

Not sure about that. It's not over yet.

'Tis for you, mate. Lucky sod.

The soldier smiled, gestured for another puff.

It's not bad here, is it? said Drake, looking around. Sun's out. Flowers are out. Birds are singing.

What kind of flowers?

Drake picked a yellow trumpet close to his boot and held it up in front of the soldier's face.

Cowslip, said the soldier.

34

Cowslip, repeated Drake. He held the cigarette to the soldier's lips. So, what's the first thing you'll do when you get back? he said.

Swim.

I fuckin' hate water, said Drake.

We're sixty per cent water. Our bodies, that is. Did you know that?

Probably why I'm not good with people.

The soldier smiled. Dougie Arnold. Please to meet you.

Francis Drake, said Drake.

Ahoy there!

I've heard it all before.

You're kidding, right?

My father was a sailor.

Gets better.

Never met him, though. The name was my mum's idea. Still romantic about the sea by the time I came along. Drake placed the cigarette between the soldier's lips. He began to cough. Easy there, Drake said. Come on, slow breaths. That's better.

Will you do something for me? said the soldier.

'Course.

In my pocket, in the front, there's a letter. I can't reach it. Can you get it out?

Drake stubbed out the cigarette and leant over Dougie Arnold. He pulled back the blanket carefully and the smell made him gag. Where arms should have been were tied-off stumps, ragged and charred above the elbow. He held his breath and hoped his face gave nothing away as he gently unbuttoned the tunic pocket.

Here, said Drake, lifting it up. It's to Dr Arnold?

Yeah. My father.

Cornwall?

My home.

Never been.

You'd like it. Lots of water, and Dougie smiled.

Drake pulled a small hip flask out of his kit and waved it in front of the soldier's face.

The soldier said, Fucking marvellous, the Cavalry's arrived.

There you go, said Drake as he poured the liquid in.

Cheers, said Dougie.

Cheers. To better days.

Better days, and the soldier gently closed his eyes.

Drake stared at him. They were about the same age, he thought. Wondered if he had a girl. Probably not. The letter was to a father, wasn't it? He undid another button on the soldier's collar. Noticed a faint pulse at his neck.

Deliver, said the soldier weakly.

You what? said Drake, leaning in.

Deliver.

Deliver? Deliver what?

You deliver the letter.

Me?

To my father. In Cornwall. When it's all over. When you get back. Tell him I was all right –

– you are all right –

– tell him good things.

Tanks rolled past, soldiers began shouting. On the move again. Allies taking back France.

Promise me, Francis Drake. I can't hear you.

I'm here, said Drake. He leant in close.

Promise me, said Dougie Arnold.

I promise you, said Drake. I'll deliver your letter.

5

FROM VICTORIA STATION DRAKE TOOK THE UNDERGROUND
to Farringdon and came up the stairs into a chill misty dusk. A
large rat passed in front and looked at him with indignation.
Yeah, I'm back, said Drake and he walked up Turnmill Street
with the constant rumble of trains to his left, the ever-watchful
dome of St Paul's behind. The air smelt grubby, tasted dusty.
He'd forgotten what it was like. So many people rushing
towards him heading for home. But he hadn't forgotten, not
really; it was in his marrow, this city, and had given him life.
The air stirred as a dark cloud-front moved briskly across the
rooftops. He picked up speed and crossed the road into
Clerkenwell Green towards the streets beyond. He managed to
get to the lodging house moments before a heavy rain fell.

He waited at a small table in the hallway as damp traffic
clambered past. Overhead a body fell upon a bed and the ceiling

creaked and the light above him swung to and fro, casting him intermittently into shadow. The smell of wet wool mingled with the smell of overcooked shepherd's pie and he could feel the rise of nausea again. A young woman passed him and he tried not to look, she tried not to smile. His face was coloured by two summers of a French sun, his body shaped by war and building. His hat was French, his cigarettes too. He travelled light; at his feet a small suitcase carried all the necessities accumulated along the way. He watched the woman climb the stairs. Good legs. In the living room behind him, Louis Armstrong sang low from the wireless.

He glanced at the telephone next to him and realised there was no one in this world he could possibly call. He felt his chest tighten, felt the languid motion of liquid beneath his feet. He leant forwards and breathed in a deep slow lungful of air.

Room's ready, said Mrs Marsh, the landlady, coming down the stairs and handing him a set of keys and a wad of cut-up newspaper.

Lavatory's outside, she said. Don't use too much.

Ah, England.

The room was shabby but the sheets were clean. The reading lamp cast a pitiful light across the bed and he went to turn on the overhead light but saw that the bulb was missing. Blue flock wallpaper peeled away at the ceiling edge where a haze of mould had made its home, and a garish picture of chrysanthemums hung above the headboard. He crouched down and switched on the electric fire; one bar blushed but little heat came. He went to the window and looked out on to a dirty night made dirtier still by the drab buildings that huddled either side of him, some boarded up, one derelict. He pulled the curtains to. He took the letter out from his jacket pocket and placed it on the mantelpiece in full view. It seemed different somehow, looking at it back in England, the first part of its journey complete. What he thought was mud was actually old blood, and he caught himself apologising for not coming back sooner. It sounded like someone else's voice. It was just all a mess, he kept saying, and he had never heard himself say that before and it shocked him because he sounded like a child, all those sorrys.

He sat on the bed. The mattress, an unwelcome lump beneath his arse. He took out a packet of Gauloises. His hands were shaking again and he wondered when that had started. He lit a cigarette and blew the pungent smoke towards the mottled shade above. In the dingy light it swirled and hovered, thick like mist. He closed his eyes and lay back; imagined he was warm, not cold. Imagined he could hear the sound of seagulls rather than the argument next door. Imagined he was anywhere else other than here in this dismal room.

It was after the war that he had stumbled to the south of France where the light was soft and the welcome real. He smiled, seeing again his café at sunrise, chairs laid out in the square, a small black coffee as thick as dirt, fishing boats returning to port, selling their catch of octopus and urchins on the quay. Pastel shades of fishermen's cottages, so beautiful in the syrupy dawn light. He had hauled vegetables from vans, he had served drinks and built decks and fishing sheds, fuck, he'd done whatever they'd wanted him to do and there was always work for him, the Liberator of France. Women had kept an eye on him too, sprayed perfume in intimate places just in case, but he stayed away from the women, seeing that his dick was as soft as brie.

Days off, he walked aimlessly around, pretending that nothing bad had happened, that the violence he had seen, the violence he had enacted on men like himself, on women like his mother, had been worth it and had left him untouched, with a heart still capable of care. War had been his first experience of violence. He'd run bets for violent men as a kid, who hadn't? But they'd seen something in him, a fissure of gentleness, of innocence, and had taken him under their ample wings and protected him as if he was the mirror of their own lost souls.

Days off, after rain, he built sandcastles on the beach. Soon, castles turned into villages, ruddy intricate things with moats and boats, fairy-tale imaginings that soothed him. Digging like a dog, he made sure that everything unpleasant – everything fetid – was buried like shit in the sand.

Oh, he could have lived there all right. Sitting at a table in the outside for ever and for ever unknown, never thinking about the letter or returning to England because in his mind it was as far away as the moon and just as blue. It was perfect. For a whole year. So bloody *parfait*.

But then his mind began to play tricks. Memories had taken root in the cool of that bottomless dark and had broken through like marram grass, binding and enduring, and soon he saw faces again and smelt the acrid stench of burning hair, and so he took off in the night. No goodbyes, no thank yous. Just him running from what had been good.

He kept away from stations and ports and headed inland and further north to the hidden hamlets and farmsteads in need of men. He slept in barns and the movement of the cows was good company in the twilight. He lived like a monk, quiet and alone. Did his job and ate bread and cheese and the occasional stew, and he never spent the money that came his way. And then one night, outside Tours, the daughter of the house crept to the barn and bedded down beside him. She unbuttoned him and took him in hand. He was embarrassed, blamed the proximity of livestock with all their snorting and all their pissing. But she knew a lot for a girl of eighteen and she bent down and took him in her mouth and he grew hard in her mouth and that seemed to quieten the cows. He came quickly. He didn't move and she didn't move. He stroked her hair to see if she had fallen asleep. She lifted her head, her mouth glistening and inviting. Nobody had ever done that to him before and he doubted anyone would again, so he kissed her hard and even the discomfort of tasting himself couldn't halt the strange peace he momentarily felt.

They sat side by side, backs against the old barn wall. Strangers. Not talking, not hoping. She left at the sound of her father's call. *Adieu*, she said. Farewell. Alone in the stall, the fetid stink from the straw softened and became for him the smell of a rimy cheese, and he felt so hungry he could have chewed his fucking hand off. He ate the last of his bread and realised that it wasn't hunger that he felt but loneliness. It was an empty space where a heart should have been. That's when he decided to return to England. He needed to find something that belonged in his chest, if only to stop the hunger.

Drake stubbed out his cigarette. He got up from the bed and pulled back the curtains. The pavements glistened but the rain had stopped. He lifted his suitcase on to the bed and flicked open the catch. He took out a half-drunk bottle of gin, put it into his raincoat pocket and was about to open the door when his sight was drawn back to the letter. Tomorrow, he whispered. I promise you, tomorrow. He left his room and the argument next door and headed down the stairs, out into a darkness unadorned by barrage balloons and crisscross shafts of searching light. Headed out into the sweet silence of a world at peace.

6

THE STREETS WERE EMPTY. NIGHT HAD DEVOURED THE living like an ancient plague. Faint outlines of buildings and people could still be seen in the desolate maws where daisies now grew. Ghosts had never bothered him, only the living had, and occasionally he heard footsteps behind but on turning saw his own edginess startle in a streak of gaslight. He veered down St John Street where St Paul's rose in the distance. A city of saints run by sinners, that's what the aunts used to say. Maybe they were right about that, he thought. The loading bays of the meat market were deserted. Just him and paper bags swirling in the gathering breeze.

He wasn't shocked by the devastation. How could he be? He had witnessed the bombardment of Caen. Waves of bombs had blasted that city until nothing was left and they had marched into the narrow rubble-choked streets, undercover of the dust and smoke, and the air was corrugated by the winds of fire, by the scream of falling masonry, and the pathetic cry of the invisible injured. The dead affected him less as war went on but the decimation of homes choked him. Hundreds of years of brick upon careful brick gone in minutes. And when civilians climbed out blinking and trembling from the cellars, gradually they began to clap and to cheer and it fuckin' did his head in – was he supposed to take a bow? He hadn't thought it at the time, of course, but he had afterwards. That was why his hands shook, he was sure of it. Everyone had a limit.

He picked up his pace now and hurried on down past the hospital, down towards Old Bailey. He didn't know what he was expecting to see but when he caught sight of the old pub on the corner and the grubby tenement next door, he felt dizzy, seasick almost. Something caught in his throat, something good, he knew it had to be because his eyes were stinging and his nose was snotting. That's where he had spent his first eleven years, with his mum, of course. Two rooms for two people; it had been enough. And he wished he could have turned back the years on that fast-moving clock and told her that. He heard chatter and laughter inside and he stood by the window and peered in. No Mr and Mrs Betts tending bar, no Mr Toggs playing on the piano, no Iris, no Lilly with their grubby stories of sex and men. Sixteen years had passed and everyone he had known there was long gone. But he knew it wasn't war that had taken them, simply life because that's what it does. No, he wouldn't go in, not that night. He closed his eyes and listened to the familiar sound of a train and a trolleybus rumble by.

He walked aimlessly through the streets where he'd played as a kid, where he'd waited for the neighbourhood men to return from factories or pubs so he could latch on to them and imagine them as older brothers, and sometimes fathers. They were his lemon drop moments: sweet-sour moments that had made his mouth water, and later, his eyes too. For when light would fade and tea was called, those same men would prise him away like a bur and head inside to the light of their own families. And he would stand and watch through the windows the scene of this drama, sometimes for minutes, sometimes longer, and when time was called and the curtains were drawn, he would turn away gutted, embarrassed even, at the burning realisation of all he didn't have. Of all he would never have. And those moments buried down into his legs and stopped him working right, for when he should have run he stayed put. And when he should have stayed put, he ran and the running felt good to a fatherless boy.

Missy was the only person he had ever told about this and she said that moments like that make us stronger. An *antigen*, that's what she used to call it, like an inoculation, to protect against the loneliness of the future. Missy said a lot of daft things, except the things she should have said and then she wasn't there any more, and no one, he realised, had ever invented an antigen to protect him from that.

He'd last seen her – Jesus, when was it? – autumn of '39? Could it have been? Just come out of the Savoy, she had, all done up like a movie star with hair so perfectly waved and a waist so small you blinked you missed it. On her arm a man as flashy as a bracelet. When she saw him she beamed and shouted, Freddy! because she was the only one to call him that, and she unpeeled herself from Flashman's grip and headed over to him with arms out wide with a smile so red, so genuine, so bloody wide. She said, You've turned into a right looker, Freddy.

Always knew you would, and she touched his cheek and felt him blush.

He said, I'm nineteen. I'm getting out of here as soon as I can.

What d'you wanna do that for?

Someone has to fight. Why not me?

A hundred reasons, doll, and Freddy laughed.

Flashman hailed a taxi. Missy let go of Freddy's hand and began to walk away.

Where you heading? he asked.

Café de Paris. Ken Johnson and his band.

I like to listen to him.

I'd say come with me, but—

Say it and I will.

Oh Freddy.

He followed her to the waiting door.

Not dressed quite right, am I? he said.

Good enough for me, she said, and she slid into the back seat as smooth as the silk she wore. You make sure you come back safe, you hear me? Keep your head down, you little idiot.

I will.

And come and find me, Freddy.

Where will you be?

Café de Paris, of course!

Drake was running now. Down past St Paul's, islanded and adrift in its sea of dust. Down Godliman Street and across Queen Victoria. His collar was up and he knew where he was running to, could run it blindfold. The salted muddy smell of boyhood rang a hundred bells and it was a good sound even though he didn't feel so good. Down the narrow cobbled lanes

45

towards the wharfs he went, a single feeble gaslamp lit, and his breathing was loud and his memories were too, as he neared the wet steps calling him down towards the Thames.

There! The river! The beautiful, the beautiful river.

And that old dog of a river watched him come. Had watched him cross in the tail lights of a passing motor car. Lit up briefly, he was. Collar high, and shoulders hunched, blowing warm nicotine breath on to his cold calloused hands. Brow furrowed. Eyes lost. Old Thames wept and the waters rose a sad mucky inch. So different from the boy I knew, said river.

Drake stopped at the edge of the warehouse wall. The water was bloated, shimmering in the gloaming. Silver crests licked light from the night and splashed against the stairs, caught the front of his shoes. He felt the familiar heavy pounding in his chest as he crouched down towards the current. The river slowed in his presence, made him lean in, made him listen.

Don't tempt it, he could hear his mother say. Stand back! It finds its way into the strongest of things and rips 'em apart – a wall, a jetty, a *family* – it ruins everything including love. You keep away now, Francis Drake. You keep away.

His mother had a lot to say about water, had a lot to say about most things except his father. Just that his eyes were blue and he was a sailor and he never came back.

He never came back and his eyes were blue, You loved him so but he never loved you. Ta dah!

Drake opened the bottle of gin. He grimaced as he swallowed the first mouthful.

What was his name, Ma?

Stop asking me questions.

What was my father's name?

Lucky.

What kind of name's Lucky?

The only one he had. Now sleep.

The power station was pumping out muck and a fine mist was drawing over the city. Mist or smog, he wasn't sure which, but the lights looked pretty in the haze. The familiar cranes that rose opposite stood mute and melancholy like tired old men keeping watch over the city. Drake took off his raincoat and placed it in the shadow of the wall. He sat down, wrapped his jacket more tightly around himself. It was a damp world and it crept through to his bones like the memories themselves. He lifted the bottle of gin to his lips. He sees again his mother creeping through the fog to this very shore. He is eleven and he watches her from this same spot and he watches her call out for his father who never comes home and he doesn't understand because he is too young and he doesn't tell anyone in case she is mad. For a whole month she did it. Backwards and forwards to the calling of the river. Then one morning she never woke up and everything changed. Something wrong with her heart, that was what the doctor had said. But Drake knew there was nothing wrong with her heart. It was just too heavy so it broke.

The sound of a brewer's cart echoed in the mist as hoofs clopped their way across the bridge. Drake finished the remains of the bottle. He stood up groggily and threw it into the black river. He watched it bob briefly on the surface before the tide carried it down to Silvertown, to Wapping, to the open sea beyond. He felt spent. Fuckit, he was drunk, his stomach was on fire. He climbed back up to the streetlights above, to the sober majesty of St Paul's Cathedral, to a cold lodging house with a garish painting of chrysanthemums above the bed.

He stopped. Turned back for one last muzzy look.

And that old dog of a river sighed.

7

THE NEXT DAY, DRAKE AWOKE TO THE SOUND OF A VACUUM cleaner in the room next door. Jesus, even the mornings were closing in. His head pounded, his tongue as rough as brick dust, his bowels hot with liquid. He stared at the blue flock wallpaper until he realised where he was. He picked up his wristwatch. Shit. He had slept past lunch.

Are you still in there? shouted Mrs Marsh, her fist hammering against the door.

Still here, Mrs Marsh, he mumbled.

He paid for his room and headed to Paddington Station to try to salvage something of the day. He had decided to buy the train ticket first then find a room around the corner for an early start to Cornwall the following morning. That was about all he could manage. His hangover chewed at his brain like a rat and he felt the sticky wash of anxiety welcome him back.

He had missed the busy hours of day-trippers and passed through the ticket hall with relative ease. Clouds of steam rose as a train came to a halt, and he stood back to let the passengers and porters pass. He looked up at the clock. It pointed to hunger so he made for the tearoom to his left.

He had eaten little since breakfast the day before, and most of that had joined him on the deck of the car ferry. He asked the waitress for tea and a bacon roll and she noted his rudeness, said, A *please* wouldn't hurt. God, if only she knew. He fumbled in his pockets for the right amount of money. He wasn't rude, just economical with words. He was struggling not to slur, not to shake. It took both hands to get his tea over to a table without spilling it. It was strong and dark, English tea – the French couldn't make tea – and he drank a mouthful straight away. He went back to the counter. Here, said the waitress. Your bacon roll, *sir*.

Drake looked at her. He knew she didn't like him, knew she wasn't fooled by him. Not by the French clothes nor the peppermint breath. She knew what lay underneath that clammy sour sheen.

Thank you, he said. And I'm sorry. Bad night.

Bad morning by the looks of it.

Bad everything, he said, and he managed a smile. Now that didn't hurt, did it? he thought.

He sat down and ate quickly. Watched the waitress clear the table opposite and his headache was momentarily soothed by the tilt of her breasts, by the rise and fall of her hips. She disappeared behind the counter and his sullen mood returned. He watched passengers tick-tock past the window and let himself be drawn into the hypnotic state of motion. He ate the last of his roll and lit a cigarette. He started to feel clearer.

It was then that a blonde hurried by. It was brief but he caught her none the less, because she slowed as she passed, slowed to take in her reflection in the steamy glass. Not a moment of vanity, but a simple one of recognition, as if she was a ghost seeing herself with a body once again, seeing herself *alive* once again.

Missy? Drake stood up and knocked over his tea. No, it couldn't have been, God his head was so fucked. He righted his chair and tried to mop up the tea with his handkerchief. He sat back down, tried to get a grip. He lit another cigarette but stubbed it out straight away, it tasted all wrong. He jumped up. Fuck. It was her, he was sure of it. In the doorway, an elderly couple blocked his way with an oversize suitcase, there was no need for him to have sworn at them like that. He noticed the waitress's pitiful look as he ran past the window.

Two trains pulled in and the station was awash with passengers and noise and steam. Missy! he shouted. Missy wait! But his voice was swallowed by the constant din of chatter and the clatter of luggage and trolleys and the soot dust in the air. He stopped to catch his breath. She was nowhere to be seen. He took a punt and ran down the stairs towards the underground. He was quick at the ticket office, and staggered breathlessly towards the platforms. Eastbound or Westbound? He heard the familiar rumble of an underground train approaching. Come on! East or west, Drake? The noise of the train got louder. East or west! He began to run. East. She had to be going east.

The platform was packed. It was difficult to move through the crowd without drawing comments and looks. He couldn't see her; she must have gone west. He leant against the wall and felt the first swoosh of air rush through the tunnel, before lights appeared and finally the train itself. He lost his hat in the tumult and was resigned to leaving it there amidst the jig of jostling legs but as he bent down to retrieve it, that's when he saw her. Getting up from a bench without a care in the world, looking into a compact mirror, adding more red to already perfect red lips. He felt restored and he began to laugh. She looked so bloody good.

Bodies entered close. She took the left-hand door, he was swept towards the right. A man offered her a seat and a cigarette at one end of the carriage – she accepted both – and she placed her small valise on her knees. Drake stood at the other end of the carriage watching. It felt wrong and delightful. The brim of his hat pulled low. Peering out through the years, a latent buzz pressing against the front of his trousers.

He could remember it so clearly, the day he had first set eyes on her. He was eleven, and it was after his mum had died when he was living with the aunts. She had burst into his room without knocking, all sixteen years of cheek and beauty, and she had said, I'm Missy Hall and I'm your third cousin. Don't worry, we can still marry, and she laughed a deep laugh, and took a pack of cigarettes out of her school blazer. She went over to the window and opened it wide. She lit up and exhaled a stream of smoke. Said, Stick with me, Francis. I'm an orphan too.

He hated that word. Wasn't ready for that word.

She said, One more year of school then the world's my fuckinoyster. By the way, Francis is a girl's name, you know that, don't you? I'm going to call you Freddy, if that's OK? And it was OK and that was that. And when the aunts' backs were suitably turned, she marched him down to the River Thames where she shed her clothes effortlessly under the grateful eye of Tower Bridge.

Come on in! Missy had cried, as she ran splashing into the water. Freddy would have given anything to have followed her in, anything to have been braver, to have been older, but he kept his clothes on instead, and anchored his toes ever deeper into the safe damp shingled shore. He watched pale scrawny bodies run and jump into waves as steam tugs passed. He thought it looked like fun.

Whassa matter, Freddy? Can't ya swim? said Missy stumbling towards him.

No. Not really.

Want me to teach you?

Nah thank you, and he bent down and handed her a towel.

He watched the costume dry upon her and noticed her body brought to life by the occasional breeze that blew across her skin and made her gasp. He watched her reach for her packet of Players cigarettes. He beat her to the matches and, in his cupped hands, he gave her light. In the brightness of her smile, it could have been *life*.

An exodus at King's Cross Station forced Drake to make a quick decision: stay and be seen or move to an adjoining carriage. He moved and watched her through a jammed window. Watched her cross her legs. Pat her hair. Pull at the hem of her perfect tweed skirt.

It had been a dare. About a year later, Missy had called him to her room, and when he got there she was lying on her bed in a shaft of yellow lamplight. Blouse undone and breasts exposed, a single coin was balanced on the left nipple.

Take it in your mouth, she had said. Take it in your mouth and it's yours, Freddy.

He was nervous. It felt wrong and a bit mucky and he was scared at first, but he knelt by her bed and lowered his head and

52

opened his mouth and kissed the warm line of her skin. The coin came away easily but she held his head down until his tongue flickered over the coin, until flesh and metal and warmth were one. They stopped as the aunts' footsteps neared. Breathed out as the aunts' voices passed. And only afterwards in the dark did the dare give way to a simple need.

This is the size of your heart, Missy had said, tracing the area of his palm with her index finger. Love just enough, Freddy.

What's enough?

Enough to hold. When it hurts, you're loving too much. Just enough to hold. Anything more than a handful and you're in trouble. Got it? Are you listening or are you asleep?

I'm listening.

What did I say, then?

You told me to never let go.

He heard her laugh. That'll do, she said.

He gave her the coin. Can we do it again? he said.

Say please, she said.

Please, he said.

He lingered at her breast, and when he raised his head, the sixpence gripped between his teeth, he dared as he had never done before and his mouth dropped the coin and his mouth found hers and tasted, for the first time, what he believed to be the life that existed outside of those solemn walls, outside of himself and he loved her and that was everything.

She kissed him back – passionately, to start with – he felt her tongue exploring his mouth and the sensation felt fine, the sensation pulsed between his legs until she suddenly shuddered and pushed him to the floor. She stared at him, shocked. It wasn't the taste of promise that coated his mouth, but that of first milk. That's how she knew for sure and that's why she left.

That cold morning in March when life all around was beginning, his was ending. A piece of paper hurriedly slipped under his door, the drawn outline of her hand in the middle. *Not too much, Freddy,* she wrote. But it was already too much. *Never forget me.* Never. Never. Never.

Liverpool Street. Drake stared at the station sign but nothing registered. Only when the doors were about to close did he notice that Missy had gone. He lunged with his suitcase at the narrowing doorway and forced the doors back once again. He caught sight of her not too far ahead. The platinum hair bobbing upon a lake of black and grey. He straightened his hat, took deep steadying breaths and walked a safe distance behind her.

Missy veered right across the concourse, heading towards the Bishopsgate stairway. When she reached the top, just out of view, Drake ran up two steps at a time into the dusk and caught her as she was about to cross the road. She slowed at the police station and seemed to change her mind and she headed up Brushfield Street and the fruit market. But then she stopped. He turned away, bent down to tie his shoe. She took off again and he followed her to Commercial Street, saw her wave to a woman at the Ten Bells. She looked as if she was about to cross the road but hesitated and stopped again as if she had forgotten something. With each street the years peeled away. She turned left quickly, almost a run now. Doubled back down Folgate Street, back down . . . Jesus, thought Drake. She can't be. But she was. When he got to the turning, the street was empty except for her.

She was standing in the middle of the road, looking at a house. It was at a tilt, it seemed, leaning on the ruin next door, wounded but still standing, it was, and that's what she liked to call it when she was a bit drunk and a bit sad: Still Standing. It was a gas leak, and not a bomb that had almost taken out what Hitler couldn't. Careless whispers cost lives, careless cigarettes just as many, thought Missy, lighting up. She picked up a stone and threw it at a boarded-up window. She didn't know why she hated the house so much, it had been a home of sorts. But it had made her feel useless and dirty when all she had ever been was young.

The footsteps behind sounded loud and sinister against her thoughts. She didn't turn. Just pulled her shoulders back, stood taller and said, What do you want? I know you're following me. I could of gone to the police, but I'm not that type, never been that type. But I've got a knife in my pocket and –

Missy, said Drake quietly.

– I'll bloody use it.

He called her name again. And he walked out of the shadow of childhood and into her light, and she said, Freddy?

And he could say nothing because his heart was in his mouth.

8

THEY SAT AT A TABLE IN THE CORNER OF A PUB AS NIGHT grew through the window behind them. The sounds around were generous and soothing. Men chattered, glasses clinked, jokes coasted and a fire crackled, and now and then someone let out an almighty laugh and it was catching and circled the room like a kid playing tag. And they were grateful for distractions like that because really they didn't know what to say. They looked tired and they looked worn but neither of them would mention that because their joy was so loyal. And they held on tight to that beautiful silent moment before words transported them to the realm of the ordinary, to the realm of the inarticulate and mundane.

I just can't believe it, she said. You're here.

Freddy grinned. He lifted his glass and savoured the first

taste of a pint of Truman's. God, that's good, he said, and wiped his upper lip.

You saw the world, Freddy!

I saw the world.

And not a scratch on you.

He smiled, kept his shaking hand under the table.

When d'you get back? she said.

Yesterday.

Yesterday? Blimey. What took you so long?

Dunno.

Most got back last year. Some before that.

Yeah, I know. Didn't know what there was for me to come back to.

Not even me?

I thought you were dead, he said.

What? Why?

Because of the Café de Paris. When I heard it had taken a hit, I thought about you. Thought I'd lost you.

Missy went quiet.

That's where you told me to find you, said Freddy.

Did I?

Don't you remember?

Long time ago, Freddy.

I know.

Lifetime.

Yeah. Freddy drank his beer.

I bet you fell in love, really. I bet that's why you never came back, said Missy.

Freddy smiled. Nah.

Don't believe you.

Wouldn't be here if I fell in love, would I?

57

Things end.

Not with me, he said, and looked into her eyes. I never met no one, Missy. No one who counted.

That's a pity. Would of done you the world of good.

You reckon?

I know you.

And he smiled because she did know him and it felt good all of a sudden to be known by someone, cared for by someone, and he felt warm and expansive, and loosened his tie and rolled up his cuffs. He reached over and lightly touched Missy's cheek.

You look good, he said.

Me? You're bloody daft.

You never seem to change.

Is that a fact?

When I saw you at Paddington, I thought, Cor she looks all right.

Cor she looks all right? What are you? Twelve again?

Freddy laughed. You did, though. Where were you coming from?

Oxford.

How come?

I was visiting someone.

Someone who? said Freddy.

Not what you think.

What am I thinking? said Freddy, grinning.

Look, three days a week I work in an office on Fleet street. Nice. Rest of the time I do a bit of modelling.

Magazines?

She laughed. Said: Ten years too late for that! No. I sit for an old bloke who likes to paint me. Pays good money too. Don't look at me like that, Freddy, I know that look. You're making it mucky and it's not. I'm a life model and that's respectable. And he's respectful. He's never touched me, just looks at me. Only once did he ask me to pull down the straps from my slip or bra.

Did you?

Yeah.

And?

And nothing. I sit in me nightgown mainly, in front of an electric fire, next to an old tabby cat, and he drapes things round my shoulders.

Freddy smiled. Like what?

Scarves mainly. A fur stole, once. Anything. And when I look at the painting, the room I'm sitting in has gone. The fire's gone, the bookcase. All gone. He's painted a completely different world. The painting he's doing at the moment is of a farm but it's not a farm here, it's somewhere far away. Big horizon and strange trees and a red earth all around, and a sun so bright it hurts to look at it. In the distance, the bluest sea. He calls it an *ocean*, though. And I can smell that sea. That's the power of what he's painted. And d'you know what? I really like who I am in the picture. What he's captured. He's put a scarf round my head and I've no make-up on and I'm looking out towards something, but he hasn't painted that something. Can you imagine it, Freddy? It's fascinating. And as he watches me, I watch him now. I watch the world he enters, the world he never really wants to come back from. Art: it's about some kind of order, I reckon.

Order?

Yeah. Or reorder perhaps. He's bringing rightness back to his life. The life he thinks he should've led. It's just like dreaming, really, but with paint. He doesn't think he's Picasso,

59

he's just lonely. I reckon I would've made a good painter, Freddy.

Missy finished her half. Another? she said. My shout, she said, and she wiggled free from the table and surfed across a sea of eyes towards the bar.

Freddy was aware of men watching her because he always had. But that evening he noticed the blokes looking his way, too, checking him out, seeing who she was with. He turned round to smile at her, just so they could see him. He knew he was being an arse but he couldn't stop himself, he felt a little too good and that was rare. He pulled the table out for her as she slipped back in to the bench. He lit a cigarette and grinned at her.

French cigarettes, said Missy, winking at him. Bit sophis for a place like this.

Want one? said Freddy.

Why not?

And he offered her his lighter. She held his hand to stop him shaking.

Builders hands, she said.

I was apprenticed after school. Carpentry mainly.

Well, you'll never starve. People always need a table.

Is that a fact? And he laughed.

So tell me, said Missy, awkwardly. What happened to the sisters? Where'd you all go?

Northumbria. Moved there three years before the war. They took a cottage and some land.

Missy said, So that's it? That's the end of the story?

'Fraid so.

Nothing better than that?

No. It ends in a field.

No, *we* end in a field, Freddy, they were our story. *We* end in a bleedin' field! And they drank their beers and laughed.

I'm glad you're back, and he said, Me too. And there was a flash of the old Missy when she stood up and wrote on the foggy windowpane behind: 'FReddY home 1/11/47'. Now it's official, she said. She turned to face him and as she did, a face from the past appeared over his shoulder, standing in the doorway. *Jeanie?* It was instinctive, her desire to move towards her friend, but they weren't friends no more, were they? Jeanie hurried on through to the lavatory out the back. Was that the new secret code? Shit or leave?

You all right? said Freddy.

Better than all right, said Missy brusquely.

Look like you've seen a ghost.

They're all around, Freddy, and she gathered her things quickly, quietly cursing her choice of pub. When they left, beads of condensation rolled down the windowpane.

9

THEY GOT TO MISSY'S LODGINGS BEFORE THE RAIN hammered down and the first of the thunder roared through the streets. Missy took his hand and quietly led him up the narrow staircase to the second floor, without Miss Cudgeon catching them and causing such a fuss like she had the week before.

What happened the week before? asked Freddy as casually as he could. But Missy didn't answer him; she said, I'll just tell her you're my brother. The word irritated him.

She opened the door and motioned for him to be quiet and to take off his shoes. She placed them on an old *Radio Times*. She took his coat and hung it on the back of the door.

Make yourself at home, Missy whispered.

There was a single bed or a chair so he sat down on the chair. She went to the stove in the alcove by the window and lit a gas ring. Warmth came surprisingly fast. She rinsed her hands and filled the kettle from the sink. She unclipped her earrings and danced around him with ease. She was familiar with this scenario, with a man in her room. Her hips were practised. He felt a spasm of jealousy even after all these years.

Swap places now, she said, and she squeezed past him to get to the wardrobe.

She told him to turn round while she changed, so he turned round and took in her life. A framed photograph of Clark Gable had pride of place opposite the steel-frame bed – she obviously liked waking up to a leading man. And over by the window hung a birdcage inhabited by silence rather than song. There was a small bookshelf, too, that held shoes not books and a Philips utility radio and that week's edition of *Melody Maker*. A large bottle of perfume sat on the bedside table together with an ashtray and a reading lamp. Under the table a hot-water bottle and a thick pair of socks and an opened can of Bartlett pears. Practicalities hidden away. This was a life that had never known a husband. A life that had never known children.

Talk to me Freddy. It's weird you just sitting there after all this time.

I don't feel weird.

Well, I do.

What's the bird called? he asked, gently putting his finger through the bars.

Buddy, said Missy.

Hey, Buddy, said Freddy, and he clicked his tongue.

He doesn't sing, said Missy.

How come?

Dunno. Just stopped one day. Never told me why.

Freddy looked at the cowering bird, huddled against its

63

mirror. The cage was a fancy cage, more for a cockatoo or a parrot rather than a linnet. Its crimson and brown feathers looked ragged and dull next to the yellow plastic model of a perfect canary.

Well, the other one doesn't say much. What d'you expect? said Freddy.

Missy came into vision wearing a simple green house dress, and the kettle began to whistle. You're bloody daft, she said, ruffling his hair. He leant down and dragged his suitcase beside him. He flipped the catch and took out a bottle of brandy.

I was saving it, he said.

For what?

For a good day.

Then let's make it an even better day, she said, and she took the kettle off the stove and handed him a bone-handled corkscrew. You look happy, she said, as she took two cups from the hooks and placed them on the side table positioned between the bed and the armchair. He uncorked the brandy and poured.

To us, she said.

He thought those two words tasted beautiful.

Missy pulled the curtains on the world outside. In the harsh glare of a bulb, next to the semi-decent hang of her dress, the curtains looked tired and ragged. Everything was coated with the dust of better days, herself included. She looked over at Freddy dozing on her bed.

She had asked him what he wanted for his supper. Surprise me, he had said. She had gone to the stove and from the cupboard underneath pulled out a real egg and she had held it up to him and said, Remember when these were like gold dust? And they'd both laughed because there was just too much to say and where do you start? Those war-drawn days, those nights, when she ran around doing a little bit of this, a little bit of that and plenty of the other. She felt a deep stab of shame. It was seeing Jeanie again that had done it. It always affected her and she placed her hand across her stomach. The feeling never really went away, did it? because it lived in the dark and was uncovered by the glare of light. And him over there on the bed, dozing like a child, he was light. Missy stopped preparing supper. She sat down and poured herself a large glass of brandy instead.

She couldn't remember who had mentioned the bomb shelter first, her or Jeanie, but they had both been as bad as each other, goading each other on like a couple of kids. But the place was already notorious by the time they got to set foot in it, and then they couldn't quite let it go. It was their ritual and none of their other friends knew. They kept it to themselves, like the knowledge of an infection you get down there.

The first weeks after the shelter had opened, it was chaotic and disorderly and thousands had queued outside the Exchange even before the sirens had gone off. Her and Jeanie held hands and used to walk in silence through the front doors. Other people chatted, some goofed around, families kept up the front of normality. But her and Jeanie, they didn't talk because they knew where they were going to. Down the stairs they tottered, all made up they were, spiralling down into the dark basement where miasmic smells of old fruit and veg mingled with every type of human smell.

Families and oldies used to stay in the bounds of torchlight where songs and storytelling jollied people along. Others ventured towards black holes that governed themselves, where cards and money were lit but faces weren't. That's where her and Jeanie used to go. Shuffling steps towards an unsecured darkness. Towards a rare freedom. Towards the compulsive thrill of ever-ready touch.

They always knew when they had reached the area because they could smell the strong scent of perfume and cologne and cum. Missy was all nerves and weak knees. She had to empty herself before she came out because she couldn't trust herself, not there where anything could happen.

She could never tell if Jeanie was near her because nobody spoke. But you could feel breath and sense movement behind, in front, on either side of you. Nobody lit matches or flicked lighters or switched on torches. Darkness reigned. Anonymity was respected. It was everyone's dirty little secret and no one wanted to give it up.

She could always tell the men who had been there before. Always started with hands on hips and arse then quick up to the breasts. Jumpers were lifted high, and mouths found mouths. Mostly people tasted of booze but once towards the end, she tasted onions on a man's breath and it was strangely lovely because she hadn't had an onion in a while, and she had kept his mouth still and breathed in that sour, queer delight. She'd learnt not to wear knickers in the shelter, just stockings and a belt, it was easier that way. Clothes to lift up, unbutton or pull aside, nothing to be left behind on the floor. It never took long for a skirt to be raised or for a hand to reach between her legs, strange fingers soon inside her and it was a mix of shame and excitement, fear and disgust, and it was a fluid feeling that made her legs give way just as she was lifted up on to a stranger's cock that ate at her with a desire fuelled by the constant nearness of death. She had bitten hard on suit jackets and greatcoats and tunics and had made no sound, and when it was done, when he was gone, she used to clean herself up with a perfumed handkerchief and wonder who the man had been. Not wonder if he was a soldier or anything like that, because most were – they headed straight there on leave. But wonder whether he was handsome or plain or ugly. Or whether he was a man she would never have looked at in daylight. A man who might have revolted her, in fact. In the privacy of her mind, she liked to think that he was.

And her and Jeanie weren't friends no more. How could they be? They hadn't expected to survive and come face to face with the other's knowing. Fuck, she missed her. But Jeanie was respectable now. She was married to a policeman and had a kid. So her and Missy crossed the road if ever they saw each other. Or they left pubs, or raced to the lavatory. Better that way. Shame's shame no matter what perfume you spray on it.

Freddy stirred. Missy stubbed out her cigarette and got up. She felt weary. She opened a tin of Spam and began to cut it into thick perfect squares.

10

FREDDY RECOGNISED THE SOUND OF AN EGG BEING BEATEN, a can being opened, a brandy poured. He listened with eyes closed to the sounds of the kitchen because they were comfortable sounds, sounds of home and companionship. When eventually he opened his eyes, he was careful not to shift or disturb Missy's solitude. He watched her lost in thought, drinking. Watched her chop the Spam and spoon breadcrumbs into a bowl. He watched her go to his suitcase and carefully lift out shirts and a pair of trousers, a razor and soap. He watched her unfold a piece of paper, watched her place her hand against the faint outline of her hand, hurriedly traced on a March morning a lifetime ago.

You all right? he said, sleepily.

Missy started. I was looking for some matches –

– they're at the bottom –

– and then I got distracted, she said.

It's all right, he said.

Nosy, actually –

– there's really nothing you can't see.

And she looked back down at the paper before refolding it.

I always wanted to ask, said Freddy. Where'd you go?

When? said Missy.

When you left me, he said, nodding towards her hand. I was just a kid.

Me too, said Missy and she put the folded square back into the suitcase. She said, I went to a place I wasn't known. A place I'd never go back to.

And then?

And then I came back. Lived south and got a job at a press-cuttings agency in Fleet Street not far from where I work now. Nice job, too, it was. Made a good friend there, a woman called Jeanie, and she got me to move back east with her. That's it, really. By the time I did, you'd all gone.

The matches are at the bottom, Missy, said Freddy.

Oh yeah, ta. She dug deep and found them hidden under a fold of amber lining. Found the grubby, creased envelope addressed to Dr James Arnold, too.

Monk's Rise, Chapel Street, Truro, Cornwall, she read. Imagine living in a place called Monk's Rise. Sounds nice, doesn't it? What you got this for?

I promised to deliver it. That's why I was at the station when I first saw you. To get a ticket.

To go to Cornwall?

That's right. Freddy adjusted the pillows and sat up.

Who's it from?

The man's son.

Is he dead?

Yes.

Was he your friend?

No. I'd just met him.

And he just handed you this letter?

Sort of. He was dying and we got chatting, that's all. I think he knew he was dying. Wanted to make sure the letter got to his old man. So he asked me.

To post it?

No, to *deliver* it.

What's in it?

I don't know.

Aren't you tempted?

It's private.

You should do it soon, you know, said Missy.

I know, he said. I was going tomorrow.

That would be the right thing.

Or the next day. Monday, I reckon. Monday'll be the day I go, he said, and he rolled his legs off the bed and ran his fingers through his hair.

What's this? asked Missy.

Freddy stopped.

It was a picture she held up. A composite. A collage of lips, eyes, nose, beard and hair, all cut out from various magazines, stuck together piece by piece to form a man's face.

Careful with it, Missy.

Who is it?

No one really. But it means a lot.

Looks a bit like you.

Now you're being daft.

Missy studied the picture. Actually, it looks like a Wanted

Poster, like in those cowboy films. Stick 'em up, mister!

He raised his arms but felt uncomfortable by her laughter. It's just a silly picture, he said, smiling. A kid made it for me a long time ago. It's like a lucky charm, goes everywhere with me. Always has. Put it back, Missy, please.

I never knew you were so superstitious.

Yeah, well.

Who was the kid? asked Missy.

Doesn't matter. The kid's long gone.

Sorry, she said, and she handed him the picture.

He folded it up and put it carefully back in his suitcase. When he turned round her lips were on his.

I'm sorry, Freddy.

He leant in to the kiss, but as soon as it had started she pulled away as if the impulse was already forgotten.

They ate in candlelight. The dingy room was transformed by soft flickering light and they, too, were transformed by the semi-darkness. They sat at a table surrounded by shadows and ate Spam in breadcrumbs, served with boiled spuds and tinned peas, nothing fancy. But Freddy said, What a feast, and not even a pea was left on his plate. I could eat it all over again, he said, and he kissed her hand and she didn't pull away because the gesture was sweet and boyish.

Freddy cleared the table and washed the dishes in the tiny sink. Missy turned the radio down low. Dance with me, was what she said. I'm no good at dancing, he said. We'll rock from side to side, everyone knows how to rock, even you. And she lifted his hands out of the suds and he left traces of bubbles on her waist. And they rocked. From side to side. To a song about memories, those foolish things. And Missy hummed and Billie Holiday sang.

Never forgot you, Freddy.

Never forgot you, Missy.

And they rocked from side to side, eyelids closing at the familiar comfort and smell of one another. A sudden knock at the door made them freeze. Missy placed a finger on Freddy's lips.

You got someone in there again Miss Hall?

No one, Miss Cudgeon, just me dancing with a few memories. You know how it is. And Miss Cudgeon did know how it was, because some nights her memories were loud as well, and that's when she drank – why she drank – just to quieten and steady them a bit too.

11

THE EXPLOSION WENT OFF JUST BEFORE MIDNIGHT. FREDDY
awoke with a start and slammed his elbow hard against the lino
floor, quietly cursing as his heart pounded. For a brief moment,
he could have been anywhere – the disorientation was so severe
– on any floor in any room in any city; he'd slept on a few. He
sat up and rubbed his eyes. The sound of rockets echoed outside.
He reached for a packet of cigarettes, searched his trouser
pockets for a lighter and came up with a handful of coppers. He
stood up and went towards the stove. Matches were on the
window-ledge. He looked through the nets as the flutter of
cascading blue and green lights fell against Christ Church spire.
The cigarette felt good. He noticed his hand was shaking again.
He picked up a newspaper and scanned the date. Ten days
before Remembrance Day. He startled as another rocket tore
open the sky.

Don't worry, Buddy, he said to the bird. Be over in a minute, and he pulled the tea towel over the cage.

He stood by the bed and watched the rise and fall of Missy's breasts, the soft sound of her sleeping. She was lying on her back with both arms tucked under her head. He studied her face. Deep furrows tracked across her brow and he could have followed each one to the land of What Might Have Been. And he knew she knew it. Her self-consciousness was rasping. The way she moved her hair now, how her hand paused by her forehead when she frowned. She had a face that was born knowing. As if she had always known the story of her life and there would be few surprises. Beautiful still, and ever would be, but things had passed by now, and those lustrous dreams of youth had tarnished under a familiar low sky. He wondered if she really knew the end of her story. That there was no prince, just a damaged soldier with a hole instead of a heart. But I'll take care of you, if you'll let me, the soldier whispered.

Missy rolled over and stretched.

You all right? she said.

Yeah, I couldn't sleep, that's all. I think I might go out, he said, putting on his trousers and buttoning up.

Out where? she said.

Out there, he said, and he ground out the cigarette in the ashtray. Someone's setting off fireworks. Kids, probably. Just need some air.

I'll come with you, she said.

He crouched down by the electric fire and looked for his shoes. He noticed her pyjamas were now in a pile on the floor, and he caught her nakedness in the shine of the metal surround. He watched her pull on dark blue slacks and the grey cable-knit sweater that he'd left draped on her bed-frame.

74

Missy coughed. Freddy stood up and buttoned his shirt.

You can stop looking now, she said, smiling, as she began to line her lips with red. You're blushing Freddy Drake. Yeah you are. Come on, let's go. Bring the rest of that bottle and don't make a noise.

She picked up her coat and torch and headed towards the door. Freddy took a slug of brandy before following her into the dark. He felt done in. Head and heart together.

A mizzle of rain played in the November sky. They sat on the roof, huddled and daunted like kids on the run, the bottle of brandy passing from mouth to mouth, taking his words to her lips, his warmth to her cool. Roof tops and chimneys strung out ahead, irregular and familiar to the east, an occasional break where the wind gathered and swirled with the restless ghosts of a family cut short. A rocket shot into the air and exploded. White stars falling.

People are trying to fucking sleep down 'ere! A lone voice echoed across the brickwork. Freddy buttoned up his coat, anything to mask the pounding in his chest. Missy leant into him and she smelt good.

I used to come up here during the war. I'd only say it to you, Freddy, but it was beautiful. Isn't that crazy? The fires all along there, like a burning sunrise, over there out by the docks, and you could smell 'em, too. Wind in the right direction you could smell burning sugar, even cheese once. Planes overhead dodging crisscross lights, guns pounding, I tell you, Freddy, it was the movies and Christmas all in one. Once I sat up here with my friend Jeanie and it was a test of faith, well that's what she said, us blind drunk on knocked-off spirits, out of our wits really, but alive. So bloody alive. And I felt lucky. Like everything I'd ever dreamt of was within reach. That I was being saved for something. The all-clear would sound, and I'd never felt such a thrill. And nothing touched me. Not really. Jeanie used to say I was a cat with nine lives.

Got any left? asked Freddy.

Dunno, said Missy. Be nice to think there was a couple left, and she grinned, and he looked at her and he was that twelve-year-old kid again – confused and eager with jump leads stretching from his balls to his heart.

I was there, you know, that night, said Missy, softly.

What night? What you talking about?

At the Café de Paris. The night it happened.

Jesus, Missy.

I was dancing. Well away from the band, strangely enough for me, and the band was playing *Oh, Johnny! Oh, Johnny! How you can love! Oh, Johnny! Oh, Johnny! Heavens above!* And then it went silent. Everything slowed down, d'you know what I mean? Just smiling faces and this sort of blurred movment and the sweetest silence. And then a blue flash. That's what I remember. Beautiful blue. And then I woke on the floor with a body on top of me and saw sheet music fluttering down like snow, and fragments of glass like stars. And then the screaming began. Parts of bodies and limbs everywhere. A woman wandering about, dazed and still singing "Oh, Johnny! Oh, Johnny!" All I got was a cut to my head. I did my best to help. My dress was already ripped so I ripped it some more and made tourniquets. And I cleaned people's wounds with champagne. I often wondered what they must of thought, lying there dying, listening to the sound of champagne corks popping. It wasn't right really, was it? Not that. I never cried, Freddy. Still haven't. Jeanie reckoned I was a hard cow, but the way I see it you can't cry for everyone and I'd done my crying before the war. Punctured me ear drum, that's all. So I'm a bit deaf. Won't be such a surprise when I'm old, eh?

Come here, said Freddy and he went to put his arms around her.

No. I don't need that, I'm all right, and she pulled away from him. You'll have to get used to this. This is what you've come back to. Everyone here has a story and that's just one of mine.

A rocket screeched into the cold air.

Oh, look! Let's hope this one's blue. I still love the blue ones! The rocket exploded and flared. Cascades of red and green.

I wanted it to be blue.

Maybe next one, he said. But there wasn't a next one. Stragglers below wandered off and calm fell across the London sky.

It did us all in, really, didn't it? said Missy. We're all a bit different now, aren't we?

And he wanted to tell her just how different he was, and he wanted her to hold that difference and for her to tell him he wasn't so bad, and that's just what war did to people. But he lit a cigarette instead and handed it to her. She took a puff as the first of her tears fell on his hand.

Don't look at me, she said, and turned away. Please don't look at me.

Freddy did as he was asked, looked away towards Truman's chimney stack, and the roof tops, and curtained windows of bedrooms and bodies and warmth, and the stars, and the ever-obvious gaps more and more intrusive along the cityscape. This was his city once. He couldn't even remember what was there or what should have been there any more. A bit like his life, he thought.

They crept down to the strange quiet of her room with the sound of rockets still ringing in their ears. Missy bent down and switched on the fire. They sat opposite each other in the orange glow from the electric bars. The warmth made their cold faces flush. They were alone. Their bodies were alone. Freddy led her over to the bed and began to kiss her. She leant across and felt for the safety of the light switch. He took his trousers off in the dark. She began to touch him as if she were blind.

12

SUNDAY BELLS PEALED ACROSS THE CLEAR DAWN SKY. Missy awoke abruptly. Her head throbbed and her breath stank and a man's body was pressed much too close. She moved his arm away from her waist, his leg off her leg, mornings-after she just wanted space in her own bed, was it really too much to ask? She looked up at the ceiling and gently blew at the fine grey webs clustered in the corner.

She got up and crept towards the sink. She ran the tap and cupped her hand, ran the excess across her face. She bent down to the mirror and thought she looked a horror, the early light being so cruel. She pinned her hair hastily and roughly and tied a scarf about her head. She reached for her pack of Players and drew a cigarette towards her mouth. She struck a match and took two pulls on the cigarette: one for sorrow two for joy. Better, she felt. The tightness in her head was easing.

She drew back the curtains and squinted against the clear metallic light.

She ran water into the sink, lifted her foot on to the narrow porcelain edge and soaped between her legs, down her thighs. She rinsed with a flannel, dried off with her housedress.

Mornin', sweetie, she whispered, as she lifted the tea towel away from Buddy's cage. She poked a stale piece of honey bun into the cage. The bird stared at her. What is it? she said. What am I missing, eh?

She ground out her cigarette on to the stubs of a dozen others and looked out over the eastern sky. She filled the window with her nakedness and it was an unconscious act, one that spoke softly, said, This is who I am, not This is what you're missing. She watched the tide of life below. People doing their very best, trying so hard to make it better. And she took to wondering, like so many often did, what it had all been for. The triumph of two years ago hadn't gained access to wallets or purses or homes. People were poor and the city was crumbling. She lifted the window and a blast of chill air blew in. The birdcage swayed. She shuddered. She wedged her thighs under the sill and leant out as far as she could, arms out wide. A couple of lads laughed and shouted and pointed at her but she didn't hear. She felt the breeze stir her hair, felt it in the musk of her pits. She closed her eyes and felt as if she was moving above it all, away from it all.

She pulled herself back inside and rubbed vigorously over her arms and legs until warmth flowed through her blue and green veins. She unclasped the birdcage door and opened it wide. Go on, Buddy, she whispered. Off you go now. Go on, be happy.

The bird was unsure, cautious. It didn't budge.

Go on. Missy blew lightly on the linnet's feathers. Fly.

She almost missed it. A sudden flash of ruddy feathers fluttered against the cloudless azure sky and then he was gone. She closed the cage and replaced the linen coverlet. She crept back to the warmth of the bed and gently lifted the covers. She noticed Freddy's erection and moved away from him but he followed her. She felt him hard against her thigh but she kept her legs together. He whispered her name but she pretended to be asleep. Not that last night had been a mistake, but she wouldn't let it happen again. It had felt awkward, truth be told, and now all she wanted was to be alone. Freddy came quickly with a muffled groan, but she didn't move. She stared straight ahead at the coffee percolator and couldn't believe that she hadn't put it on because she could do with a coffee right now, that more than anything. Just a little something to help her on her way. That was what she was thinking whilst he was thinking of love.

Freddy sat up in bed and smoked. He watched Missy unpin and brush out her hair. Her fingers were deft and sure and she didn't even need a mirror twisting ends into a curl. He'd be all thumbs, but he'd like to try it, he thought. Do something for her that no other man had done. He lifted the ashtray and tapped the cigarette free of ash. He couldn't believe she was dressed already. As if she'd had the morning without him and he felt jealous of that space and time. Navy slacks and a Fair Isle jumper. They suited her and brought out the red of her lips but it was quite a homely look for her, he thought, maybe that was what she wore on Sundays. God, there was so much to learn. She looked into the mirror and caught his eye. He smiled, and she did too after a beat. Why didn't she smile straight away?

Why wasn't she next to him when he woke up? All he wanted to know was whether he'd been all right last night. You know, as good as the others?

What do you want to do today? said Missy.

Whatever you want, he said.

And Missy went quiet thinking about what she wanted because what she wanted was to be alone. She wanted to go downstairs to Miss Cudgeon's and have a bath, and come back up and lie in her bed and read a magazine. But she didn't know how to ask for that, so she said, We could go for a walk.

Is that what you normally do?

I don't have a normal, Freddy. Walk's as good as anything right now.

What was he missing? Long time since he'd been in this situation. We could stay here, he said, and he patted the bed.

No, she said. We're going out. Come on, she said, we're missing the day. And her words were set in a fog of hairspray.

It was clear that the mood of the night before had evaporated at sunrise. He slid from the bed in embarrassed silence, turned away to pull on his underpants. When he was dressed he began to straighten the bed but Missy stopped him, said she wanted to change the sheets; that's how he knew he wouldn't be sleeping with her that night. He repacked his suitcase and closed the lid. He watched her pick up the empty brandy bottle and place it in the bin. He saw her shake her head as if it was the booze that had lowered her standards. He tied his tie badly and pulled on his raincoat. He picked up his suitcase and said, I'll take this with me. Head over to Paddington later on for an early start tomorrow, and he half-hoped she would have said, Leave it, Freddy. I'm sorry, don't know what's up with me right now, 'course you can stay tonight. But she didn't. She said nothing, in fact, just waited for him by the door, immaculate and perfumed. Let's not go out, he whispered. She kissed him on the cheek and placed his hat on his head. Out, she said. He felt like a schoolboy.

He wanted to dawdle but she marched ahead through the competing shouts and crowds gathered to buy birds and animals along Club Row. Cages were piled one on top of the other window-high against the shops. Linnets and canaries, parrots and finches, dogs, kittens, all life it seemed, for sale. Look at this! Freddy would shout. But Missy wasn't near, and he had to run after her and relay what he had seen.

She held on to Freddy's arm as people pressed close. She felt dizzy and trapped. She tried to lead him away from the throng, looking for clear water and a chance to breathe. Blisters had begun to bubble at her heels and she felt calmer when they finally burst and bled.

From Shoreditch High Street they took a number 6 bus and they climbed the stairs and rode on top. He thought they were going to Trafalgar Square, but when the clippie shouted, St Paul's! Next stop St Paul's Cathedral! Missy said, Come on! and they jumped off into the thunderous peal of cathedral bells. The air was smoky and a faint chill tugged at the edge of the City. Freddy frowned as brittle sunlight reflected off a motor car and fell across his sight.

This way, Missy said, and she took off in the direction of salt and mud. Across roads they marched, across bomb sites towards the familiar wharfs and warehouses, towards the river. Silent they were, and shy, their come-and-go shadows stretching dark behind them, elongated fingertips trying desperately to touch.

And that old dog of a river saw them come and he closed his watery eyes and tried to turn back time but tide said no. And

Old Thames, he must've known something but he didn't say something. He just kept rolling, oh he just kept rolling along.

Freddy climbed down the stairs on to the muddied foreshore. He felt uneasy. Clouds from the south began to encroach on the afternoon sun. Missy held up the hem of her coat and carefully left the slippery stairs for the damp riverbed. Her small heels disappeared immediately into the mud. The bells stopped and the air rippled with silence. It was eerily deserted. Only the sporadic rumble as a train rode the Blackfriars tracks.

They stayed in the cool shadow of the warehouse wall. Nubs from barge-beds rose from the shore like rotten teeth and a close-by barge stayed sunk in the ooze. They watched funnels and chimneys spew dark filth into the sky. A chain swayed overhead. Freddy put down his suitcase and lit two cigarettes. He drew heavily on the first and offered her the second. She took it without looking at him. He asked her if she could smell the salt from the river and she said she could, and she said, Let's close our eyes and pretend we're by the sea, and the sun came out from behind a cloud and they closed their eyes and felt the warmth spread across their faces, and they pretended they were by the sea.

Freddy loosened his tie. Come away with me, Missy. Come with me tomorrow.

I'm working.

Where?

Missy didn't answer. Freddy began to laugh.

For Picasso? Hardly wor—

Fuck you, Freddy! and she moved away from the wall down to the water's edge where a shimmering line of muck and rubbish had collected. The wavelets were weak and lapped against a small lugger, moored close to shore.

Years ago, said Missy, my old nan told me a story about a mermaid. Said her mum saw a mermaid in there. Well, that's what they called her then. Maybe she wasn't, not a real one, but who knows? My nan said she was real—

Missy—

No listen to me, Freddy, I'm talking.

There aren't any mermaids.

You gonna tell me there's no Father Christmas either?

There's no Father Christmas, said Freddy, and he reached for her but she pulled away.

My nan said her mother saw it when she was a kid, when she was out on the river with her dad. All the lightermen knew about her. She was a beauty. A real beauty in that river of shit and the smell didn't seem to bother her because she was beyond all that and that gave people hope, that did. And sometimes people went down to the river just to see her, and make a wish. Because if you saw her your life would change. That's what people said. Imagine that, eh? So they threw in whatever they had and mostly it wasn't money because they was poor. But she wasn't right, my nan said, not in here, and Missy tapped a finger to her temple. My nan said she was sad and her mum could see it in her eyes and she sang sad songs. Why do you think she was sad, eh, Freddy?

Freddy pulled her towards him, felt her arm against his arm, her body against his.

She'd seen too much, said Missy. Too much to be happy. That's what my nan said.

But he didn't care what her nan said, he cared what he said, and he said, We could go away. Anywhere you want, he whispered.

You're not listening.

85

It's a stupid story, Missy. And I'm trying to tell you something about us.

So am I.

Don't you get it?

Get what? said Missy.

Us. We fit. You felt it. I know you did.

You really don't understand, do you? said Missy, and she picked up a stone and threw it into the tide. I always wonder what happened to her, she said. She died probably. Bloody dirty in there, she said.

And what if she got away with a handsome sailor? Or soldier, eh? Someone like me.

No one gets away. Not really.

Maybe she did.

Not from this.

Let me take you away, he said, and he pressed his mouth against her mouth. I love you, he said.

Don't. That's not us.

Not what you said last night.

Last night was last night.

Wasn't it any good?

Grow up, Freddy.

Fuck you, he whispered quietly, and he walked back up the shore and crouched next to the moored barge. I could make you happy, he said.

She had to stop herself from laughing. She had heard those words time and time again. Never made sense, not now not then. Trapped, that was what she was. Trapped by her past and he was her past. Everything was suffocating. And she looked beyond the Blackfriars bridges and imagined running the riverbank all the way down to Hammersmith, and she imagined doing something different – really different – like running the Thames to its source in the Cotswolds, where the river water is fresh and clean and all salt washed out. To its beginning. Run, she urged herself. Run and don't look back.

Missy! Him shouting at her: Bang! The needle in her balloon.

She turned towards him and shaded her eyes.

This is supposed to be a good day, he said.

Then let's make it a good day, she said. Turn round.

You what?

I wanna play a game.

Freddy grinned. What kind of game?

Like hide-and-seek.

Kiss me first.

Turn round.

Kiss me.

She kissed him. She took his arm and led him back to the mossy wharf wall.

Don't turn round, she said.

What am I supposed to do? Count?

No, sing.

Not doing that, he said, picking at a wooden fender.

Yeah you will. That hymn you used to sing at the aunts'. Come on, I know you know it.

I don't sing, not since the war.

War's over didn't they tell you? Come on, I liked it when you sang that. It made me happy.

The sound of her shoes on the pebbles was loud.

And it's Sunday, she said. Never a better day for a hymn.

Jesus, Missy. Why can't we be normal? One day of bloody normal.

Because we aren't normal, Freddy. Come on, she said laughing, and she began to sing the hymn.

Forgive our foolish ways.

He heard her move away.

Where are you going?

Nowhere. I'm still here. Don't turn round. Come on, sing, Freddy.

Freddy faltered. Then Freddy sang.

Reclothe us in our rightful mind, In purer lives Thy service find.

Keep singing!

In deeper reverence, praise.

It takes me back, Freddy. Takes me back to that day when I first saw you. You were always so kind to me even then. You made them be good to me. They weren't always but you made them be.

What are you doing? he shouted.

It's a surprise. Just keep singing.

Beads of sweat glistened at his forehead. He wiped his hands on his trousers, began to feel dizzy, feel unwell. He noticed his hand had begun to shake again. He fucking hated the hymn, but he'd do anything for her.

Keep singing! she shouted.

So Freddy kept singing.

Take from our souls the strain and stress . . .

And Freddy noticed as he sang, that where the sound of a train should have been, where the sound of a river lapping at a shore should have been or where the sound of footsteps on pebbles should have been, was now just silence. A heavy impenetrable silence.

The beauty of Thy peace.

No, it wasn't the sound of silence pressing against his ears, but something different, something else. Something that made his guts stir, made them twist. What was it? Eh? What was it? He felt his heart lurch. Oh Jesus God no. He stumbled as he turned. It wasn't the sound of silence, but the sound of *absence*.

Oh fuck, Missy. No!

And Missy's head went under just as he reached the water's edge. And then there was nothing. And the sound came back and it was loud because it was him and he was screaming, but there was no one else around.

And overhead, a linnet flew free with a chest full of song.

13

MARVELLOUS AWOKE SUDDENLY. SHE COULDN'T BREATHE. Outside, the wind chimes were tinkling, the wind picking up. She fumbled with the matches, managed to light a candle. She slid from her bed and looked out. The sun was failing and clouds were racing; the light dark light of an angry whiplashed sky. She put on her oilskin and left the caravan. Strong smell of decomposing weed full on the nose, silage too from across the valley. She heard the *beat* of wood; saw the boathouse door flapping in the wind. She stood on the riverbank, her crabber jigging high on the spume. Something was beginning. A crow crowed from the opposite bank. The end was beginning.

III

III

14

DRAKE OPENED HIS EYES. DUSK OR DAWN, HE WASN'T SURE which, the birds were giddy. Leaves were pressed close to his face and he felt the crawl of damp and insects. He could smell sick, the faint whiff of faeces. He had a body that couldn't move, his breathing was shallow. He didn't know why he was crying and could only think that it was because he was still alive.

There was no strength in his arms. Wondered if his bones were broken, the ones in his legs, too. His throat sore, his arse sticky but he felt no shame. The temperature was dropping. He would feel warm soon – that's what happens with the deepest cold – he would feel warm and then there would be nothing and he would dissolve into mulch and maybe from his remains a tree would grow. A willow. Something good. The wind gathered and moved through the branches and it sounded like the sea. He drifted off with the rise and fall of waves.

He had come silently in the end. There were no starfish, no rumour, no birdcall, no footfall, his pain had made him invisible. But Marvellous had heard his trespass through the bare prongs of trees and had found him conversing with Death. She had held him and rocked him and had given him her breath. She had dragged him down to an elder bush to shelter him from the gathering wind, and so exhausted was she now that she could do little more than sit in her caravan and stare at the door, wondering about the fractured life that lay outside. She buttoned up her oilskin and pulled her hat down low. She took a swig of sloe gin and held a flame to the wick of a hurricane lamp. Her caravan flared with light.

Darkness now. So it had been dusk. Drake listened to the screech of an owl, relentless in its call. He called back but the effort made him cough again and he held his hand against his neck. It was the light he saw first. Saw the creature coming towards him with a lantern. Big eyes like an owl, and yellow feathers, that's what he saw: an owl in a hat. He thought he was laughing but felt as if he was dying.

Hello, Mrs Owl, he said weakly.

The old woman put down the lamp and helped him to sit up.

I've been waiting for you, she said quietly. Waiting a long time now.

Sorry, owl.

The owl went ahead with the lamp, she gave him her stick and it took his weight and led him through the woods, until the ground fell away to a river. The shallows flickered like a million stars and he had to shield his eyes because of a majesty he simply thought was bright. The owl put down her lamp on the mooring stone. Stand still, she said. She began to unbutton his shirt. Arms, she whispered. She dropped the shirt on to the ground. She unbuckled his belt, unbuttoned his fly and helped him to slip out of his trousers, out of his underpants. The smell of shit hit his nose. Owl didn't flinch. He kept his head down so she couldn't see his tears. His penis looked small and frightened and wormlike against his thigh. He cupped his hand around it, didn't want owl to see it.

Owl took off her yellow coat. She had long waders that came up to her breast. Clever owl, he thought. Come, she said, and took his hand and led him down into the sandy shallows. He shivered. He stopped as the water lapped his ankles. No more, he said. A bit further, she said. But he would go no further than his knees. He stood, shaking, terrified, one hand tight under his armpit, the other holding his shrunken balls.

Fear rose as bile and sick burned his throat as he retched and spat what he could into the river. His chin and chest glistened with pukefilth. Owl handed him a bar of soap. He took it without looking at her and wet it. He crouched down into the water and rubbed the soap hard between his hands and soon it lathered and the smell dug into him and he couldn't remember the name of the smell – it was violet – but it was too good for him, that he knew. He washed himself all over once, all over twice, rubbed that lather into his hair, into his mouth and spat. He rinsed the soap and handed it back to owl.

He crouched down up to his chest, and watched the soap scum float downstream. Come here, said owl. He waded carefully over to her and held on tightly to the grass bank. Lean forward, she said and he did. She cupped her hands and poured water over his head. Rinsed his hair. He took his hands away from the bank to cover his eyes.

The blanket felt rough but was warm upon his skin. Owl led the way, lantern aloft. He heard her wheezing. Old owl, he thought. They stumbled along the riverbank following the scent of wood smoke until a boathouse blocked their path. They climbed up and around it until the ground leant towards an open doorway lit by a second oil lamp.

In, said owl.

In the hearth a fire burned steadily, a cooking pot suspended over the flames. Firelight settled on his skin. There was a bed made up and on the bed there was a pile of clothes: heavy woollen trousers – like sailors' trousers – socks, linen shirt, jumpers smelling of salt and lanolin. A pair of leather boots, newly polished. Pyjamas. Underpants.

They belonged to a friend. Similar size, said owl, untying the ragged bandage that had held her hat in place. She placed the hat on a chair. He saw newspaper stuffed around the rim, and some of the print had come off on her forehead, words like *war*, *waste*, *peace*, *health*. He lay on the bed and drifted off.

The sound of cooking brought him back to the room and he watched her by the hearth ladling soup. She carried a bowl over to the bed.

Kiddley broth, she said. Eat, she said.

She helped him sit up, placed a pillow behind his back, said, There, that's better. She sat on the bed and spooned the liquid into his mouth and he ate quickly. Near the end he lifted the bowl by himself and drank the buttery, peppery dregs. He lowered the bowl and handed it to her. Rivulets of broth streamed from his chin down to his neck. She took a rag and wiped carefully around the bruising that was now encircling. He didn't look at her. She took the bowl and shuffled back over to the fire. She came back and handed him an earthenware mug.

Warm ale. She noticed the shake in his hand. She made one for herself, too, and they drank in silence.

He could taste the rum hiding at the bottom of the ale. His stomach settled, and there was a coating of sweat upon his skin. The old woman knew that was the fear coming out.

It's my job now to take care of you, she said. Don't do that again.

Do what? said Drake.

And the old owl stared at him. He couldn't see her eyes, her eyes were alight with the reflection of the fire. And she stopped to think because she wanted to choose her words carefully. It took a little while because her mind was leaky.

It's precious, she said. And it's all you have.

He couldn't look at her because he was ashamed, and he lay back down and turned away as the fire and the old woman kept good watch over him. She didn't take her eyes away from him, couldn't take her eyes away from him. She guarded him like a treasured egg.

15

FOR DAYS DRAKE DRIFTED IN AND OUT OF SLEEP, THE
change of light the only sense of time passing.

Sometimes he would wake and feel the old woman's hand
across his brow, sometimes he felt the spoon upon his lips and
he imagined himself a mouth, feeding, never talking, just a great
big mouth.

And sometimes he awoke to murmurs throughout the night.
Not the flight of birds or the language of insects, but words,
as prayers, racing across the landscape like waves longing to
break. The old woman said it was the chatter of saints rising
from the earth.

What do they talk about? he asked.

This and that, said the old woman. Mostly the weather.

And sometimes in the cracks of loneliness that appeared
between the old woman's coming and going, he gave into the

spasms that took hold of his legs, the icy fear that gripped his guts the moment Missy's head went under the water. He'd tried to save her, by God he'd tried. Had reached out to her, water up to his waist and he'd half expected her to rise again, shoot up like one of them dolphins at a show and laugh at him, saying, Fooled you! Didn't think I'd really do it, did you?! And he would have screamed at her, called her stuff, might even have hit her, and that would have been it for them, but at least she would have been alive. But she didn't rise. And the ripples that splayed out from her head were like the last of her thoughts, pulsing weakly, until there was nothing left of her except a pair of shoes placed neatly by the shoreline. Oh Missy, why'd you do it?

No answer, but sleep.

16

COME TWILIGHT, CALM. ATTEMPTS TO PIECE TOGETHER THE jagged puzzle of Time Lost between London and the boathouse.

He'd been so boozed he could barely remember crossing the wide estuary, the jolting movement of the train, leaving the destruction of Plymouth for swathes of green on the other side. How they'd let him on the train, God only knew, but he'd always been a trouble-free drunk, at least he had that going for him.

He'd hid inside the lavatory to drink. Nice. Came out only when visions of Missy had been coerced into oblivion, and then he took to standing in the corridor smoking cigarette after cigarette to dispel the stink that had lodged in his nose. He remembered a card game but doubted he would have played, he wasn't that lucky any more. Not since war had made cards dirty.

He got off the train a stop too early and couldn't find his hat; the beautiful *French* hat that made him look so handsome and a cut above what he knew himself to be. But when the train pulled away, there it was: waving from a window amidst a torrent of jeers.

And then he was walking, fields either side of him, with a vast horizon of nothingness ahead of him. And he begged for a sign and he was given a sign and the sign said: STOP HERE. So that's what he did. And then there was silence. A drowning silence that poured through his ears and fell into his lungs. The sound of a heartbeat – his – distant and fading, until everything went dark and he had woken up in a wood. Being cared for by an old woman who he thought was an owl.

Marvellous slipped out into the rare dry night and left the young man sleeping. Instructions to take a glass of bitters had been left on the table next to his bed. She stripped at the mooring stone and glided over to the island. Pulled herself up the muddy bank and rested against a gravestone. Clouds raced east, driven by the briny Atlantic breath, and under a glimmer of stars her body glowed, as if she was a ghost rising for a last look – just one last look – to see what it had all been about. She stood up and brushed leaves from her bottom. She padded gently into the church, the matches already on the altar waiting. She cupped her hand around the flame as a gust blew through the broken window. She lowered the glass guard around the candle only when she was sure that light had taken hold.

She looked out towards the boathouse. Saw the shifting smudge of his shadow against the flickering orange fire-lit walls. Up at last. She felt anxious. She walked out into the heavy night, dived into the river, unsure who she was any more.

* * *

Drake sat up in the chill fug and pulled a sweater over his clothes. Orange embers pulsed faintly in the hearth. He rolled his legs slowly from the bed, the pain in his side not sharp but still there. On the table was the small glass of bitters the old woman had told him to take. He drank it and grimaced.

He held on to the wall and pulled himself upright. He felt dizzy immediately and clung to the plaster, clammy handprints marking his journey to the double doors that led to the balcony beyond. He peeled back the shutters. The joints were stuffed with paper to stop the rattling, and he pulled the scraps away and opened the doors on to a star-filled midnight sky. An owl hooted.

The smell of salt was strong and the water was high, lapping confidently against the pylons below. He noticed the flicker of candlelight in the church opposite. He thought he saw a shadow move past the window but realised it could only be the movement of the trees, no one could get over there now. Somewhere overhead a robin sang. Not that he knew it was a robin because to him it was just a bird, just as he didn't know it was the old woman at first because she carved through the water like a creature. Only when the moonlight caught the white of her hair did he realise it was her. He crouched down and pressed his face to the rail. He watched her pass in front of the island, saw the pale shadow below the surface. She could have been a seal, there was a splash – like the whip of a tail – before she disappeared. He began to panic and stood up to see her better. He counted the seconds and thought of Missy. No, there she was. She had surfaced next to a boat wreck further downriver by a sandbar, now rested her head against its wooden side.

She swam back and rose in the shallows and that was when

he saw she was naked. She pulled herself up on to the shore into the lamplight that bled upon the mooring stone. He didn't look away. He studied her because he had never seen a body that old before with all its creases, all its wounds, all its flesh. He felt embarrassed, felt leery, but he couldn't look away. He watched her raise her arms, dry her breasts, between her legs. She stopped, stood quite still in the cold night air as if she could smell his gaze. He wondered how many memories and years had nestled down in that flesh. Wondered who and what it had loved. Who had loved it? Wondered why she had never given up like he had. Why he had given up so readily. So fucking easily. His shame burned.

17

RAIN HADN'T STOPPED FOR DAYS AND NIGHTS AND THE boathouse stank of salt and damp and Drake couldn't get warm. He awoke to sounds: a crackling fire, a pan busy on its chain, an old woman's night-time shuffle. He watched her cook but he didn't move. The pot looked heavy and once he thought she might drop it on to the iron rest, but he didn't move. He watched her ladle out the stew. Fucking stew again. She came towards him, a bowl of fragrant steam cradled in her knotty hands.

Here, she said, and took a spoon out from her jacket pocket. She sat on the stool next to his bed. You look better, she said.

He nodded and continued to eat. And you? he said, between mouthfuls.

Me? she said.

Yes.

I'm well.

Where am I? asked Drake.

In the boathouse.

What boathouse?

My boathouse.

And who are you? he said.

I'm no one, she said, quietly: a voice more breeze than voice.

What's your name? he said, and she told him.

Marvellous what? he asked.

Ways.

Drake spooned a large dollop of stew into his mouth. That's quite unusual, he said.

Apparently, she said.

I once knew someone called Banjo.

And could he play?

Not really, said Drake.

That's even more unusual, said Marvellous.

That's what I thought.

And he carried on eating and they fell back into a shared silence.

My name's Francis Drake. People usually call me Drake.

Fancy that, said Marvellous.

I've heard the jokes.

What jokes? said Marvellous.

That I've never gone far and I hate water.

I don't think that's very funny, I think that's a pity, quite frankly, said Marvellous. You know, it's a dying art, naming well. My father gave me my name. He travelled far, and he travelled to places where names mattered and he brought my name back from across the sea and put my name in this shell box together with my calling.

And she lifted a small box away from her chest for him to see. Here, she said. It was my mother's. My mother was a mermaid.

Drake stopped eating. Oh Jesus, here we go, he thought, his ears suddenly alive to the wind outside hurling the rain against the smooth slats. He rested the empty bowl on his lap. He was deliberate with his actions, anything so as not to look at the old girl's face. He reached for his cigarettes and lighter, he blew a stream of smoke towards the ceiling, aware that the old woman's eyes were locked on to his. A mermaid, eh? he eventually said.

Yes, said Marvellous. Apparently she was so beautiful that even waves drew back to look at her, and Marvellous got up and took his bowl back to the hearth.

I don't think I've ever met a mermaid before, said Drake.

How would you know? They don't advertise, said Marvellous.

What else do they do? he said.

Who?

Mermaids.

What do you mean what do they do? They *swim*.

Don't they sing and comb their hair?

I think you'll find they're rather more accomplished than that.

That's what the books say, isn't it?

Rumour.

Luring sailors to their deaths?

Rumour, said Marvellous a little more emphatically, and she filled two mugs with warm rum and ale and shuffled back to the bed.

Here, she said.

106

Drake took the mug and drank gratefully. Where do you live? he asked.

In the caravan. Out there.

Drake craned his neck towards the window. It was a tarry tarry night.

You won't see it, said Marvellous. It's too dark for your eyes. You've still got city eyes.

Drake fell back against the pillows. He took a drag of his cigarette and flicked ash into a scallop shell the old woman had left for that use. Did your mother come from round here? he asked.

No, no, no. She lived off the coast of Lady Island in South Carolina. *America*, she said with emphasis. My father went to a house one night for a ball, and she was standing in a nearby street surrounded by men. He said it was as if she punctured his skin and entered his veins and swam directly to his heart. I don't think he got out much.

Marvellous lifted her mug and steam rose and misted her glasses.

Did they stay there? asked Drake.

No. My father brought her back to London where he thought differences could be hidden. They took a house by the river and lived in a world that straddled the two, half dry half damp. Over time, though, my mother became unhappy because the Thames was dirty and people said she was dirty too. She became sad and lonely and took to midnight swims amongst the tugs. Her eyes became infected. I think she probably cried too much.

Marvellous finished her ale. Are you all right? she said.

Drake nodded. Smoked the last of his cigarette and stubbed it out.

You look very pale, said Marvellous. Seem tired all of a sudden.

Maybe, said Drake, and he shifted down the bed. Marvellous leant across and adjusted his pillows. She pulled the blanket up to his neck and made sure his feet were tucked in at the bottom. She had a vague memory of someone doing that for her when she was small. She began to button up her jacket.

Where are you going? he asked.

Back to my caravan.

Don't go. Stay, he said.

Three words, beautiful. The old woman sat back down. So? she said into the silence.

Drake placed his hand across his forehead. Just keep talking, will you?

What about?

Anything, said Drake.

What sort of anything?

Your parents. There you go.

What about them? she said.

Did they stay in London?

Oh no. My father gave my mother a hand-drawn map of the Cornish Peninsula and said I'll meet you here. Well, my mother arrived before him, of course, because she was half fish, and when she came across this sheltered creek and saw ramsons and bluebells sprouting from the mud, she knew instinctively that it would be her home.

Days later when my father arrived at the confluence, my mother leapt out of the water with her hands across her rounded belly and said, She's coming soon! – Me, obviously. She knew I was a she by the way I swam inside her. Boys swim in circles.

Drake nodded wearily.

My father had money and bought everything he could see – land, river, chapel, too – and he built this boathouse, and they collected food from the shore and every high water night or day, that sacred time when the river stills, they swam; because *that's* what mermaids do. And then sometime in – and Marvellous thought hard for a moment – in 1858, I believe, I slipped out like an eel and surfaced in a ripple of light, where my first breath was scented with the sweetness of wild honeysuckle. I had feet not fins, my father's brow and my mother's eyes. But, more importantly, I had my mother's heart. I never met her, though. She was shot just after my birth. I think someone mistook her for a seal.

Jesus, said Drake.

Marvellous shrugged. You should sleep, she said.

No, wait a minute, he said. Tell me. What did your father do when your mother died?

What did he do? He stopped breathing, said Marvellous.

He died?

No, he stopped breathing.

Died?

Are you doing this on purpose?

Doing what?

I said he *stopped breathing*. There's a difference, you know. It was as if a blade had shucked his heart like an oyster and stolen the beauty within. He said his heart never started beating again, it just started working and I never understood the difference, not until I was much older anyway, when I learnt that coming back from the dead is not quite the same as coming back to life. Know what I mean?

And she stuffed her thinking pipe with black twist and held a match above the bowl, and said nothing more. She waited for night to take him and it took him swiftly and deeply. His head tilted back and snores became soft growls. She rested her hand across his brow and whispered good night. She didn't leave straight away, sat and watched the rise and fall of his sleep.

18

DRAKE SLEPT SOUNDLY THROUGHOUT THE FOLLOWING DAY and only awoke at the handover of sun to moon when the old woman staggered through the door and placed the pot of steamed mussels and cockles on to the crane above the fire. The smell was divine and his hunger was ragged. He was feeling stronger he could tell, but the old woman looked weaker.

They ate the river stew with stale bread that became less stale in the salty broth. When the shells had been sucked clean, and the bowls wiped clean, old Marvellous took out a small bottle of sloe gin and filled her glass and downed it in one. Her cheeks began to glow. She slipped off her glasses and rubbed her eyes and they squeaked because they were so dry.

Are you all right? asked Drake.

Marvellous nodded and refilled her glass. Tonight I'm old, she said. Most of my life I've felt like spring but now I'm winter.

May I? said Drake and he reached over and smelt her glass. Sloe gin, he said.

Make it myself, and she raised the glass to her lips. It usually helps.

To feel young?

She smiled. No, to remember, she said.

Drake drank his ale. I was wondering, he said. Your mother. Was she buried over there? and he pointed to the church and cluster of gravestones.

Oh no, said Marvellous. You don't bury mermaids. They go back to the sea. My father carried her into the river when the waters were high and on the turn. He said a rogue wave came towards him crested by gold, and the wave enveloped them and the waters unpeeled my mother from his grip and carried her back to the warmer seas of her people and her birth.

And what happened to you afterwards?

To me?

Yes, he said.

Oh. I was sent to London to be brought up by my father's sister and her husband. It was quite clear by then that my father could barely look after himself, let alone a baby.

Where did you go?

I don't remember. But we lived in a big house and there was little light but a lot of God, and so many *things*. And they gave me everything a child could want including a new name that I didn't want: Ethel.

You're not an Ethel, I think.

No, I'm not, am I? Anyway, I didn't see my father again until I was ten years old. It was like meeting a stranger, albeit one who had the same smile.

What kind of life had he had? asked Drake.

I suppose I'd have to base a lot on speculation.

I won't hold you to anything.

That would be a good thing, said the old woman, and she nodded her thanks. She said, From what I gathered – and this is the speculation part – my father went through quite a transformation after my mother's death. He was a man who, up until then, had not even been known for rudeness. But overnight he became a man full of hate, and most of all, his hatred was for God. Which in truth, I believe, was really a hatred for his father, who was a strict man, very religious, who later became a doctor. No doubt thinking that with feet firmly planted in both camps, salvation could be secured.

Marvellous sipped her gin and smoked her pipe. Where was I? she asked.

God . . . ? Medicine . . . ? Your fath—

Ah yes. Well, either of those two pathways my father was expected to take.

So which one did he choose?

Neither. Choice didn't really come into it. On one hand he was scared of God and on the other he was scared of blood. He took his inheritance and fled to sea. Made a fortune. Indigo.

So when he woke up one morning and had as his first sight a House of God, you can imagine, it near destroyed him. Kindness made him angry. The sight of the first bluebells made him seethe. And every day at the close of day when the world stilled, the utter emptiness of life alone filled him with dread. So he prayed for a sign from my mother, prayed night and day for permission to end his life.

Did it come? asked Drake.

No, said Marvellous. What came instead was permission to *live*. One morning, he was awoken by a fearful sound coming from the coast. He headed towards the shore thinking a large steamer had run aground, but what he found when he got to the sea was the sight of a large grampus whale wedged between the rocks, tearing off its own skin in the instinctive fight to free itself. That was the sign my father needed, and the following morning he locked up the boathouse and what little remained of his heart, and he took to the road.

Three hours into the journey the rain hammered down. A mile later a double rainbow appeared over the sea. He felt no hatred, no bitterness, he noticed. Just awe. And the first pangs of what he would eventually describe as freedom.

Miles of road became inscribed on his soles, dirt grass moor and sand, a whole history of the Peninsula laid down one on top of the other, like fossils, like prayers. He walked across to Michael's Mount, around its periphery and walked back undisturbed by an encroaching tide. He walked to the Land's End, across the jagged cliffs. He often slept standing up, lodged against a wall, his legs twitching, dreaming their own walking dreams. Daybreak he kept on walking, never stopped to have a conversation, a raise of the hat maybe, a quick hello, but those legs never stopped moving.

He covered two thousand miles and had walked the periphery of that county six times. It had taken him nine years. He had seen eclipses and pilot whales. He had seen ships turn into wrecks, raging waves swallow men whole. He learnt from the old wise women who traded in ancient secrets and ways, and from them he tasted herbs and learnt what made him better, what made him ill. He learnt to find fresh water when the landscape told him there was none, and he learnt to deliver the dying. And only then, after those years of seeing so much, did his legs finally stop. He took breath at an ancient stone at the edge of the land and watched the sun fall to earth, and knew it was the end of something, and I think he would have said that something was grief.

And as the sky turned gold he felt the most glorious contentment wash over him. And he thought, Somewhere between God and Medicine there is a place for me. And he put that thought in the small shell box around his neck – this shell box, she said, lifting the one around her own neck. And that's when he slept, she said. When his legs slept. You see, he had finally caught up with his calling. He had refound his purpose. And that meant he could *live*.

That's when he brought me back from London. He had bought the gypsy caravan by then and an old dray horse and we travelled the length and breadth of the Peninsula together. In the villages and hamlets he was called upon night or day to sit with the dying. I went too and learnt from him.

I watched him whisper words – usually words that came to him there in the moment, or sometimes words from the Bible if the family requested it. And I watched him administer herbs, and he took their pain, and they thanked him by passing on unencumbered. In those early days, little money changed hands; he was offered food, drink instead. When there was no work we ate what nature provided, and it provides much. The gossips revered him.

What were the gossips? asked Drake.

Village women, said Marvellous. They were the ones who often delivered babies or mourned for the dead, they were the attendees anyway, and they called him to prepare the laying-out, whilst I went with them and learnt about the lying-in, the giving birth.

You delivered babies? asked Drake.

No, no, not at first. Years later I did, but then I just helped to boil water, and to lay out the sheets, and sometimes to tie the cord. But I watched and listened and learnt. Many died, that's what I learnt. It wasn't clean then, Drake, you see. Cuffs weren't clean and sleeves weren't rolled up. Noses weren't clean and in the depth of winter they dripped. They didn't understand how important it was to keep things clean.

Sometimes the dying begged for more time and that was the hardest, and my father would send me out under the cloak of night to release lobsters from their pots, to release lambs and pigs and rabbits from imminent slaughter. Buying life for life, he called it, bargaining with an unseen fate that played his cards too close to his chest. In many ways it was idyllic. Threatened, but idyllic.

Why threatened? asked Drake.

Because it was only a matter of time before the pain he swallowed whole bedded down and nestled somewhere warm until it grew like yeast. He kept little from me except the swelling in his legs. I kept little from him except the fear of our parting.

We need to turn back now, my love, was what he said the day he knew our adventure was over. And at the age of fourteen, I turned the dray round and made my way back to my father's past.

He was asleep when we arrived back into St Ophere. It was day but he was asleep. I secured the wagon and allowed the horse to wander amongst the trees. I had never been inside the boathouse, and the bolt was easy to pry away, the wood being so rotten. But ten years of damp had rusted the hinges and swollen the door and a violent kick was the only way to gain access to my parents' private world.

It was so tidy, with little within. The bed was made, as if it had never been slept in. And there were candelabras by the bed. And by the hearth. Red rugs carried a hue of green where mould had settled in the woollen pattern. But what I remember most was that it was a world of two: two chairs, two glasses, two bowls. I felt like a trespasser and not the natural product of their love.

Drake pointed to the soot-smudged outline above the fireplace. What used to be there? he said.

I don't know, said Marvellous. Something my father couldn't live with?

A painting?

Yes, I suppose it was. I never asked and he never said and in the end everything was quick.

The old woman reached for her glass. Three days, that was all it took, Drake. On the third and final night, a bright light shone from my father's body. And in the sublime peace of his face, I saw my mother waiting for him.

I had never seen my mother's face, and had longed beyond all longing to one day see it. I still do, in fact – that is a desire that age hasn't softened – because that night her face was hidden, covered by the thick tress of her dark hair. But I knew it was her because she used words like *mine* and *daughter* and her breath was of the sea.

My father said to her: Hello my love. You've come back to me.

My mother said: I never left.

And in those three words was a lifetime.

He said: Shall we go then?

And they both turned to me and they said: Can you let us go, do you think?

And I could say nothing. I raised my hand, a feeble attempt at a wave, I think. But I could say nothing. Because I was fourteen years old and all I wanted to say was, Please. Don't go.

19

THE NEXT NIGHT, DRAKE WAITED FOR HER. HE WAITED FOR the old woman but she didn't come. The birds quietened, the river emptied, the night passed, and she didn't come.

He fed the hearth a solid pile of sappy logs and they seemed to eat all oxygen from the room and he felt suffocated; couldn't even eat the salty broth left over from the night before. He lifted the water jug and filled the basin, splashed his neck and face, but still his mind wouldn't clear. He stood on the balcony; the candle flickered in the church opposite. Maybe he should go out and look for her in case something had happened? He went to the front door and opened it. The cold air pounced on him, fed off him as if he were prey. The trees swayed and the clouds raced north and the need for light was the rarest ache. There was nothing out there but loneliness. He closed the door swiftly. Nothing out there but the sad pull of Missy Hall.

After it had happened, after she'd gone, he'd run. Hadn't even waited for the police, couldn't face their questions nor their contempt: What do you mean you couldn't reach her? How hard did you try, eh? How hard did you *really* try?

He didn't even go back to her lodging house, heels took off on the wings of guilt and fear. Right along the Embankment all the way to Westminster he ran, kidding himself he was still searching for her, scouring the shingled banks and incoming tide for a body, at least. But he just wanted to get away from it, as far from the horror as he could.

And then as night had fallen, he had wandered aimlessly through the dark with sodden trousers and his pathetic suitcase of possessions, retracing every minutiae of their day looking for a clue, an open door she may have stepped through instead of the one leading to her grave.

He stopped at a lit brazier with the Lost and the Poor and the Broken and he was all of them so he took his place around the flames and when he had given out his sixth cigarette he realised he felt nothing other than cold, so he kept on moving, kept on wandering. He cut through to the quieter streets behind the Strand. Propositions crept from doorways, from alleyways, carried on the scent of smoke and over-ripe perfume, and those propositions were punctuated by a lazy smile and he was so tempted because he felt so fucking lonely but he passed them by, didn't stop.

He kept going east and soon the sooty tenement streets of childhood loomed familiar between the bomb sites, and his footsteps echoed loudly against the cobbles with the same displaced tread they had always had. He'd gone full circle and was back at St Paul's and that bloody river, and it was fat and dark and bloated and dozens of craft were moored near and far, and the cranes looked on and the power station puffed and the lights looked beautiful and they shouldn't have, fuck they really shouldn't have. He leant against the Embankment wall and drank from a bottle of gin. A single firework exploded overhead. The scattering of forlorn embers across a quiet London sky.

Drake ate in the flicker of firelight. He stared into the flames, looking for truth, but the truth he already knew because it came in the stillness, came as the boathouse creaked in its own sad sea. The truth was he had never known Missy Hall, not really. He had run towards a feeling and the feeling was his, and there had been little else there.

His sight was drawn again to the haunting outline above the hearth: *Something the old man couldn't live with*. He got up and went to his suitcase. He flicked the catch and took out the folded sheet of paper that had been slipped under his door when he was a boy. He carefully unfolded it. Placed his hand in the drawn outline of Missy's hand. 'Not too much, Freddy. Never forget me.' Her scrawl was erratic even then. He placed the paper gently on to the fire. It curled and danced, rose in the updraught like a small prayer lantern, and disappeared across the sky with the whisperings of childhood love trailing behind like a comet's tail.

In bed, he listened to the lapping waves and failed to sleep. He rose edgy with the early morning light and as he padded across the cold uneven floor, he looked down at the empty hearth and the dusty mound of clinker. For there, lying alone on the slate stone was the feathered remains of a small piece of charred paper. Two words stood out, dark and clear: *Forget me*.

His chest heaved and he staggered back to the bed. He held his breath and dived into a bottomless pit of sleep.

20

THE OLD WOMAN CAME BACK THE FOLLOWING NIGHT. SHE came back and Drake felt calmer. He watched her carry the same heavy pot over the threshold and he took it from her straight away and placed it on the cast-iron rest. He laid the table, spoons, napkins and glasses and ale, and put logs on the fire and the fire burned fiercely and the pot bubbled and the boathouse came alive with heat and his expectation. He even asked if she had done something different with her hair. She looked at him strangely and mumbled something about nonsense. He watched her ladle the vegetable stew into two bowls and place them on to the table. Stew! he said. My favourite! he said, and he pulled out a chair for her as she sat down to eat. Thank you, he said. Thank you.

They ate in silence, the stew thick and good, and the old woman didn't take her eyes away from her spoon and Drake didn't take his eyes away from her. Eventually, he wiped his mouth and quietly said, You haven't finished your story, by the way.

Marvellous looked up. What story? she said.

The story you were telling me. I waited for you last night but you didn't come.

I didn't?

No.

Didn't you eat?

Yes I ate. But you didn't come.

Marvellous broke off a corner of bread and dipped it in her stew.

You were telling me a story and the story's not finished. You can't leave a story in the middle.

How do you know it was the middle?

Because it wasn't the beginning. And it wasn't the end.

How do you know it wasn't the end?

Because you were fourteen years old. That's what you said. And now you're eighty-nine. There must be more.

I'm eighty-nine? said Marvellous. Are you sure?

I think so.

And Marvellous shook her head and continued to eat.

You have to finish a story, said Drake.

Says who?

Says me. Says anyone. And Drake pushed away the empty bowl and lit a cigarette and stared at her. The old woman finished her last mouthful and wiped her lips. She took out a bottle of sloe gin from her pocket and filled her glass. She drank it in one.

Stories, like nature, tend not to end, said Marvellous.

Drake flicked his ash on to the bowl and said, You got to the part where your father had just died. You had brought him back to the boathouse and had entered it for the first time. You saw what their life was like. And as he died, you felt your mother's presence and she was waiting for him. And had never left. And they turned to you and said—

Can you let us go, do you think?

Yes, he said. That's right.

And I could say nothing.

Yes.

The old woman adjusted her glasses and rubbed her forehead. She drummed her fingers upon the table and waited for the memory to return. And I could say nothing, she said again.

She remembered she had to wait for night to grow. It was a new moon, shed little light, and she wore a hat with a stub of candle secured by river mud at the front. It gave just enough light. She lifted her father's body from the bed and he was no weight at all, for all he was had passed. She carried him down to the river; negotiated her footing easily into the boat and placed him gently on to the bottom boards.

She chose the tides well and kept great pace with the outhaul of the sea. It was quite beautiful. Masthead lights rose and fell like wounded stars in the darkness. She sailed round bays and coves until she found deep water, private depths away from lighthouse beams, and there she lowered the sail and let the boat drift at will.

She whispered words her father had taught her until a fierce cloud of phosphorescence had encircled the boat. She knew then that it was time. She lifted her father and gently rolled him into the depths that immediately became the bright hold of her mother's arms.

She gripped the side of the boat and stuck her head in the

water so she could watch them go. But she was too young and it wasn't her world to see – clear sight being the privilege of age and passing time, and at fourteen years she had neither.

Sky and sea were one. Each rose and fell at the mercy of the other and she was suddenly consumed by a dark absence that sat in her guts and placed fear at the very core of life to come. She took in the sails, lay down across the seat slats and cried. She knew she was only a day away from an unforgiving sou'westerly gale that would toss the boat like deadwood and she prayed that it would come soon. She prayed that it would take her. So she could join them.

She awoke, not to death, but to the sound of shingle scraping upon the hull, and the anchored stillness of land. There had been no gale. The boat instead had washed up on a lee shore that was immediately familiar in the early morning light. She was alive. The world was still, the sea as calm as a millpond.

She uncoiled the bowline and pulled the boat along the shallow shoreline until it joined the Great River. From there she sailed the river past the lighthouse and the castles and the huge sailing vessels of the fleet, past the rotting outlines of hulls whose sailors had rotted elsewhere, until she turned towards the confluence and sandbar into the encroaching shallows. And she dragged the boat up the ancient creek, disturbing shrimp and crabs as she went, and she dragged that boat against the waters as if it was a reluctant pig going to slaughter. And turning the bend she saw the white of the boathouse and the church in the brittle light. She secured the boat and sat down on the old mooring stone. The creek was hers now and yet she felt nothing. It had been the longest walk of her life for no one was at the end waiting for her. She slept through winter. Missed Christmas and awoke to a New Year. She felt so lost. Until the first bluebells and ramsons coloured the green-brown floor of her world.

Hymns lifted the air as she dug in the river mud and uncovered a feast. She filled pails at the well and by the time the people had filed from the church she had a fire going outside, and a pan bubbling, and shells were opening their mouths but nobody looked at her.

She grew vegetables and baited lines that she cast from the shore. She ate well, sold the rest. But still nobody looked at her. And then she grew her hair and began to swim as her mother had swum, and that was when they looked at her. Water has memory. Theirs were stirred, hers reawakened for everything she needed to know was in that water. She scared them as her mother had scared them. Her nakedness scared them as her mother's had scared them. She was in bloom and everything around her was buzzing, and the men raised their nostrils and smelt her in the air and grinned before swallowing their shame.

Apple don't fall far from the tree, said Mrs Hard.

That's right, said Marvellous. Closer it falls, sweeter it tastes.

But she would let no one get close enough to taste.

Three summers had to pass before Marvellous' life would change. One morning, she awoke to a loud excited knock on her caravan door.

Betsy's about to have her baby! said a woman from the village.

Does Keziah know? asked Marvellous.

Keziah's attending a death. She said you can do it. She said, you're ready.

Five minutes, said Marvellous, and she closed the door to compose herself. Keziah said I was ready, she thought. Her stomach clenched and a cold clammy fear slipped down her back. She had never met a wiser Wise Woman than Old Keziah. She has taught me everything she knows, said Marvellous to herself. She said I am ready. She said I am ready. She said I am ready. And Marvellous repeated the sentence over and over as she gathered together the things she would need to deliver her first baby into the world.

The sun was high as she hurried up through the bosky wood. She caught up with the village woman at the start of the meadow, and together they walked silently through the cornflowers and marigolds and poppies until they got to the edge of the High Road. They saw Betsy leaning on the back wall of her cottage. Her cheeks were flushed, and Marvellous noted the steady deep rhythm of her breathing. She looked at Marvellous and said, Plug's out and water's have broke! Nipper'll have me screamin' soon.

Marvellous ran her hand down the woman's inner thigh and sniffed the clear liquid. She looked up and smiled. Come on, she said, and she put her arms around Betsy and guided her back along the road, back past the folded-arm glare of Mrs Hard, back into the expectant cottage.

Water was boiling on the stove downstairs. The air was hot and clammy and the stench of pungent yeast had stolen in from the bakehouse. The gossips were upstairs in the bedroom and the birthing sheet was in place. Betsy groaned as she lay down.

Marvellous placed her bag on a chair by the window. She took off her shirt and from her bag unwrapped a clean smock, a linen square and a neckerchief. She put on the smock and rolled the sleeves high and she took a bar of carbolic soap over to the wash basin. The water was fiercely hot and reddened her skin immediately but she scrubbed her hands and nails and dried them on the linen square. She tied the neckerchief about her nose and mouth and went towards the bed.

She let her hands roam across the bump. The baby's head was low and she could feel the slow instinctual movement of the uterus; the body knew what it had to do. Her senses came alive to each new alteration. She placed her ear against the bump and listened for the baby's solitary beat. Nothing. Her mouth went dry, she felt dizzy. She shifted her ear but still couldn't hear the tiny heart. She felt the eyes in the room watching her, felt the mother's eyes a heavy weight upon her. She ran her hands over the bump, and coughed and cleared her head and she leant down again and listened for life. There! Oh there it was, the galloping *ratatatat* of the baby's beat. She laughed with joy and the women in the room took that joy and swallowed it whole.

Just the one is it? asked the mother.

Just the one, said Marvellous.

Thank fuck, said the mother, and the women laughed.

It was all exactly as she had learnt from Keziah. Watch the face, the face don't lie. And the face didn't lie because two hours later the nature of the labour changed. The mother went into transition and the pattern of contractions changed and the cervix opened and amidst a volley of deafening screams and curses, a healthy baby girl popped her head out into the world.

Marvellous tied the cord with black silk and cut the cord and presented the mother with a gift of a girl. That's when the mother asked if Marvellous would name her baby and Marvellous said that she would gladly. The women laughed and said, Right, Gladly it is!

Hours passed. Shadows lengthened and the sun fell wearily

and still Marvellous wouldn't leave that room. Not till the placenta had come away well, till the baby had suckled well, not till she knew there was no bleeding between mother's legs. The gossips woke her in the end and said, You're done. Time now for you to go. All's good, ducky.

Marvellous left a cottage filled with laughter and a new baby's snores and a proud returning father and there was so many thanks that day – so many – it was as if she had entered the world once again holding a potential previously unknown.

She stepped out into a warm black summer night. There was a light still on in an upper room of the bakehouse. She saw the looming outline of Mrs Hard at the window. Marvellous raised her hand and waved; it was not a day for recrimination or judgement.

She cupped her hand and drank from the standpipe, ran the excess on her eyes and face. She trekked back across the meadow and down through the trees in possession of the oldest secret known to man. She sat on the mooring stone and surrendered immediately to the down of night. She hadn't slept long before she suddenly jolted awake. Thought she had heard the sweet call of a lark ascending. Unaware that it was actually the sound of her soul awakening.

Outside the boathouse, the breeze stirred. Shells and metal and bone danced against each other on the hanging twine, music of the night. Marvellous slipped off her glasses and put them next to the oil lamp. She rubbed the bridge of her nose where the plastic had left an indent. She finished the glass of sloe gin, dabbed her lips.

So? Have I given you an ending?

Drake stubbed out his cigarette. I don't know, he said. I

129

think it might be the beginning.

And she smiled and said, Good. Now you're getting the hang of things, Drake, and she got up, picked up her glasses and headed towards the door. As the night air streamed in, she stopped and said, Can you hear them?

Hear who?

The saints. They're up to mischief tonight.

Why?

Because they feel replaced. Ever since you arrived, they've felt that. And they'll keep me awake and that's for sure.

An owl hooted.

Midnight, said Marvellous, adjusting her gold fob watch and winding it well.

Drake looked at his watch. It *was* midnight.

Thank you, Marvellous, he said.

She stopped and turned. It was the first time he had called her that. She raised her arm and disappeared into the dark.

The wind picked up, and Drake looked out and saw the trees swaying. He listened to the old woman talking to herself. He thought that's probably what happens when there's been nobody around but dead saints for company.

21

IT WAS THE FIRST OF DECEMBER WHEN DRAKE FINALLY
emerged from the boathouse. Berries were bright and red and
hard. Winter had arrived.

Marvellous had woken him early and had handed him his
slop bucket and a bucket of ash and had pointed to a flattened
path up through the trees towards the outhouse and manure pit
beyond.

His eyes squinted as they adjusted to the bright morning
light. Calls from curlews and oystercatchers echoed around the
creek and the air smelt fecund and the creek was not the fearful
creek of his night-time imagination, but one of forlorn beauty,
of something ancient and serene.

Up through the trees he saw the gentle rise of smoke, then
the gypsy caravan for the first time. It was covered by wartime
camouflage netting, and the fake leaves stood out unnaturally

against the bare branches that surrounded it. Up close, the canvas was faded and patched, and once there had been writing on the side, but nothing of sense remained. A meat safe was secured to a pole at the side, and a small patch of land had been cleared behind, where vegetables now grew. A washing line joined tree to tree, and from old fruit crates a wooden shed had been built, doorless now, and packed with earthenware flagons – some with stoppers others open – fishing rods too and crab pots, tools, all sorts of tools, a tin bath and jerry cans of fuel. Secured to the side of the shed was a large metal-framed canvas kite smelling strongly of the sea.

He put down his buckets next to a battered lamp and climbed the caravan steps. A braid of damp seaweed hung from a telescope that was roped tightly to the outside slats. He pushed the door gently and encountered the strangest world he had ever seen. The room was still and warm, just the muffled sound of fire crackling in the stove, the occasional creak from the wooden wheels long embedded in decades of mud 'n' mulch. The air was clear and smelt of pine, and something else he couldn't put a word to, something feminine, something intoxicating. He went over to the bed and sat down. The wall opposite had been covered in shells: a mosaic of periwinkles and limpets mainly, hundreds of shells meticulously arranged in patterns of sea swirls and waves. And at the back, on the ledge below the window, in the dust and dark, a small bookcase housing a single book: a compact lockable ledger, hand-scrawled down the spine: *The Marvellous Book of Truths*. Drake pulled out the book and ran his forefinger down the words. He looked for a key but couldn't find one. He put pressure on the lock but the lock wouldn't budge. He put it back into the dusty chink for another day.

He crouched down to the Marconi wireless that sat on the floor next to the bed, the volume knob rubbed smooth from use. And there along the sides of the walls bags of dried leaves and herbs, and scales too, with brass weights the size of pennies. A pestle and mortar on a shelf up high. Cartons of Craven 'A' cigarettes and Lucky Strikes: the usual war bartering.

He lay down on the bed, glanced over the hand-written notes pinned to the quilted ceiling above, some new some old, but private instructions from her to her. He read:

> Egg Friday   Man outside is Drake
> Drake=Sad   Watch Drake
> Born 1858
> Money in cupboard   Blow out candle

He knew this world. Had seen this world of fractured thought before, when he was a boy. An old man used to come into the pub – a regular he was – and one winter's day he came in with bits of paper that his wife had stuck to his gabardine coat, and from a distance Drake thought the paper looked like snow, and on the paper was the man's name and address, what he liked to drink, and where his money could be found. It was in case he was having a *bad day* because that's what they called it in those days, a *bad* day. Nobody ever robbed Stanley Morris and someone always got him home, usually with a song on his lips. That was a good world, thought Drake. A gone world.

He unpinned the scrap of paper that said, *Drake=Sad*. He looked at it for a moment before putting it into his trouser pocket. He smoothed the bed cover and left the caravan as still and untouched as when he had entered.

He picked up his buckets and marched up to the manure pit

where an icy crust had formed. The cold froze the smell and it was just waste, just dirt, and even a startled rat didn't disturb his calm. He undid his trousers and entered the outhouse. Pulled his pants down and shat like a bull. He wasn't a new man. He just felt a bit kinder.

22

AT THE START OF THE SECOND WORLD WAR, MARVELLOUS had made a rare journey over to the Great Port.

Whilst sitting on a bench feeding a pigeon, she had overheard a woman talking about a film she had seen the day before. The film had been shot in colour, the woman had said, and Marvellous listened carefully because she was curious, because she had never seen a film in colour before, in fact couldn't remember the last time she had seen a film at all. From the title, she thought the film was probably about sailing. Something she would thoroughly enjoy.

Instead of heading back home straight away, Marvellous joined the queue for the pictures and soon found herself sitting in a row with courting couples, and as the lights dimmed, she looked about as heads dipped to kiss.

She had never seen so much colour, never in her life had

such colour exploded across her landscape, not even in sleep. Red and orange flames burst across the screen with the black silhouette of marching armies, and she thought, maybe, this was Britain to come. And Marvellous thought Vivien Leigh looked like Robin Hood in her curtain dress, it was war there too, it was Make Do and Mend.

But it was the image of those orange lips and those red lips that had stayed with Marvellous over the years, and she had often wondered how she would have looked with lips like that.

She had been the last to leave the cinema. They had asked her three times to go as she sat staring at the large empty screen. She only moved when the air-raid siren screamed and she saw the panic race across the usherette's young face.

It felt like a thud walking out into a blacked-out world. The sirens wailed and people ran to shelters, but Marvellous didn't go to a shelter, she carried on down to the harbour and her boat, oblivious to the shouts of the wardens and the noise of bombers overhead. And as she left the falling bombs for the dark quiet creek, she thought again about those orange lips and those red lips and thought that had she had lips like that, then maybe she might have been kissed more.

She stood in the doorway of the boathouse and unfurled the poster.

Gone With the Wind? said Drake, raising his head from the washing bowl.

I knew I had it somewhere. An American gave it to me. I thought you could put it here on the wall by the table.

Thank you, said Drake, and he dried his hands and took the poster from her.

Might brighten things up for you a bit in here, said

Marvellous. It's a young person's picture, I think.

I think you're right, said Drake, and he carried the washing bowl and emptied the contents on the briar rose outside.

I wondered how I would look if I coloured my lips, too, she said.

What?

Like her? she said, pointing to the poster.

Like Vivien Leigh? he said.

Is that the actress?

I think so.

Yes, like her then.

What colour were you thinking of?

Red. Or orange.

I think red.

Yes, I think so too.

I think you'd look nice, said Drake, and he missed her smile as he went over to the hearth where a pair of newly washed socks had been left to dry.

You have post, said Marvellous, following behind him.

Drake picked up the letter from the mantelpiece and handed it to her. It's not for me, Marvellous. See? I was asked to deliver it. To this man here, he said.

Why?

Because I promised someone, he said, and he put on his socks.

And she studied the envelope, brought it close to her eyes. She said the name out loud, Dr *Arnold*, and she felt a whiplash of memory, something sharp and brief, and held on to the table for balance. And then the feeling disappeared just as suddenly, as if the pages to the book had been ripped out and the jagged edge at the margin hinted of something that remained.

Are you all right? asked Drake.

Yes, she said quietly. Yes, OK.

Here, he said, and he led her over to the bed. You look tired, he said.

It's been all the waiting, she said.

I'm sure it has.

When are you going?

What?

The letter, she said, pointing. When are you going to deliver it?

Oh. Not today, Marvellous, he said. I won't be going anywhere today. Or tomorrow. Or the next day, I don't think.

And she nodded and said, Good, and like an echo said, Good, again. And a faint blush of colour pushed its way back into her cheeks. She didn't want him to go anywhere; she was getting used to him.

23

THE AFTERNOON STRETCHED OUT VACANTLY BEFORE HIM. Marvellous had taken the crabber round to the Other Saint's Village, as she liked to call it, to deliver winter herbs and rosehip syrup to those who still refused to see a doctor.

The cloud had shifted, replaced by an unbroken blue sky, and the shrill call of gulls and geese echoed around the empty creek. The tide was out but on the turn and the wet sand was surprisingly firm underfoot. Between the dark limp popweed, coils of lugworm patterned the riverbed, and discarded seashells too – cockles, mussels, winkles – evidence of their evening feasts. A flock of carrion crows landed over by the church and pecked at stranded sand eels in the thick blur of stinking weed.

Alone, Drake guided his thoughts back to the night he arrived. His memory was still vague, and for years it would be, the only fixed point was the strange sign that rose from the hedgerow commanding him to Stop Here. But it was what old Marvellous had said to him that night that stayed with him. That she had been *waiting* for him. How could she have known he was coming? He hadn't even known that himself.

The lowering sun shifted as he marched up through the meadow, and it took him no time at all to reach the road beyond, the road once grandly called the High Road, back in the day of God and Bread and Wealth and Men. He was a thorough scout, but an hour of walking and searching along the stretch of road by the derelict bakehouse revealed nothing. No sign. Nothing. And he noticed for that whole hour no motor cars or carts or vans passed the boarded-up cottages. No traffic at all. The hamlet was eerily deserted. It was so quiet he could hear the mercury drop in that still air of yesteryear.

He sat down on the milestone and lit a cigarette. He played with his lighter, he looked at his hand. His shakes were lessening, he was sure of it. He watched the aerial dance of swooping starlings pattern the now familiar approach of dusk. Watched as they twisted and dived in the rich eternal blue, and for that brief moment, lost in their joy, he didn't care about the sign or what old Marvellous Ways did or didn't know. He felt transfixed by something other, and the golden light shifted across his face as it edged west, and as it did, it momentarily blinded him and he dropped the lighter to the ground. He bent down to pick it up, and as he reached for it, that's when he saw it. Through his legs and upside down it was, but still he saw it. He began to laugh. And as he marched over the fields back down to the river, he left behind a granite milestone glistening in the late afternoon sun. A granite milestone, simply carved with the words:

ST opHere

24

THAT NIGHT THE MOON WAS OUT AND A SLIVER OFF FULL. Huge brushstrokes of pink and mauve had encroached upon the deepening blue. The river was filling up and shadows were forming on the bright surface and music danced hand in hand with the tide. A familiar trumpet introduction curled around the trees. Armstrong. Louis, they whispered.

A long time since Drake had heard music. Had forgotten how it stirred, how it moved him. For months he had tried to remember the name of the jazz club in Paris, the one he went to after the war. He had tried to remember the name on the ferry back to England whilst he gripped the rails and vomited on to his shoes.

He remembered following a group of American soldiers – black soldiers, they were – down a dingy staircase into a dank underground cave, full of sweat and dancing and smoke and drink, and the music was unrepentant and men, women danced freely, danced sex upright and fully clothed. A woman came and sat next to him and she was French and she leant over and whispered, *Merci*. And then she whispered, *Liberté*, and the only reason he remembered was because he thought at the time they rhymed. She got up, saluted him and left. Even in civvies he looked like a soldier.

Drake caught his reflection in the glass. The soldier had been replaced by something else. A fisherman perhaps? He went on to the balcony and saw Marvellous inspecting the pit-fire he had started an hour before.

Drake called out to her and she looked up and waved.

Caveau. That was the name of the club. Caveau *something*.

They fished in a creek still stained by the fall of day, and they watched in silence as the iridescent flow of pink and gold gave way to the solemn colour of night. Marvellous reeled in and cast her line back out towards the deep black channel. They'll bite now, she whispered.

How d'you know?

Shh, she said.

Fuck! said Drake.

Got one?

The *jab jab jab* was like electricity in his muscles and his heart beat fast and even faster still when he saw the silver fish darting just below the surface. He'd never fished before and he felt like a boy, and he laughed and thought he might even have squealed like a girl. And Marvellous said, Careful now, we want this one, and he was careful and he did what she said, and he reeled in and raised the rod, reeled in and raised the rod until panicked gills could be seen flapping at surface break and the fish surrendered with a last flick of fin on the ignominious mud, staring wildly at the idiot who had caught him, the squealing idiot who had never landed a fish before. God, what a silly way to go, thought fish.

A mullet, said Marvellous. A good size too. And she hit it on the head with a thick branch.

She stood over Drake and showed him how to gut the fish. Knife under the gills and head off. That's it, she said. Slice all the way along from its bottom. Scrape the guts out. Simple. Here's your fish, Francis Drake. And Drake took it in both his hands and he felt so proud. And he wanted to hold that fish up high like a trophy and would have done it, had Marvellous not pointed out the bright hungry eyes that watched him intently from the barren trees around.

They drank mugs of warm bitter ale whilst the fish cooked on a griddle pan in a sea of flames, butter and salt browning and crisping the skin.

The wreck on the sand bank, said Drake. Was it your boat?

No, said Marvellous, that's *Deliverance*. That was Old Cundy's boat, a fisher chap I knew way-back. Both he and his boat passed on a few months after Dunkirk, not that either of them were particularly seaworthy at the time.

Marvellous took the pan off the fire and on to the grass. It sizzled and spat. Plate, she said and Drake handed her his plate and she placed the fish upon it. There was little room for the boiled carrots.

Remember this taste, said Marvellous. It is the taste of freshly caught fish and triumph and the knowledge that you will never need to go hungry. It is the sweetest combination, in my opinion.

And from the first mouthful, Drake knew that it was.

Do you know, said Marvellous licking her fingers free of fish oil and butter, that when they asked for fishing boats to join the flotilla and go to France, *Deliverance*'s engine started all by itself?

Really? said Drake, smiling.

I know you probably find that hard to believe, but yes, it did. And Old Cundy didn't have any decision to make at all because it had been made for him: that boat was going with or without him.

Brave boat.

It *was* a brave boat, Drake, indeed it was. But it was more than that. Would you like some carrots now?

Thank you, said Drake, as a large buttery spoonful landed on his plate.

What was more than that? he asked, pulling a bone from his mouth.

Old Cundy's grandson was over there. And the boat loved that boy because it could still feel the young man's hand on its tiller. A tiller never forgets the hand that steers it. Always remember that, Drake.

I will, he said.

I waved *Deliverance* off myself. It was a moving sight. Imagine it, Drake! Nose forward through the waves. German bombs dropping fore and aft but onwards she went, until the French coast came into sight. And what a sight! Beaches packed with men, tanks on fire and oil drums too, and lines of soldiers wading into the breakwater desperate for home.

Deliverance got as close as it could because of its shallow hull and planes flew in low and dropped their bombs and boats were hit and boats went down and fishermen drowned far from home. And soldiers scrambled towards the boat and some fell just feet from safety. And that boat shuddered every time a young life was lost, but it didn't turn away, didn't shift into reverse, not until it had ten soldiers on board, and its job was done.

But then suddenly, said Marvellous, racing from the shore, came the last man standing. He dived into the spume and struck out for *Deliverance*. Come on! Come on! they shouted as bullets rained down. His comrades leant over the sides causing the boat to tilt dangerously, hands reaching for the struggling soldier, his hands reaching for them. Come on! Come on! they screamed. His hands, their hands reaching. And then they got him. They heaved him aboard and he fell face down on the deck and refused to move. He stayed there for minutes. Maybe a bit longer. And only when they reached safer water with naval gunships by their side, did the old fella leave the tiller. He knelt down by the young man and placed his hand on what he believed to be a familiar shoulder. The young man stirred and slowly raised his head.

And it was him, right? The grandson? said Drake, eagerly.

Marvellous put down her plate and lifted the ale to her lips. No, it wasn't, she said.

Fuck.

You swear a lot.

Sorry.

But it should have been him, shouldn't it? It should've been him.

Did he ever come back? said Drake.

No. Old Cundy died shortly after. Maybe it was the effort, maybe the heartache. They tried to sell the boat but the boat was like a grief-stricken dog and refused to move. It knew, you see. Overnight it just seemed to break apart. I watched it die on the ooze. Everything has its time, Drake. That's what I've learnt. Everything has its time.

The fire burned low and the cold grew and old Marvellous retired early. Drake sat alone and finished the last of the ale. He looked over to the church and thought that maybe God too had become a casualty of war. He watched insects flit feebly around the dying flames lured by the charred remains of fish bones and skin. He poured a jug of river water on the fire. It hissed and steamed, and his face glistened. The unexpected sound of a clarinet and saxophone in the early bars of a song stirred his heart.

He picked up the oil lamp and stumbled along the riverbank until he stood level to the rotting hull on the other side. And in the lamplight, as Billie Holiday sang of foolish things, Drake stood to attention and saluted the good ship *Deliverance* and he didn't feel silly – or foolish – because he was a little bit drunk. And had you been passing that clear night, you would have seen a young man saluting a wreck on a sandbank as an old song wound its way around the coast and up valleys and along creeks, falling into the ears of the sleeping, reminding them of love because sometimes that's all there is.

And as the song came to an end, back in the caravan, Marvellous Ways reached across and turned off the wireless. She lay down on her bed, her head giddy in the silence. She was about to blow out the candle when she noticed a note stuck to the ceiling, scribbled in an unfamiliar hand.

Drake=a bit happier

She blew out the candle and like a blind, darkness fell.

25

A WEEK LATER, MARVELLOUS NOTICED THAT THE BIRDS IN the creek had become edgy and their songs rushed. A flounder had beached itself during the morning's empty, given-up before sun up, it had, died in that cruel between-light. Crabs, too, had risen from the mucky ooze, looked about fearfully before thinking better of it.

For days she had felt it coming but had said nothing. Had felt it in the mar of her back, the slow build-up of strange behaviours and unfamiliar smells, smells of the dark soul, she liked to call them.

She stood by the mooring stone and studied the encroaching dark. Her barometer had fallen but not a cloud weighted the sky as yet. It was the pressure of expectation, that's what it was, because that's what happened during the Night of Tears. Her ears sifted the silence. When the dogfish barked that's when the river rose. That's when broken dreams escaped the mud and floated to the surface like bobbing wrecks.

Once, Mrs Hard's pram had floated wheels up and wedged itself in the eelgrass. The pram had never felt the weight of a child, only bread, and there'd been talk back-along of Mrs Hard carrying a child but whether it had entered the world breathing, no one quite knew. But Marvellous knew and knew that it hadn't. There never was another child and the pram remained the dream she couldn't quite let go of. That was when her name seemed to change from Heart to Hard, and Marvellous knew nothing good could come from a heart turning hard. It was Mrs Hard who had told Marvellous that tears ran out like women's eggs. When you no longer bleed, you no longer cry. That's what Mrs Hard had long-back said.

Drake awoke suddenly to the light drum of rain and the sensation of a clinging wetness around his body. He opened his eyes, sat up. The room was moving, had become one with the river; a continuous plane of shimmering black. A shaft of moonlight snaked across the floor as strong as a lighthouse beam. Drake rolled out of his bunk and his toes disappeared into the chill salt water. Panic gripped immediately. He rolled up his trouser legs and waded across to the balcony door and looked out. There was no more riverbank, no mooring stone, the world was water. The tide had won.

So cold he began to shake. He grabbed his oilskin by the door and stumbled out. A step to the right was the rising tide, a step to the left woodland. He stepped left and saw the light. It was just a flicker at first, hazy in the drizzle, but it got bigger and came towards him like a large firefly, and as the firefly drew near, so it turned into a candle, stuck above the brim of a dirty miner's tull, worn by an old woman carving across the creek in a canoe, her stroke slow and majestic.

Get in! shouted Marvellous as she reached his feet. Get in and paddle!

And he got in nervously and did.

He pushed away from the bank and let the vessel glide in the current around the island and the dark outline of the church. He looked back to where the white of the boathouse merged with the waterline at the balcony edge. The strange disorientation of it all. Trees were reaching out for the opposite bank, branches reaching up from the depths like fingers, everything reaching suddenly for him, and the image choked him and the first wave of puke shot from his mouth.

An owl hooted, and the clouds pulled away. And suddenly, there was the moon, fat and orange and low, directly above the roofless church. Shafts of light poured from the broken windows like bright tentacles reaching out, highlighting the tops of the submerged headstones: *Sacred . . . In Loving Memory . . . In Peace Perfect Peace.*

Drake stopped paddling and held tightly on to the sharp fronds of a palm tree.

You all right?

Yes, he said, wiping his mouth with his sleeve. It'll pass, he said, shivering.

This way then, said Marvellous, pointing ahead.

As the way became narrower, Drake used his hands to guide the craft towards the open door of the church. It was just wide enough to get through.

It had been years since he had been in a church. Years since eyes of stained glass looked down on him and wept. His heart felt heavy as he ducked under the doorframe and entered a still world that time had long forgot.

A lit candle rose from the submerged altar slab casting fierce light on to the crumbling walls, and what walls! They near took his breath away, for clinging there like crabs were model boats of every shape and size – yawls, cutters, gigs, luggers – perfect, every one of them, in care and detail, made from matchsticks and cork and whittled twigs.

Who made these? asked Drake.

I did, said Marvellous.

When?

I don't know. I've had a long life.

He manoeuvred the craft to the wall and read out some of the names of the boats: *Gladly, Douglas, Audrey, Simeon, Peace.*

Peace, said Echo.

Children I delivered, said the old woman. Ships of souls.

The canoe drifted back to the light.

They say Jesus came to this land as a boy, Drake. The old woman's voice was measured, and echoed in the submerged ruin. He came with Joseph of Arimathea. They were on their way to Glastonbury. Imagine that, Drake! Jesus here. That's why they call this land a blessed land, blessed by the tread of Holy feet. And people over the years have spent a lifetime trying to walk in the exact confines of that tread and people were so busy looking down that they forgot to look up. Forgot to see what it was all about.

Marvellous took out her pipe, lifted the glass guard around the altar candle and lit it. She said, Where you are now was where the young Breton saint who founded this hamlet in the sixth century sat and fasted and prayed. He dragged a granite stone all the way from Penwith with a thick rope held between his teeth, and he walked in silence. And he placed the stone here and from this stone rose a church. From this stone rose the faith of thousands.

Drake looked up through the broken roof. The sky was starlit and directly above him, the moon cast its beams directly on to his face.

Once upon a time that would have signified you were the chosen one. Maybe you are the chosen one? What's your story, Francis Drake? What stone are you dragging behind you?

I don't have a stone. Or a story, he said.

Everyone has a story.

Not me.

Hmm, she said, looking at him disbelieving, and the drizzle turned once again to rain and carried moonlight with it.

She said, The young Breton saint was called Christopher – or Christophe, I expect, as the French say. 'Course he wasn't a saint then, just a hermit monk with great ambition. He couldn't actually be Saint Christopher anyway because the Catholics had that one, so his name became corrupted just as he eventually did. One day he bartered a thorn from Christ's crown for waters from the River Jordan – holy relics were like cigarette cards in those days – and he fasted and prayed and his prayers led him to pour the River Jordan into our river and it became a cure-all for those who swam. He went into the woods and cried and from his tears rose a spring – just up there beyond my caravan – of the purest, freshest water. I've drunk from that well all my life, Drake, and I've never had worms.

Drake took out a cigarette and placed it between his lips. Marvellous dipped her head and he leant towards her candle and took a light. The brief sensation of warmth calmed him.

You know, she said, even when the roof was long gone and

the rain fell like this, they still held services in here. They became known as special services.

What happened to the roof? said Drake.

Blown away in a gale probably. Yes, it was, in fact, destroyed by the storm at the end of the last century. The Great Blizzard, that's what they called it. Brought snow and wind and death to the Peninsula. I saw sailors stuck to mainsails out in the bay. Spread-eagled like this. Arms reaching skywards. Mouths frozen in prayer. No atheists at sea, Drake. When the waves are the size of mountains even the godless kneel.

Do you think that's what I should do? Kneel? asked Drake.

No. To kneel you have to believe you might be heard. I don't think you've ever believed that.

Small spirals of smoke rose from her pipe into the moonlight. The rain had ceased and Marvellous dipped her hand in the water and watched a shoal of young mullet file slowly up the aisle.

What was I talking about? she asked.

The services in the rain, he said.

Ah yes, the services in the rain. Yes. They liked the rain, that's why they never bothered with a roof again, thought it was a sign of God's grace falling upon them. And God was very important then because He'd blessed the Cornish Trinity – The Copper, The Tin and The Holy Fish – with prosperous and far-reaching breath.

Who's Jack? asked Drake.

What's that?

The other night I heard you talking to Jack. Was he your sweetheart?

The old woman sucked hard on her pipe.

Yes. He was my love. My *great* love.

Was he your first love?

No, he was my third love, my last. My first love was a lighthouse keeper: unexpected, that was. Then came Jimmy: that one was expected.

Why expected?

I saw him coming.

In a dream?

No, in a glass.

In a glass?

Are you repeating things just to annoy me again?

No. Sorry.

And then came Jack.

So was he expected or unexpected?

Good question. He was neither. He was my always. I have had three loves, Drake. At the time I thought it was enough, but looking back I think there might have been room for more. I've seen life expand like a womb to accommodate love.

Love, said Echo.

One was my beginning, one was my middle and one became my end.

Drake looked down at the still water.

So it all started with a lighthouse keeper? he said.

Yes, I suppose it did, said the old woman. All love starts with the flicker of a flame.

26

I WAS IN A TAPROOM IN FOWEY BY THE WATER. MY EYES were set on the pages of my book, but even though my eyes were occupied my ears were not and I heard a fisherman talking about an old sea captain he once served under, a man he dearly loved, a man who now kept light on the Eddystone Rocks. And the fisherman said the lighthouse keeper was close to death and needed help, and even though I was young I found the image distinctly profound.

I followed the fisherman out on to the quay and introduced myself. The fisherman explained that he was looking for someone to witness the ending of the lighthouse keeper's life. The old sea captain, he said, wanted to die peacefully in his tower and be buried at sea, so no doctors were to be called. However, his two children who kept light with him were fearful to dispose of his body in case they were later accused of murdering him. I said I'd be the witness and help his passing, and days later we were in his boat waiting for the weather to turn.

The first morning we headed into a strong south-easterly wind that turned into a gale and sent us scurrying back with our hearts in our mouths. But then April arrived and the first morning of that month brought us a steady north-westerly breeze, which was the most favourable wind for a landing, and with sails full and hope billowing, we set our course for the famous tower in the sea.

I sat at the bow and focused my telescope on the horizon, that incandescent line that tugged at me as strongly as the moon tugged the earth. I was seventeen years old when I spied my first love standing at the base of the Eddystone light with a fishing rod in hand and his cap pulled low and us still a mere speck in his peripheral sight.

With an hour's journey left to go the sea became as smooth as glass and the men rowed the remaining miles with seals at our side and gulls at our heads, and what was once a fissure on the horizon soon became the lighthouse itself. I never took my telescope away from that young man fishing on the rocks. Closer he came, closer, until the lens became a face and the face looked up and the man became a girl.

Hello! she shouted.

You've caught a fish, I said.

I've caught three!

We anchored the boat fore and aft and then I jumped. And she caught me.

The lighthouse keeper was days from death. He was in between worlds, sleeping mostly, but then he would wake suddenly, staring, as if he was looking back to his world from a very distant shore. The son never said a word. He stayed next to his father like a loyal dog, slept next to him too. Three little bunks in a simple round room: one small one, one medium, and a large one. I chose to sleep with the mice on the kitchen floor below.

As dusk approached the weather turned rapidly and the winds picked up and we had just enough time to bolt the door when the first wave hit us from the south-east. The lighthouse shuddered and rocked like a tree, and a wall of water hit the window and obliterated any daylight that still remained.

The daughter took my hand and led me up the stairs to the lantern gallery. It was a small room, with iron cross-bars at the windows. We cleaned the windows and lit the oil lamps as the waves pounded and the lighthouse shook. We were so high up and the night stretched out before me desolately. Every minute felt like an hour as the Channel swallowed the tower and the wind shrieked in joy at my terror.

And that night I never left the light and she never left me. It was so hot up there and it stank of oil, and we unbuttoned and sawdust and grime stuck to our clothes. And we listened to the lamps turn and the boom of waves and the squeal of the wind, and she halted my gasps of fear with a kiss, and I never stopped her. It was my first kiss. It lasted till dawn.

The son paced round and round the room and the lighthouse keeper continued to fade. I gave him water that rested on his lips and placed my hands across his heart, and under my palm I felt the last rhythms of life play out, the last bar of a song brought to its end by the half-time beat of a solitary drum.

And with his final breath the lighthouse keeper said: *He is the light of the world. Whoever follows him will never walk in darkness, but will have the light of life.*

We buried him at sea, as was his wish. In return, the sea gave two weeks of calm for the sacrifice. The gales abated and the sea lowered, and the birds were busy overhead, cawing and diving into the fertile depths, and that sun flickered brightly across the crests of waves like young promises of love.

The grimy lantern gallery became our bed, and as the wind shrieked so did I. In the depths of night I would stand outside on the balcony with sawdust stuck in my hair. I held tight to the rail and watched the sweep of light carve through that infinite blackness seeking something greater at the horizon edge. And sometimes migrating birds, stunned and disorientated by the glare of beams, would smash into the glass and fall dead on the balcony floor. My girl would take the birds down to her brother to give him something to love.

We were the centre of that liquid universe, for we were the night sun and we said to ships, Do not come too close, we have rocks at our feet. And the crash of waves sent white spray flying, and I am scared and exhilarated and a little bit in love too. I gripped the handrail and inched slowly around the balcony searching for that small channel of calm on the opposite side to the wind, and she came out and did the same – in the opposite direction – and we met at the back and there was no room to stand side by side, so we stood face to face until it became face on face until the only breeze there was, was warm, and came from her mouth, and smelt of sweet china tea.

She was the one who taught me to smell the air. So high up the air is clean and undisturbed, and when a strong south-westerly wind blew fierce, my senses bristled as it deposited sounds and smells from America, from another time, from my mother's time. And there was a lament on the breeze as the songs rose up from the rivers and fields.

Two days before I was due to leave, the sky was cloudless and as blue as I had ever seen it. The sun was so warm, my arms were out, my trousers rolled high. The wind stirred fresh and a ground swell sent waves billowing over the rocks at low tide depositing frothy spume that, from such a height, looked to me like fallen clouds. The boy hadn't moved from his bunk. He slept with grief surrounded by dead birds. She left food and water by his bed, then took my hand and led me up to the gallery.

I watched her smell the air. She was like an old-time fisherman scanning the sea for the dance of fish, feeling for the mood of the currents. The sea was her mistress – not I – and she would never leave her mistress. That's why I never asked her to. Everything has its time. Ours was fourteen days of nights and tides.

She brought out a large kite. It had a metal frame and was covered by heavy white canvas. The tail was a thick cord a good fifty, sixty feet in length and attached to the cord was a dozen or so hooks ready and baited. She secured the handling rope around the balcony rail and when the wind was in the right direction she launched the kite off the balcony and guided it beyond the reef and steered it like a craft so that the tail and the hooks dipped into the sea. Up it swooped, down it swooped, and that bait came alive to fishy mouths.

It didn't take long for her to shout and for me to help pull in the kite, and on my word, seven fish were hooked and flying through the air towards us. Oh the weight of it, Drake! But we pulled it in and unhooked the fish, and an hour later the kitchen was filled with the smell of cooking and the son lifted his head off the bed and out of grief to the unmistakable smell of freshly caught sea bass cooking over a burning stove.

The morning the boat came to pick me up, she gave me a coin. It's always with me. I have it here, somewhere in my pocket. Wait a moment. Here, and she handed the coin to Drake.

An old penny, he said.

Yes.

Why a penny?

But she didn't answer him straight away. She said: When I got in that boat, Drake, I never looked back. I couldn't. I was seventeen and I loved her. And I had had my first taste of sex and it was wonderful. Even now I still shudder. She was wonderf— Now, why have you just turned away from me?

I didn't.

Yes you did. Oh yes you did. Does this embarrass you –

No.

– an old woman talking about sex?

Of course not, he lied.

I was young once. Hard to believe, isn't it? For most of my life I've *felt* young, but of course I haven't been. I took being young for granted. That is a statement that can only be made when one is old. I know it may not look it, but this tired old body has loved passionately. It has done things that would obviously make you blush.

Blush, said Echo, emphatically. Drake blushed, scolded.

Why a penny? he asked, after a while.

I'm getting there, said Marvellous. Don't hurry me. Especially not *now*.

She said: Waves fell over the stern and with full sails we surfed those waves and made good speed back towards Fowey. But then I could bear it no more. My heart ached and pulled my sight back to the rock and the tower now fading into the horizon. But there was a flickering light coming from that tower, a glint, like sunlight on a mirror, and I realised it was her light to me, and I knew she would always give me light and always get me home.

I felt cold then, yet the coin burned hot in my pocket. I brought it out and warmed my hands, and looked at the coin and saw the picture of Britannia ruling the waves, and I thought, That's her, really. A little bit her. And then I noticed it. Positioned behind Britannia's shoulder. The lighthouse. Smeaton's lighthouse. And everything we had was in that lighthouse. And this coin was the key to that particular door of time.

I can no longer remember her name. And I can no longer see her face. Such is my mind now. Often I am left waiting at the entrance whilst ghosts of my life are ushered to the exit. Many times I never had the chance to say goodbye, but then again my father would have said, Sometimes you never do. *C'est la vie*, say the French. But what I do remember is the *feeling* of her face and it was a *good* feeling and from that I know it was a good face. We never saw each other again.

Never? said Drake.

No, she said. Never. I never knew what happened to her, but I often wondered, of course, whenever I saw a light flashing in the distance. But it wasn't until the night of the Still-Talked-About Storm many years later, when the new Douglass lighthouse sat upon the reef instead, that I really got to know.

Got to know what? asked Drake.

That she was still alive, said Marvellous, and her face lit up.

How'd you find that out?

Through something quite incredible, really, she said.

Go on, said Drake.

And Marvellous relit her pipe and said, Well, that night, I'd just got past The Point when the weather suddenly turned. The sky became bruised and waves hit the boat sideways in patterns of four of ever increasing size. I thought it was a dark cloud at first, Drake – it looked like a cloud – until this wave bore down on me and the boat was sucked up against its spume-crested wall. Higher and higher we went, until the wave pulled back, and the boat hung in the darkness for a moment before falling and hitting a sea as unyielding as wet sand.

I awoke dazed, looking up through a portal to a star-drenched sky. And beyond the stars bands of milky light stretched out to the hush of infinity. It was beautiful. The boat was floating in the middle of a disc of calm. The storm had pulled away, was encircling but not engulfing, and I watched as waves crashed against an invisible wall thirty yards away. And I realised I had fallen upon a grave of lost seamen, a grave not marked by a cross but by this prayer-sodden peace.

Ten yards away now, the waves were gathering and my boat was drifting mastless and rudderless towards that unmarked boundary between Life and Death. And all the while, I never took my eyes away from the sky, never took my eyes away from that narrowing portal that gave a glimpse to the other side.

And that was where it came from, Drake. The *kite*. Out of the dark like a falling star, hurtling towards me, its long tail skimming across the mountainous sea. I stood up and when that tail fell just above the boat, I jumped and reached for it. There was a moment of suspension before I felt the rope wrapped firmly between my hands, before my feet lifted off. And when the kite felt my weight, up it swooped just as the waves crashed down and engulfed my boat below.

Up I flew and my stomach lurched. Then sometimes the kite

would plunge and my feet would disappear in the froth of waves and sometimes I saw the lights of other ships appear and disappear in the towering swell, and sometimes birds flew at my side, gulls and cormorants mostly, and a small flock of redstarts with the African sun still warm on their feathers. And sometimes the half-moon appeared, and I felt half glad, half scared.

It was just before dawn when the wind abated, when the billows of grey cloud dissipated and became part of a black starless sky. The battered kite drifted into the shadow of a quiet shore and I descended.

I felt the earth beneath my feet again. I listened to the silence that lived the other side of the falling waves, where a line of moon jellyfish had washed up on the wet shingle and pulsed and glowed like footlights.

And the silence melted me. I stumbled up the beach to where the cliffs rose, to where thick clumps of dry grass grew from the sand. My arms were worn ragged, but I managed to pull up great handfuls of the stuff, picked up driftwood too, that looked like severed limbs in the nibbling dawn. I struck my knife against a piece of quartz and using the grass as kindling lit a fire. When the fire took, I walked along to the rocky outlay and prised limpets from their anchor and ate them from the shell.

I untied the guide rope from the kite and dragged it back down to the shore where it disappeared like an eel into the watery dark. And there I waited. With gulls by my side and a fire at my back, I waited.

Sun high, a boat appeared, lured by the spiralling smoke. The fisherman threw me a rope and landed easily at the shore, and in no time at all I was aboard. The boat glided lazily on the swell and I sat back and said nothing. Just held the kite tightly in my arms.

Eighteen sailors died last night, said the fisherman. How you got here, God only knows. Something must have been watching over you.

And you know what? said Marvellous at the end of her story. Something *was*.

You going tell me it was God? said Drake.

God? Good God, no, Drake. *Love*. Don't confuse the two. Love. It's the only thing to have faith in.

Is that right?

Oh yes, she said.

Or the moon, she added.

The moon?

Yes. Something that turns up every day when you can't. The sun. The moon. Anything. You have to have faith in something.

Why? said Drake.

Because it makes you more interesting to women, she said.

Drake laughed.

Women like something behind the eyes, said Marvellous.

I have plenty behind my eyes.

Yes, but you don't have *light*. Faith gives you light. Jack had light, she said.

What did Jack have faith in?

Me, of course, said Marvellous.

27

THEY DRIFTED OUT FROM THE CHURCH ON THE TIDE. Drake paddled against the current and came to a halt on the bank below Marvellous' caravan. He gripped hard on to thick clumps of exposed tree roots as Marvellous rolled from the flimsy craft on to the shore. He told her to go on ahead, the yellow of her back rising on the steps, disappearing into the warm and dry. Drake groaned and crawled on to land and dragged the canoe in his wake. He was still on all fours when a final purge of vomit left his body. He looked across to the shed, to the canvas kite tied to its side, and he shook his head. Inside the caravan, a paraffin lamp flared, and he heard a popper pulled from a bottle of gin. He staggered up. Wiped his feet against his trouser legs and climbed the steps.

The gypsy wagon felt close after the wide breadth of night. They sat in silence, huddled around the lamp, and they drank sloe gin and they listened. Listened to each other's breathing, to the welcome crackle of the stove, to the slow move of salt rising travelling falling as the water made its journey back out to sea. They listened to the confused call of an owl, the splash of water voles amusing themselves in the grooves along the bank. They listened to the creak of the caravan releasing whispers from its weary well-travelled joints. Drake pointed to *The Book of Truths* on the shelf at the back and asked what it was about. It is what it says it is, said Marvellous, a Book of Truths. Can I read it? he asked. No, she said, you're not ready for the truth, and she turned away and rested her eyes.

Drake stood up and took off his oilskin. Empty bottles on the shelf flickered in the lamplight and caught his eye; the glass magical and alluring in the eerie glow. He leant over and lifted one to the light. Inside was a coil of paper.

What are these? he asked.

Marvellous opened her eyes and frowned.

Messages. I collect them from the shore. Always have.

What do you do with them?

Read them. Answer what I can, said the old woman.

Do you rescue people from desert islands?

Don't be obtuse. Not on a night like this.

Sorry, he said.

Marvellous picked up a gin bottle, label long gone. This was yours actually, she said. November 2nd 1947. River Thames.

I never sent you a message, said Drake.

Yours was silent.

He took the bottle and the date bore down on him and a fist of grief travelled from his guts to his throat. Marvellous rested her hand upon his back as the story of Missy Hall limped out on his tears. She listened to him speak. She lit her pipe and refilled his glass. And she listened to him speak. I loved her, he finally said. I know, she said.

And he so wanted to talk about the war but the sun was creeping high over the trees, and his memory of that day in France wasn't for the light. He lit a last cigarette and stood up. When he got to the door he stopped. He was about to ask Marvellous a question but she surprised him with the answer: You, she said emphatically. I have faith in you.

He walked on down through the trees towards the boathouse. The still morning air reeked of saltmud and echoed with the sorrowful sound of curlews.

The sun was bright. Skimmed the tops of trees and took them out of shadow. The rippled sand glistened and leftover pools were squatted by terns or gulls.

And for the first time he was aware of the possibility of not settling but living once again. And as the sun shifted it turned the river into a silvery molten flow and it looked beautiful and for the first time in weeks he knew he was going to be all right, and because he was going to be all right he knew he was ready to leave.

He looked back to the riverbank and there she was watching him. As if she could read his thoughts. He raised his hand, she raised hers. He turned away so she couldn't see his eyes. It had been a long night.

28

HE DIDN'T PLAN THE DAY HE WAS LEAVING. HE SIMPLY ROSE late with the winter sun, apprehensive of the day ahead. He looked over at the letter addressed to Dr Arnold and knew that today was the day.

He got dressed into his civvies; Collar and Cuffs felt stiff and strange to touch. He looked down and saw turn-ups falling neatly across a polished leather brogue. This was the life he had left. He wasn't sure it was the life he wanted to go back to. He had got used to the routines, the funny ways of this life, and he wondered what he was going to do when the letter had been delivered and an open road lay ahead of him. He neatly folded the clothes the old woman had given him the night he had arrived. He stood back. The fire was doused. The bed stripped. The little touches gone. It was as if he had never been there. No smudged outline of his presence on the white-washed wall above a hearth.

He had never said goodbye to anyone before. Never had the chance to say goodbye to his mother, nor to Missy, had never left anything he'd cared for. Maybe that was why he was hovering. He'd got used to the old woman and her ways. He cared what happened to her. He quickly put on his raincoat and picked up the suitcase before his nerve failed.

He found her at the riverbed ankle-deep in mud, her knees thick and muddy below her rolled-up trouser legs. He watched her, unseen for a moment. He watched the life she had had before him, the life that would go on after him, just her and her solitude, orbited by a lifetime of stories and irritable saints. And he wanted her to be all right because she had always been all right, and he had to believe that, else he'd never go. That's when she looked up and saw him. That's when she put the palm of her hand across her chest.

He walked downriver and waved a big so long salute with his suitcase, just so she'd know and there'd be no mistake, but of course she knew. She didn't wave back. She stopped her digging and came towards the riverbank. He knelt down to her.

I'm leaving.

She nodded. She lifted up her bucket and said, Lugworm. He couldn't be sure it wasn't an insult.

Will you come back? she asked.

I don't think so.

And the old woman nodded.

Thank you for everything, Marvellous, said Drake. Really. *Everything*.

She nodded. She said, Good luck, Francis Drake. Live well. Love again.

She offered her hand and he took it. Took it in both his hands. Her hand felt cold and small.

Don't look back, don't look back, he said to himself, but he did look back and she was still staring at him. His eyes burned. A thousand goodbyes were etched on to her face: those were the lines of age. As he walked away the clouds opened and a gentle rain fell. Her grace falling upon me, he thought.

29

HE RODE WITH BUTCHER DEWAR TO A FARM ON THE outskirts of Truro. He said he would be passing back that way in three hours if Drake needed a lift. Drake said he didn't think he would and waved him goodbye.

He was glad of the walk into town. The rain had eased and the smell was now of dirt and hedgerows, the sweetness of grass, and it softened his anxiety; he was glad of the peace.

So much had happened towards the end of the war, and this letter, this request belonged to the chaos of that time. Drake wished he could have burned it, forgotten about it, no one would have been any the wiser. He didn't even know Dougie Arnold, not really. The letter had been shoved into his hand by a dying man and Drake couldn't walk on by, had said those two words, I promise, and he was bound to the task by conscience because his conscience was so stained by then, he needed something to whiten it.

What if the man asks me about his son? Lie. Be a good soldier and lie. He was a great friend, loyal, who died bravely. Lie. Never a day goes by blah blah blah. Lie.

Drake checked his pocket to make sure the letter was there. The letter felt hot against his hand.

Weeks had passed since he had last been in a city. There were people, motor cars and vans, the to and fro of life and women in make-up clicking their heels, and noise! The cathedral spire came into view, glistening wet in the sunshine. He followed the sight and leant against the granite wall and listened to a fiddler string out bright tunes. An Austin 8 pulled up in front of him. His reflection grotesque and unmistakable in the large side window.

The barber placed the warm towel over his face and around his neck and Drake felt his skin open and relax to the sensation. He felt cleaner than he had felt in months. He looked in the mirror. His beard was groomed, his hair cut. Old Spice was patted about his neck. The transformation was complete. He stepped back out into the keen afternoon air knowing he should have felt better.

Chapel Street?

Second turning on the right, then take a left.

Thank you.

He was hurrying now. Stopped at the top of the street and lit a cigarette to ease his nerves. He made it last till the gate of Monk's Rise where he stubbed it out under his shoe.

A detached house. Front and rear garden. Trailing roses against a white-washed front. A neatly edged path to the door. A doctor's house. No doubt. Drake rang the bell and waited.

No answer. He tried to look into the front room window before ringing the bell again. He was about to push the letter through the letterbox when the door opened quickly and a kind-looking gentleman greeted him.

I'm sorry, the man said wiping his hands, I was out the back. In the garden, burning leaves.

The smell of bonfire clung to his body.

Dr Arnold? said Drake.

Yes that's me.

My name is Francis Drake. I have a letter for you.

Drake watched the man through the French doors. This was a father. He was sitting on a bench reading the letter from his son and he didn't move, and the only movement was the alternate shift of shadow and sunlight falling through the shedding trees. The peace of the scene was overwhelming and Drake wondered what he would have written to his own father. What his father might have written to him. The clock chimed two. He noticed he wasn't impatient to get away.

He stood up and looked about. It was an orderly room, a family room filled with photographs on tables and sideboards. Drake went over to the hearth and picked up a photograph of the son in cricket whites, fifteen – sixteen at most – with a Labrador by his side, when life was yet ahead.

Thank you, said the doctor, entering. Thank you for bringing this into my life. And he placed the letter on the mantelpiece behind the photograph of his son.

The clock ticked loudly. The doctor carried in a tray of tea and biscuits and placed it on the table in front of Drake. May I? said Drake, before lighting a cigarette.

Yes, yes, of course. Milk?

Please.

Drake lit his cigarette.

Sugar?

No thank you.

Neither do I. Lost the taste for the stuff after all the rationing. Here.

He handed Drake a cup of tea.

My wife's not here. She'll be very sorry to have missed you. She's often away at our daughter's, so I'm well-practised at looking after things. I know where the tea and biscuits are.

They sat quietly, smoking, drinking tea. The clock ticked loudly between them.

It never used to work, that clock. It chimed out of the blue two or three years ago after I learnt of my son's death. People often talk of clocks stopping don't they, Mr Drake? Well, mine started. I haven't the foggiest what that means, but it gives me comfort. Inexplicable moments give me comfort. Like you turning up. With a letter I never expected. Inexplicable moments.

The doctor drank his tea.

Do you have family, Mr Drake?

No.

No one?

No.

No one who cares about you?

Drake shifted in his seat. I don't really know, he said.

The clock ticked loudly.

Sorry. Too direct?

No. Not at all. No. I have been cared for, Dr Arnold, so . . .

So you have answered my question. Good. Good.

Dr Arnold sipped his tea. Had you known my son long?

173

Yes. Long enough.

He never mentioned you.

No? Drake reached for his tea. Keep your hand steady.

He was a good soldier, he added. You should be proud of him.

I am. I was. But he wasn't a good soldier, I don't think. And he hated every minute of the war. And we disagreed about the war and in that disagreement was the seed of our estrangement. So. You see. You're either a bad liar, or you didn't know him.

Drake's heart thumped loudly. The clock ticked. His mouth dried.

I didn't know him, he eventually said. I'm sorry. I don't want to cause distress.

No, no you're not, said the doctor. Please sit down. Please. But how did you come by the letter?

I was passing a wounded man who had been left on a stretcher at the edge of a field hospital and he asked me to deliver it.

And you didn't know him?

No.

But you promised to deliver it.

I did.

The last wish of a dying man?

Yes, I thought it was.

Then for that I thank you. The doctor drank the last of his tea.

We drank brandy, said Drake. And the flowers were out. And that day didn't feel like war because it was summer, and the sun was out and it was normal. And for a brief moment we were normal. Your son said he wanted to swim.

The doctor smiled, said, He was a good swimmer.

He wanted me to tell you he was all right.

The doctor coughed, cleared his throat. So? What happens to you now, Mr Drake? he said.

I don't know, really.

Back to London?

No. Not London. I may go back to France. To the south.

A free spirit?

Something like that. I've been living here the last six weeks.

In Cornwall?

Yes. I've been living by a river in a boathouse: a strange set-up for someone who hates water.

An ideal set-up, in many ways, for someone who hates water.

Yes, maybe. I think that's probably what the old woman would have said too.

And what old woman is that? said Dr Arnold.

Old Marvellous. Lived down there for years.

The clocked ticked loudly.

She's still alive? said the doctor.

You know her?

Knew her. Yes, I did. A long time ago now, and Dr Arnold got up and went to the drinks cabinet. My God, he said. How is she?

Drake thought. Remarkable, really.

Does she still swim?

Drake smiled. Yes. Every high water.

She told you her mother was a mermaid?

She did.

The doctor raised a bottle of Scotch. Will you join me?

Please.

No water I would guess, said the doctor.

No water, said Drake smiling.

The doctor handed Drake his drink.

Good luck, Mr Drake.

To you, sir.

The sound of two glasses touching. The sound of a clock. The sound of the doctor sitting back heavily in his armchair as a sigh from the past brushes his ear.

Do you believe in fate, Mr Drake?

I don't know. I haven't thought about it.

No, and neither did I at your age, the question was probably rather unfair. But looking back now I can quite honestly say that I do believe in fate.

I met your old woman – Miss Marvellous Ways – twenty-five years ago. And to this day I count myself lucky to have met her. For years there had been rumours about her. My predecessor had warned me about the Woman in the Wood. Said people were uncomfortable with her, scared of her even. But most doctors tolerated her. One even had his children delivered by her. Strange times, Mr Drake.

When I was called to visit her, she had been living rough in the woods for weeks. Naked, whatever the weather. It was not long after the First War I think. It was 1922 maybe? People said she had gone mad after burying her lover. Well, that was the story that brought me back to her door one spring afternoon, twenty-five years ago.

I remember leading her back to her caravan saying something unbelievably trite, something along the lines of, Life goes on. I was young, my only excuse.

She was oblivious to her state, thank God. She thought our meeting was a meeting of like minds: doctor to doctor, the linking of science – me – with her the traditional. Or so she believed. She had cuts on her hands and feet and sores around her mouth. She had a rasping cough, if I remember rightly. I asked to listen to her chest and she told me it was grief. I said I thought it was pneumonia. I said, Open your mouth. She said, Open your *mind*.

The doctor laughed. *Open your mind!* I told her she could die if she didn't go and live somewhere dry and stop her daily swim. I swim because I have to, that's what she said. It's what keeps me well. And I said, Can't you just swim in the morning? And she said I swim at high tide. It's who I am. My mother was a mermaid. Blame the moon. I'd never met anyone who talked the way she talked. Who saw the world the way she saw it. And I was transfixed, if not professionally curious, as well. I saw her every day for two weeks. And every day she told me about her life and the river. Took me into the boathouse and told me the story of her mother and father. And on the last day I took out my stethoscope and listened to her breathing. There was no pneumonia, no hysteria. Just the sound of deep sorrow. It was the first time I had ever made such a diagnosis.

Melancholia. That's the term the Victorians used. Grief. Depression. Unassailable loss, choose what you will, but I too understand the madness that ensues when someone you love dies. But I kept mine clothed. Respectable. I kept mine hidden so as not to frighten people. But it was there, behind my job, behind my eyes. But because I was respectable, people would come to our house with food, or a cake, or kind words. My grief – because I was respectable – was not misinterpreted. I too went mad, Mr Drake. But I still polished my shoes.

You see, this, he said, picking up a Y-shaped tree branch that stood with tongs in a brass holder next to the hearth. On my last night she sent me away with this dowsing rod tucked under my arm, which she promised would find me love.

Drake smiled. And did it?

Oh yes, it did as it happens. The following weekend at a colleague's wedding. I was so taken with the beautiful Belinda Faulks that three days later I held that very same dowsing rod above her head like a sprig of mistletoe, and kissed her. We got engaged shortly after. Then married. All the things we are supposed to do. I worked hard. Children. Back to London. Back to Cornwall. And I forgot about Miss Ways.

The doctor ran his hand over the old gnarled branch of hazel and he saw his hand again as a young man's hand with a lifeline barely explored. And he remembered again that last night in the caravan. Remembered how the sun lowered, how the fractured colours breached the leafed canopy above and streamed before his eyes, that golden light – the light blues, the rich deep blues, as if its majesty that evening was just for them. And how for the first time in his life, he was flooded by an implacable and overwhelming peace. *Somewhere between God and medicine there is a place for me.* That's what she'd said and that's what he'd never forgotten. And he could taste again the sweet sloe gin that loosened his tongue and softened his heart, and the perfumed warmth of the wagon that gave him courage to speak his fears. His eyes prickled and were burning now as he remembered how she enfolded his hand in her own, turning it over, studying it, how she ran her finger across the scar – from a scalpel, he said – and he never pulled away when her gaze ran across his palm. And he remembered asking anxiously, What do you see? Because in her eyes there was a shadow, and years later he understood that that shadow was his son: a beautiful line that suddenly dropped off a cliff.

What do you see? he asked again. And she had said,

Happiness. I see years of happiness. And she knew that's all anyone wanted to hear. And she had followed him out into the darkness and the air was damp and earthy, and the smell of salt was strong and wafted on the breeze. And she had led him through the damp ferns towards the roadside where they stopped by his car. Marvellous had looked up into the starry sky and pointed to a bright white star. That's your star, Dr Arnold, she had said. Take your bearings from that star and it'll always bring you home. And it always did.

Dr Arnold shook out a clean white handkerchief and said, Excuse me. A day of ghosts, I'm afraid. Or should I say memories? People prefer memories to ghosts, I think.

The clock chimed.

She delivered Douglas, you know.

What? said Drake. But how? I don't—

Douglas was my stepson. I engaged myself to mother *and* child. His father had been killed in the First War. That's how, Mr Drake.

There are many more things I would like to say, said Dr Arnold. But it's a question of time. Your time, obviously because you have given me so much already and my gratitude is beyond anything. But there is something I'd like you to see. Something interesting, I think. Something I wished I had seen before. Maybe it would have helped. I don't know.

And Drake said that for once he had all the time in the world.

30

THEY WERE QUIET BY THE TIME THEY REACHED THE Museum. Drake let the doctor go on ahead while he stood outside in the falling dusk. He needed time to think about the strange coincidence of Dougie Arnold, time to think about everything the doctor had said to him. He lit a cigarette and watched the ebb and flow of people along River Street. So many lives. All unknown. Drake looked back up to the building. He flicked the cigarette into the gutter and with a heavy feeling in his chest, climbed the steps expecting nothing.

He had never entered a museum before. The close hush of the building was a surprise, a strange comfort. The air was cool, the mood strangely profound. As a church should be. He thought about Marvellous' quiet declaration on the Night of Tears. I have faith in you. That's what she'd said.

His footsteps echoed across the ornate stone floor and the

fall of his London tread sounded clumsy in the vaulted room as he made his way to the staircase, to the level above.

Dr Arnold was waiting for him. He led him into a small gallery on the right and took him over to a painting on the far wall. Light snaked over his shoulder and lit the face in front.

Here she is, he heard Dr Arnold say. The young woman William Ways fell in love with. This, I believe, is our mermaid.

Drake became aware of his every breath. Aware of every beat of every pulse at his neck at his wrist in his groin in his heart. He noted the size of the frame ahead of him, absorbed the beauty of the face staring back at him, eyes deep and black and sad. An evening sun had caught her right cheek, enriching the dark honey and brown tones of her skin.

Drake turned to Dr Arnold and before he could speak the doctor said, Not what you expected, is she? Imagine her *here*, Mr Drake. Imagine people's fear, their incomprehension. Their *suspicion*.

There were some free men and women back in the American South in the 1850s, Mr Drake. I have done my research. Not common, but not rare either. But whether she was free or whether William Ways bought her freedom we can only speculate. Her desire to swim – to *cleanse*, if you will – is not that hard to understand, given what probably happened to her. A form of baptism, you could say. Purification by immersion.

Drake turned back to the canvas. Globules of water diamonds hung upon her brow, masking a scar. Her hair, dark and dripping, running down her back. Her bosom, heavy and full. There was gold around her neck, a small shell box too, holding her daughter's calling. But there was no smile, no song on those thick reddened lips, merely history; a history stolen and brought across seas and sold to the highest bidder. Those lips that had launched a thousand sailors had buried themselves into the neck of William Ways like a prow full steam into waves, and he had promised her freedom and she had given him life. The boathouse was there behind, and the river, full and bloated, nibbling at her hem, teasing her with her not-nice history whispering, Wash it off. Wash *them* off. And those eyes would not let him be.

For here she was: *Lady of the Sea*, Approx 1857. Artist: Alfred Warren. Donated Anonymously.

For here she was: the missing piece that matched the smudged outline, etched upon a boathouse wall by smoke and time. A false window to yesterday.

31

IT WAS LATE, DARK WHEN THE CAR PULLED UP AT THE TOP of the meadow. Drake got out, waved as he watched the doctor pull away. He sat down wearily on the milestone and looked at the dowsing rod. It held everything he had heard today and everything he had seen, and it felt heavier than when he'd first held it. He hadn't wanted to take it, but the doctor had insisted. Said you never really own things like this, you merely borrow them.

Come on, he said to himself, no more tonight. And he rolled up his trousers and made his way through the wet grass. He'd decide what to say to old Marvellous when he saw her in the morning. He was too tired now to come up with a story, because today had been a day when he just couldn't lie.

As he came through the trees he saw that a lamp had been left outside his door. How had she known? Every gesture weighed heavy and he wanted to go straight inside and smoke and drink more but he heard her call out his name and he could never refuse her calling. He left his suitcase outside by the steps.

When he entered the warmth of the wagon, he could barely see her under the pile of blankets, and what he could see was just two large eyes full of longing.

Here, said Drake, peeling her glasses away from her head.

Must have fallen asleep, she said.

Yes, he said.

Waiting for you to get back.

I know.

Silence.

You went to the barber.

I did.

You look nice. Very smart.

Then she pointed to his hand and said, What you got there, then?

He lifted the dowsing rod into the light. The old woman ran her hands across the grain.

Is it one of mine? she asked.

It is. You gave it to someone a long time ago.

I did?

Yes. Four years or so after the First War. A doctor came to see you. Do you remember?

A doctor?

Yes. A Dr Arnold? The man I took the letter to?

The old woman's eyes clouded.

I don't think I remember him right now, Drake.

That's all right.

I don't have to, do I?

No, you don't. You really don't, and he pulled the blanket up high.

I was thinking, said Drake.

What?

I don't think I'm going to leave. I'd like to stay –

I'd like you to stay –

– for as long as I can, if that's OK.

The old woman nodded and smiled. She reached across and patted his hand.

Ten days till Christmas, she said. Have you thought about what you'd like?

No I haven't.

I was thinking you need a crab pot.

Do I?

Yes. Because the shops keep running out of food.

That's true.

So you never go hungry.

A crab pot it will be, then, said Drake. Night, Marvellous. And he stood up to go.

What you going to get me? she said.

I don't know yet. He smiled. What would you like?

A surprise.

All right.

It better be good, mind, she said.

It will be. I promise it'll be unforgettable.

Promises, promises, she said.

Night, Marvellous.

When Drake got to the door, Marvellous said, That dowsing rod. It won't find you water, you know. Only love.

Drake stopped. He went back to the bed, leant over and kissed her for the first time.

What's all this then? she said.

But he had no words. He would never have any words for what happened that day, and she held his hand and whispered, It's all right. And that between them would be enough.

32

IN A FORGOTTEN CHAPTER TORN FROM TIME, A KEY TURNS loudly in a lock and a young doctor – newly married – is shown into the fading light of a grey room. A woman sits on the bed. She is not yet old but she looks old, fiddling with a shell box hanging about her neck. The air is still. About her, scores of model boats cast adrift on the brown institutional floor: boats of various sizes, some complete, many not, made by love and a careful eye, and the secret component of endless time.

The woman sits patiently, shudders as the raw December night whispers across her skin. She is naked beneath her yellow coat. Time passes, somewhere the tide rises. The moon shifts across the bars, and as night slips in, so her fear slips out.

She is slow off the bed. The young doctor attempts to go towards her but he is held back. The woman crawls towards the wall, feels in the dark for the rugged line where wall meets floor. Her fingers reach for the joins between the brick. There it is. She gently pulls at the ragged strips of stuffed paper until the brick slips out free. She lies on the floor now, her face pressed close to the opening where a faint draught crawls across her cheeks, across her brow. She breathes through her nose, sifts through those other smells until she finds the one that will take her home.

The salt is thick in the air, the river high. She swallows hard as her mouth waters. Heavy with the weight of longing her lids close, just in time for her to stumble through the trees to where the water is still, to where the ripple of riversong breaks the surface as it escapes from the depths of time. And it calls her and she hears that song, the song of Return.

The young doctor kneels down by her side and whispers her name.

She looks at him and sees no one.

33

IT HAD BEEN YEARS SINCE DRAKE HAD ALLOWED HIMSELF to remember a boyhood Christmas in the pub.

He used to help dress the tree and make paper chains until his tongue was dry. And late at night when the pub was locked, he would come downstairs, and the men gave him sips of booze and drags of their cigarettes but only when his mother or Mr Betts weren't looking.

And he remembered the old women in the snug drinking port and stout, and he always thought that Mrs Betts looked like a glass of stout in her black dress and her small white lace cap, but he didn't tell anyone.

And they were good memories.

And there were women there too, women who walked the streets. They were tired of the poverty, tired of the scarcity of food, and tired of men, but they were kind. His favourites were

Iris and Lilly and he thought they were lookers and they always made a fuss of him, draping their arms over him, marking him with the scent of their strange love. At night they changed their names to Peaches and Cherry because in the darkness that's when flowers turned into fruit.

Mr Toggs played the piano and sometimes Drake sat next to him to press a key, but mostly he sat next to him and sang. And everyone cheered when he sang, and his cheeks reddened but that may also have been from the sips of beer and whisky. But whatever it was, it was a good feeling, seeing all those smiling faces and listening to those singing voices and looking out the window and seeing the comfort of those grubby streets outside. And Drake thought that life was magical and his life was the best life ever, and it didn't matter that he didn't have a father that Christmas because when it came to the Christmas pudding and he found the silver threepenny bit in his mouth, he didn't wish for a father like he usually did. He wished for that day to last for ever. Just him and his mum. And that day for ever.

And that was a good memory.

He stared at the photograph he had tucked away in his wallet. She was a good memory again, his mum. He hung the dowsing rod above the doorway, decorated it with a long sprig of berried holly. Slipped the photograph behind the rod. Happy Christmas, Mum.

Drake placed a log on the low flame. He stood up and looked at the smudged outline above the hearth, and he saw again the mermaid's face, how she would have watched over William Ways, over the boathouse and their life. He went to his suitcase and took out the picture collage of a man's face. It was easy to smooth, the paper was soft. He pressed it against the outline on the wall – it was a perfect fit. He held a candle to the fire until the wax was soft and pliable, and he broke off four small rounds and pressed each to the corners of the picture. Stuck the picture against the outline on the wall, it framed it well. He stood back. It looked right. In a boathouse on a stranger's shore in a forgotten creek, it looked so very right.

Who's that? asked Marvellous.

Drake turned with a start. Jesus, Marvellous!

Who's that? she asked again.

And he looked back towards the picture and for the first time in his life, he told someone.

It's my father, he said.

How I imagined him to be, he said. Daft, eh? I was nine when I did it. When I asked my mother the questions. What colour were his eyes, Ma? What colour was his hair? How was his mouth, Ma? What about his nose? And I asked and didn't stop until she gave me the answers. I didn't know how hard it must have been for her, being made to remember something she probably wanted to forget. And when she went downstairs to the pub to earn extra money I cut up old magazines she'd been given and took parts of faces that matched her answers. Until I was left with this. With *him*. I just wanted something like everyone else had a something. I wanted a face that would watch over me when I slept. Because I wanted what my mother had. Because she was only ever happy when she slept.

The boathouse creaked.

I have his hands, though, said Drake, looking down at his fingers. And do you know how I know that?

Tell me.

Because they weren't my mother's, and Drake turned to her and smiled.

And you have his eyes, said the old woman looking at his smile.

He turned again to the picture.

Yes, he said. You're right. I *do* have his eyes.

34

THE TEAROOM WAS WARM AND FULL OF CHATTERING couples. The sounds of china and teaspoons and gossip competed in her ears, a rare symphony she seldom heard. But Marvellous felt so alive and smiled at everyone and spoke to no one. She had taken off her hat and it sat with the newspaper stuffing on the chair beside her, in front of the window framing the sight of Truro Cathedral. The waitress placed the bill down on the table and looked at her. Everybody watched. Marvellous laid a crisp one-pound note next to the sugar bowl – a one-pound note! somebody whispered – and she said, Thank you, dear, the cakes were lovely. My compliments to your chef.

The flush of a toilet. The feeling of hot running water through his fingers. Hot running water at the turn of a tap! Drake closed his eyes to savour the luxurious feel of convenience. He dried his hands and smoothed his beard in the grimy mirror.

He opened the door and stopped suddenly. He saw, for the first time, what other people saw: a small old woman with large broken-framed glasses in a grubby yellow oilskin, with a man's trilby two sizes too big. He felt his fists fizz, as he saw their snatched glances, and better-than grins as Marvellous gathered up her hat and newspaper stuffing. He marched into the room and pulled out the chair for her. He offered her his arm, she looked so proud. Thank you my boy, she said. She put her change into her pocket and said goodbye to everyone around. No one said goodbye back. She was oblivious to the eyes that watched her leave, but he wasn't. He glared at the comments that fell in her wake. She had always been talked about, she was like the weather: a constant source of speculation and disappointment. When she left they found a small mound of mud under her chair.

Where are we going? she asked, on the way out. But Drake felt too protective, too angry to speak.

They wandered up River Street, the old woman and young man. Now and then she stumbled on cobblestones because she refused to look down at her feet, there was just too much of life to see. Drake slowed and said, Here we are, and Marvellous said, You've brought me to the bank? And he said that it wasn't a bank any more. Then what is it? she said. You'll see, he said, and he took her arm and led her past the columns through the large wooden doors into the sonorous surround of the grand room. There was no one else about, all was quiet. Just the faint sound of an old woman's heart beating in wonder.

Drake led her up the staircase to the small gallery above. He told her to take as long as she liked, he'd be waiting downstairs, and when he left he didn't dare look back because had he looked back he knew the something in his chest might shatter.

And so it was, that in her ninetieth year, Marvellous Ways saw her mother's face for the first time.

She said nothing in those first few minutes, but Drake would later say that a sigh could be heard throughout the corridors and the displays of the museum. The old woman stood as close as she possibly could and in the dingy light she introduced herself. Soon words tumbled over words. And as those secrets passed from lips to ears, she would later remember carols being sung outside and the first fluttering of snow falling past the arched windows causing tiny shadows to flicker down her head then down her face like tears, on to the gallery floor. And when the attendant called time, she didn't protest but quietly said, Goodbye. Said, See you again soon, and left through the heavy doors back to the wintry present.

Once outside, the snow fell heavily and settled. Perfect flakes of symmetry. The choir sang 'In the Bleak Midwinter', and she put money in the tin. And she sang loudly, *Snow is falling snow on snow.*

That would be her memory, because it was magical. For others, however, it was the previous winter that snow had fallen so. And Marvellous would remember a brass band playing with the carol singers, even though for others the dark streets reverberated with nothing more than the frantic pace of pre-Christmas shopping.

And she would remember that she and Drake walked all the way home that night and she wouldn't remember the vans and the ferry and the carts that had picked them up and put them down, because she remembered walking down familiar lanes and for her there was no moon that night (even though there was) because her eyes were now so clear she could see everything that she had ever wanted to see. And she would remember that her pace was brisk because her feet walked on elation, and that was in fact the word she tried to remember but it had long-gone so she settled for happiness.

The snow fell deep around them. Hedgerows were covered and soon they walked through a white landscape like two shadows playing truant. Silence greeted every crunch underfoot and a smile never shifted from the old woman's lips.

Hours later, they reached the High Road by the meadow and Drake said, Stop here, because he could never fail to do so now. So they stopped there. Thick misting breath swirled from their mouths. He stamped his feet hard on the road, banged his hands against his sides.

Here, he said, and he handed her a small badly wrapped present that he took from his pocket.

Wrapped it myself, he said.

It's not Christmas yet, the old woman said.

Think it might be, he said.

So she peeled off her mittens, untied the ribbon and unwrapped the paper until a small black tube sat in her palm. She held it up to her face and twisted slowly until a perfect finger of pillar-box red emerged into the white tumbling sky.

And the snow fell. And the snow fell. And the snow fell. And it was beautiful.

35

JANUARY CAME AND DUG IN LIKE A STUBBORN MULE.

Marvellous looked out from her caravan on to the night. At first, she had thought it was a saint on walkabout, now that the evenings were so bitter. But when she looked through her telescope she saw that it was Drake down by the riverbank, looking over at the church. He had become restless again and she'd noticed that his shakes had returned, something he tried to hide. His appetite was scant and his words few, and the notion of living well had been replaced by a trenchant need to survive, nothing more. He turned and looked up towards her caravan. That's when she saw the great big troublesome dream buzzing around his head, a dream as loud and dripping as a dragonfly.

She quickly locked her windows. Maybe it was the action or maybe it was the noise, but that dragonfly-dream turned right round and headed straight for her locked-up glass and the sound was like a pistol shot, and the sound threw her to the bed, shocked.

It had always been a matter of time, she knew that. From the night he had arrived when she had lifted him from the tree, the weight of his soul had left an indelible print upon her arms, and she had always known it was a matter of time before she began to dream his dreams.

Two weeks before, a little past midnight, a breathless exhaustion and dense black had fallen upon the wood. There was no sound. Nature had surrendered and even the stars had dimmed. The moon was the tiniest sliver and for most it went unnoticed. Marvellous couldn't sleep. Truth be told, she *wouldn't* sleep. Instead, she sat up drinking as the haunting ate at the periphery of her world. When she lay upon the mattress it engulfed her, when she sat in the chair and extinguished the light, it laughed. It was a dark fear, male. It wasn't hers.

Then two nights after that she awoke to the sound of screaming. She went outside. All was still. Drake rushed from the boathouse disorientated.

I heard screaming, he said. Are you all right?

She froze. That's when she knew for sure.

Probably a dream, she said. Go back, all's well here. We're all safe here.

And he turned to go. What woke you? he asked.

Bladder, she said. The usual.

And last night: a card game. She wasn't playing, she was a card instead. There was laughter, and he was there, Drake was there. When she awoke, she was sick on the floor. She knew she wasn't ailing.

And now night had come again. Marvellous got up from the

chair and walked out into the freezing air. Fear made her colder still, and she had layered all her clothes upon her skin. She had tightened her trouser belt, had barricaded herself against the outside world and it was only when she reached the water's edge that she realised how odd that was, that only the skin on her face touched the air.

Nothing felt familiar, the creek no longer felt kind. Bushels of dark knotweed suspended below the surface became black clumps of feeding shadow. It's here, she thought looking around, slashing at the night sky with her stick. The dream is here. And she felt herself suddenly pulled to the ground, the air forced from her lungs. Oh my God the weight.

Drake found her the following morning. A small, motionless heap covered in mud and frost, and as he got closer, he saw that her clothes were ripped and dishevelled. He lifted her into his arms and carried her to the caravan and placed her in her bed. He had never cared for anyone as he cared for her in that moment. Hot roundels of slate he put down her sides and upon her back and he tended a stove that he never let go out. Pans of kiddley broth awaiting only her appetite. And he held her hand and whispered words he'd last spoken as a child.

Two days later, Marvellous awoke. She looked frail, looked older. She said nothing for days, didn't even swim, locked herself in and locked out a world that confused her. Drake left food on the wagon steps. He lit the church candle for her every night when he realised she hadn't. He sat outside in the cold at both high tides waiting for a sign. It came a week later.

She found him downriver collecting firewood a little before dusk. She handed him a playing card. He turned it over. It was the nine of Diamonds. He looked up and began to shake. Tears streamed down his face.

He sat with her that evening, his back against the mooring stone, her legs to his side. He couldn't face her, couldn't face himself. Gulls swooped downstream at fish breaking the surface and the call of a sandpiper urged him on. The tide was almost in. He didn't know where to start so he started somewhere.

36

HE REMEMBERED THE DAY AS A PERFECT SUMMER'S DAY and the beauty of the day seemed so important, so unkind, looking back.

It was the last year of war. The last day of friendship for the men who had lived through horror, but not the last day they would all be together because that's quite a different thing. But the last day they would all be able to look each other in the eye.

Four of them had been playing poker. Drake remembered it was good fun and he'd won a lot of money, which was rare because he never considered himself a lucky man. They heard laughter coming through the trees, and in the summer air it sounded pleasant and a good thing to hear. Scribbs and Johnno turned up with a woman. She wore a fur coat and carried a suitcase and looked as if she was going somewhere. She didn't speak English so Scribbs didn't have to be careful what he said.

He said she'd been one of the women who had kept company with the Germans. He shuffled the cards and turned to the men and told them to pick a card. They all did. Then he said, Highest goes first, and they showed their cards and he cheered and said that'll be me, I've got the King, and he flicked the King at the woman's face and then he raped her. Johnno and Hunch were lined up ready to take over. It happened so quick. Drake was still holding the Nine of Diamonds when he lunged for Scribbs, tried to pull him off. Bloody hell mate you're eager, I'll be done soon, said Scribbs laughing. Drake shouted at the men but the men ignored him, just stood in a queue as if they were waiting for a bus.

They told him to fuck off, and by God he should have picked up a gun and forced them to stop. But he didn't. He did as he was told and he walked away and left something behind that would be for ever lost.

The woman stopped screaming after the third and he kept walking. Kept walking until he came to a village and there was a church there, and singing came from the church, and an old man sat on the front steps drinking from a bottle of wine. He looked up and offered Drake the bottle.

Drake sat down next to him and felt soothed by the young voices and the full sweetness of the ink-dark wine. A young woman walked past and the old man smiled and raised his hat and the woman swished her skirt and she smiled too, both at the old man and Drake, and Drake almost forgot that just over the crossroads in the lay of the forest a woman was being raped by five men.

The choir sang and the old man sang and Drake couldn't sing, and suddenly he began to cry because of the music, because of the sound of the boys' voices, because of what they might turn into. What *he* had turned into. And he wanted to be comforted and the old man patted his arm before getting up to leave. But Drake wanted to be held. And most of all he wanted his father because somewhere he knew that his father would forgive him and his father would make the indescribable pain go away. That was the moment he felt his father's death. When he finally grieved for a man he had never known. That was the moment he longed for his father to tell him that it would be all right.

The choir stopped singing and he sat on the steps with an empty bottle of *vin rouge* between his legs. The heavy oaken doors creaked open and a handful of boys ran out, and the birds sang and the sun cast deep shadows that sprang out from the boys' heels. But when Drake stood up he had no shadow and that's how he knew that something had died.

He stumbled back through the trees and the woman came towards him on the way. Her lipstick was smeared and she was limping but it may have been because she carried her shoes in her hand and there were twigs on the forest floor. He stood aside and wanted to say something, but his French wasn't that good, didn't know the words for *wrong* or *ashamed*. So when she passed by all he managed to say was, *Je m'excuse*, and she spat in his face, which he knew he deserved.

She pulled that fine fur coat tight around her and walked on tiptoe as if she had heels, and in the dappled light that fell through the trees she was a goddess – for a brief moment a goddess – because three days later as the village rounded up collaborators she wore tar and jibes and her golden hair was shorn and burned with the locks of others, and the smell – fuck! – the smell. And she was marched into a crowd of men and they kicked her and he never saw her walk out the other side.

The battle moved east into Belgium towards Germany, but the others never watched his back after that because they couldn't trust him any more. He wasn't one of them, he was a fucking poof-nonce-commie, take your pick, they gave him other names too.

And then war was over and streets were lined with cheering and gratitude. Soldiers marched by and collected a woman in one arm and a drink in the other. Battalions were reassigned, some headed home, most stayed, demob was achingly slow. But what did Drake care? He had nothing to go back to.

Thirteen months passed before kitbags were packed in bitter silence and soldiers headed for troopships waiting at the coast. And amidst the chaos of departure Drake quietly slipped away. He never got his discharge papers, would get them later from a man who knew a man and they'd be as good as real. Never got his ration books either or shitty little suit. Slipped away instead, he did, and headed back to France. Down to the south where he was told the sun stayed high and stayed high for hours on end, and where he hoped the warm sirocco wind would melt those frozen, irretrievable years.

Dusk was falling when Drake finished the story. He felt light but it was becoming dark. He heard Marvellous sigh but he couldn't look at her, felt his face tight with shame and guilt. He felt her warm hand rest lightly on the top of his head.

The sound of the river filled the silence. Two gulls called to each other from bank to bank. In their cry he heard his name.

Listen, said Marvellous. And he listened beyond their call and that's when he heard it, really heard it.

Tide's on the turn, she said. He knew what he had to do.

They stood on the shore and he climbed down the bank and

waded into the river. The ice-cold water reached his chest and his shirt and trousers clung to his limbs. And where once was a dark life-long fear, was nothing now: an absence filled only with sorrow and the past. He crouched down and the water flooded his nose and ears and he was overcome by a pressured silence. His shirt billowed and his hair rose and broke the surface like weed, and he felt an overwhelming peace as he lifted his feet off the bottom and floated with the tide and fish, lungs full to bursting.

He surfaced downriver by Old Cundy's boat. And he held on to the slats as he took in great mouthfuls of air and he was aware that he felt different. His hands looked young against the vibrant green moss that coated the hull, and he leant his head against the boat and closed his eyes, and amidst the hush of nightfall he heard the boat say, It'll be all right, and he heard it say, It's over now.

IV

37

A BATTERED VAN THAT HAD ONCE BEEN AN AMBULANCE stuttered along the High Road and stopped outside the bake-house. The young woman behind the wheel didn't turn the ignition off right away, but sat staring ahead at the quiet desolation that was now her home.

She arrived that morning with a wireless, a rocking chair and a jar of sourdough starter. She had come with her mother's blessing and an old man's faith. By the age of twenty-nine, Peace Rundle knew that the winds of Fate preferred her to travel light.

She cut the thick purr of the engine, opened the door and nervously stepped out. The morning sun rested warm on her back and she breathed air she had last breathed as a baby. The cottages stood miserable and forlorn but the hedgerows were well-decorated by spring. She picked a trumpet of cowslip and slipped it into her cardigan.

She stood in front of the bakehouse door and rested her hands against the weather-beaten wood. No turning back now. Key in the lock and the door gave way easily. On the stone threshold she listened carefully as dust settled and sabres of sunlight cut oblique lines across the gloom. She heard the bakehouse expand a little and welcome her in. It was as simple as that, their union, and when it came to pulling back the shutters and undressing the windows, the building gave up its modesty easily.

Inside was a vast space with a large oak table dominating the middle. The air smelt of age and damp and the faint whiff of sourdough. The oven took up one side of the wall, a proving cupboard the other, and beyond, extending to the outside was a parlour for the moments when she wouldn't be baking. There was no electricity switch, no overhead light, and she would wait until the following month to be connected to the cables that lined the roads and fields outside.

She crossed the ancient flagstones and unlocked the back door. The garden was overgrown but with her large enthusiastic hands she knew she could clear it in a week and eventually keep chickens and grow her own vegetables. There were apple trees, too, and old raspberry canes that might flourish again with a little cajoling and care. As her mother had once told her, she was a Doer and not a Quitter.

You're a Doer, my love. That's why God made you so big. So you could do everything yourself. Girls like you don't quit till you're dead. That should be a comfort.

And in a way it was. Her mother had told her to do things once and do them well. Things like building a dry-stone wall or getting married. Once and well (wonsunwell) was her motto. Wonsunwell became her daughter's.

It was her mother, too, who had given her a detailed map of the creek, hastily drawn on the back of a white cotton handkerchief moments before she died. That, for Peace, had been encouragement enough.

Peace unfolded the map, and like a strong desire to eat, felt an immediate hunger to reacquaint with her past. She didn't bother to lock up but headed straight out, across the road into a meadow still glistening with dew and pockmarked by the ghostly tufts of dandelions. She ran most of the way, and before long was enjoying the cool of the wood, and the luring scents of ramsons and bluebells and salt. The creek was deserted, and the boathouse and caravan stood quiet and still. Piles of wooden planks rested on the bank. Peace called out to Marvellous, and a flock of collared doves flew off to the east. She thought about leaving a note on the caravan but when she searched her pockets, all she could come up with was a creased photograph, a bent teaspoon and a handful of roughly-milled flour. She would come back. She would come back bearing gifts – a loaf maybe? – and she clambered down the riverbank and began to remove her shoes and socks. She rolled up her trouser legs and waded into the water.

Her mother, she remembered, had always referred to the secluded church as the Church of the Sacred Heart and it didn't take a bagful of brains to know why. Because as Peace straddled the doorway – left leg on the holy, right leg on the pagan – she rested her ear against the rotten frame and listened for the faint sound of her brother's war-scarred heart. A woodpecker quietened and signalled for the other birds to cool it too, and they all watched intently, watched her with curiosity. *Ta-dum ta-dum ta-dum*. There it was. She pressed her heart against his. They beat in unison. Her and her brother. Together again.

She sat with her back against his gravestone, unaware that the carved sentiment *In Peace Perfect Peace* rose unobtrusively above her head. She looked about at the small cemetery decimated by time and tide, and thought about her mother and felt something she had never felt before, and that something was her mother's youth, and she learnt more about her mother and her mother's dreams in that moment than she ever had in her lifetime. Because they were her dreams now: simple dreams about living well and loving well, things she had once thought were out of reach. She had only ever known her mother in the clutch of grief, but once it had been different. Once she had been free. Like her.

She took out the photograph of a young soldier awkwardly holding a baby. It was her brother, Simeon, of course. He had just returned from war and he was holding her in his arms. She had never known him, he had never known her because they had been the bookends of their mother's fertility – he came too early and she came too late and nothing came in between. He didn't look right then, but people had clothed him in heroism and clothes like that were too bright to show the rags of misery underneath. She put the photograph back in her pocket and noticed the fine dusting of flour around her fingers. She closed her eyes and tasted the flour, and the years fell away. Thank you Wilfred, she said, quietly. Thank you.

Peace was still a baby the day her mother and father left St Ophere, so was too young to remember the horse and cart piled high with pans and chairs and mattresses and an heirloom table. Too young to remember the neighbours' faces that turned away and didn't bid them well as they made their way towards St Austell with its glistening mountains of china clay spoils. The day was never talked of again but hung about in their new cottage like worn curtains blocking light.

But what Peace did remember was a childhood of waiting. She was either waiting for her mother's grief to subside or for her father's drinking to stop. But neither did. She was either waiting for her growth spurt to stop or for the other children to catch up, but neither did and she remained an ostrich in a yard full of ducks. It didn't bother her, at first, this growing difference, but then a shyness took hold, a shyness so acute that at the height of summer even her shadow refused to go out and play. Eventually the waiting wore her out and she took to her bed like a large warming stone.

One night, however, the smell of freshly baked bread stole in through her window. She followed the scent out of her house across the terraces, past the pub and past the church until she came to the doorstep of Wilfred Gently's Bakehouse. The windows were as fogged-up as the old man's eyes, so she knew he was still baking. She knocked lightly and Wilfred opened the door and waved her inside.

He drew up a stool for her and told her to watch and learn as he began to knead the shining pale grey mound. Peace did as she was told and everything that was wrong disappeared in the muscular folds of kneaded dough.

There was no money to go with her apprenticeship but there was daily bread and purpose – something the Preacher told her mother would please God – and Wilfred set about teaching her everything he knew.

He taught her how to add moisture to the oven to help the bread rise and form a good crust. He taught her to listen out to the songs of rising bread and cooling bread. He taught how to use a paddle efficiently and safely, and what baskets hold bread the best. He showed her how to keep a proving cupboard free from mould. He handed down to her his life-long work and she devoured it.

Three years later he changed the bakehouse name to Gently with Peace. A year after that, he taught her about flour. How it varies according to the season, and sometimes even air pressure. Beware when you bake during a storm!

Finally, the last thing he needed to tell her about was his recipes. He told her something he had never told anyone: that his secret ingredient was the life he had lived.

Peace stared at him. What do you mean? she said.

Wilfred leant in close and whispered, *Everything* goes into my bread. Names. Songs. Memories. Every batch comes out different to the next but what we are looking for is not consistency but excellence. You have to risk failure to become excellent.

Peace began to laugh. So what happens if you add songs, Wilfred?

Dough rises quicker. Produces a light loaf.

Now you're teasing me.

Not at all!

What do memories do then?

Add a *sweet* taste, said Wilfred, smiling. But beware of memories, he said. Other things can creep in with memories.

What other things? said Peace.

Things like regret.

What can you do about regret?

Add currants! said Wilfred proudly.

Oh Wilfred! said Peace, wrapping her arms around him. You are daft.

Here, he said. Try this, and he went to the table and from

under a linen cloth produced a small saffron bun. I call it my Peace bun, he said.

Had a child been named after her, Peace couldn't have been prouder.

Baking taught Peace patience. It taught her the value of waiting. Nothing could be rushed because everything had its own time: time for the dough to prove, for the bread to rise, for the bread to cool. Like life itself, baking was its own master. She, merely, its loyal handmaiden.

One day, however, whilst Wilfred Gently was flouring a new batch of dough, Death crept up behind him and laid its bony hand upon his shoulder. Wilfred fell forwards into the soft beige mass. Not only had life gone into his baking, but now his death had too.

He died a rich man, and when his Will was read out, his savings were divided amongst his loyal customers. But to Peace he gave no money at all. To Peace he gave five years paid up on the bakehouse lease and the last ever batch of his famous sourdough starter.

You need to find your own recipe for bread, he stated in his private instructions to her. *I have given you five years to hone your craft. Then you must fly free, my love, and discover your own secret ingredients.*

She immediately knew what he meant and she cried into the flour, and that night baked a mourning loaf that sold out the next morning. It was a solemn loaf with a rich taste and reminded people of . . . of . . . but no one could ever say exactly what it reminded them of, though it went perfectly with cheese, everyone agreed. But Peace would never create that loaf again.

Why not? cried the village. Because she had baked it wonsunwell.

Peace rose from her brother's grave. Trees, she noticed, were tipped by an abundance of green clusters, and wrens bobbed nearby and sang just for her. Home, she thought. This really is my *home*. The word tasted good in her mouth. She would take that word and put it in the first batch of St Ophere bread. The word promised something excellent. She stood up and began to wade back through water that had now risen to her knees.

38

MARVELLOUS DISAPPEARED A LOT MORE NOW. SHE ROSE
with the sun and took her boat up the Great River until she got
to her mother. There was a chair waiting for her, and the staff
were used to the sight of the small yellow figure shuffling
through the large doors, stick first. She had a greeting, a wave
for everyone, and many people commented on her rouged lips
and she often didn't hear what they said but she said, Thank
you, all the same. And she wore her lipstick every day, and
sometimes her hand was steady and sometimes it wasn't. Sometimes the colour smudged and sometimes it didn't. But she
didn't notice these things and neither did her mother because in
front of her mother she was beautiful.

When she returned to the creek, Drake saw she was different,
as if the tendrils of age were pulling her down, and he began to
imagine the inconceivable; the inconsolable.

He, once, found her on the mooring stone, sitting upright and immobile like a statue carved from that sacred granite and the sight nearly stopped his heart. Once, he found her fast asleep against the tiller, the engine running, the boat going round in circles, burning miles but going nowhere.

He began to do things to make her life easier. He cut steps into the riverbank, reinforced by thick planks. A rope handhold he secured around the mooring stone that took her weight when her knees refused to. He learnt to forage along the shoreline and he learnt to cook – stews and broths, foods like that – and he registered at the grocer and butcher in the Other Saint's Village and brought back weekly rations of meat and butter. He scrubbed pans on the riverbank and pegged sheets between the trees. And yet every night, whatever the state of the river, dry or full, he watched as Marvellous struggled over to the church to light her candle, whoever it was for.

That was why he started the bridge the first warm day of April. It was to be a simple wooden bridge spanning mainland to the island. He had made one before in France on a farm, and would construct it on the bank like a ladder: two long horizontals with slats in between and deep troughs dug out on both banks to anchor it. It was makeshift, he knew, but it would be sturdy and enough.

A boat builder delivered the oak planks cut to Drake's specifications. The horizontal lengths would overlap each other to stretch the twenty feet required. Holes had been drilled and bolts and screws provided. All he had to do was to fit it all together. And to dig out the deep trenches on either bank.

He started island-side, on the east side away from the graves. The digging was tough going because he was out of condition and tree and shrub roots were as thick as his wrist. After a couple of hours, he sat down with his back against the church wall and lit a cigarette. He ran his hand over the dull edge of the spade and wondered if he'd find a whetstone in a dark corner of the shed.

The sun had eaten the wind and a tender quiet hovered over the creek stifling the caw of crows in the smudges of nests high in the pines. His spirits lifted when he saw the familiar yellow oilskin traverse the dry riverbed, two cups of tea held aloft in her hands.

Help is here, help is here, she cried.

He met her at the bank and took the tea from her. He took her arm, and pulled her up the slope.

I'll be dead by the time you've finished this, she said, and she lowered herself into the deck chair. Tea please, she said, and Drake handed back her cup. She took a sip. Lovely, she said. Who made it?

You did, he said. Lovely, she said, and closed her eyes.

He watched her doze. The silence oozed and dripped as thickly as syrup and emotion caught like pollen in his throat. He became aware of the majesty of the landscape, of the hard work and lives that had toiled before, hands that had left dirt and blood on spades and cups. And there, a bee clinging to the pink trumpet head of a foxglove, not resting, not feasting, but dead. A connectedness to all, that's what he felt. A rare earthed feeling of belonging. A burst of sunlight fell upon trails of shimmering web, linking all – the dead, the living – to the earth.

39

THE CHIMNEY SWEEP ARRIVED AT THE BAKEHOUSE THE NEXT morning to remove a swallow's nest that was blocking the oven flue. Soot and webs were swept clear from all stacks and no mortar and bricks fell and the structures rose safe and clean and ready to smoke into the blue Cornish sky.

The proving cupboard and the table were bleached, the windows cleaned, the floors swept then scrubbed. Peace went upstairs to the two bedrooms and had the uneasy feeling that a large black spider dominated the corner of each. They were sad rooms full of whisperings and she had trouble opening the windows. It's not that they were locked, they just wouldn't give in to her: stubbornness inherited from the previous owner, she thought. She took a while to decide which room she would take as hers. She chose the front room that looked out across the High Road and meadow down towards the wood and river below. She scrubbed the sloping, uneven floor and cleaned the windows but the sadness remained. She didn't know what to say to her room because the room stayed deaf to her words. For the time being she would sleep downstairs in a chair.

The moving van arrived early afternoon and soon a bed and a chest of drawers took position in the front bedroom. Two suitcases of bedding and clothes. A rug and a side table were positioned expectantly in the back parlour. But it was into the kitchen that a whole new world arrived: boxes of pans and baskets and cutlery and notebooks. Bags of flour and two baths and a wash basin and logs and candles and lanterns and coal. The last thing to be delivered was the old bakehouse sign: Gently with Peace. It was dented on the way in.

Peace worked throughout the night, feeding the oven until it glowed orange, then glowed white, and kneading and flouring and watering the shiny mound of greying dough. She cut the lump into a dozen rounds and oiled and basketed those rounds and put those rounds into the blistering heat until magic happened and a dozen loaves were rising and crusting perfectly. Sun up, the kitchen was fragrant and humid with the smell of sourdough and yeast and freshly baked bread, and the dewy scent of morning air.

She went outside and positioned the rocking chair in a shaft of morning light. She sat down to watch life pass but life didn't pass, so she got up and filled pans with water from the communal tap opposite. She drank from her hand and the water was cool and sweet, so perfect for baking.

She sat back down in her rocker and again waited for life to pass but nothing passed except a slow-moving hour. She got up and went over to the hedgerow and picked two bunches of oxlips and pink sorrel, one she placed on the war memorial, the other in a small vase on the kneading table. She was about to sit back down again when she caught sight of a tarnished bowl in the corner of the kitchen. She thought it was a bowl but when she pulled it clear she found it to be a ship's bell. She tugged on the thick rope and listened. It made a good sound. She rang the bell louder this time, and upstairs and out of sight four windows unexpectedly unlatched.

40

A WIND BLOWS HOT, A DRY DUSTY WIND THAT CARRIES scents in its arms, scents Drake could never know, ones of baked earth and eucalyptus and frangipani, a collision, too, of salt and muck where sea meets farmland. It's not called the sea, says a woman, it's called the ocean.

Drake clung on tighter to the heat of the dream as he felt the bed once again, the firm horsehair mattress with its lineage of damp. Crows aggravated outside. He rolled over. Christ! his muscles were sore. His palms were tight and raw, and the dream slipped through his blistered fingers like an oily cord.

He sat up dazed, with an acute taste in his mouth. He got up and poured water from the pitcher, rinsed his mouth and swallowed hard. He went to the door and opened it wide. Butterflies were busy dusting themselves in the sweet honeysuckle blossom that crowned the doorway but that wasn't what he could smell nor what he could taste. He dressed quickly and marched barefoot across the riverbank up into the wood. He stopped and sniffed the air. Unmistakable now.

He knocked loudly.

Marvellous? he said, excitedly. He heard a groan, then a shuffle. Marvellous? he said again.

The door opened. What do you want now? she said.

Have I just died and gone to heaven?

You won't be going there, she said, firmly.

Can't you smell it, though? said Drake.

Smell what?

Bread, he said.

Bread? she said.

Freshly baked, he said.

And the smell fell over the creek like spring itself, heralding change and – more importantly – *new life*. And in that moment, it was as if they were castaways, and the scent of bread was like a sighted sail closing in on their uncharted shore.

It was slow going through the trees as Marvellous refused to tread on any flowers, and thousands of blues and yellows and whites now coloured the woodland floor. Across the meadow they went, through daisies and sweet lush grass until there, up ahead, they saw the curl of grey smoke spiralling from the bakehouse chimney stack. The stone building was alive again, it was breathing again, and its breath smelt heavenly. A blue van was parked outside. The words on the side, scratched and faded, read: Gently with Peace.

They slowed as they came towards the High Road and they stopped at the standpipe to drink the sweet, cool water. Wooden boards had been taken off the windows and the glass glistened in the sunlight, and behind the glass was a shape moving busily in the dark within. A battered rocking chair took position to the left of the doorway and next to it, on its original cleat, was Mrs Hard's ship's bell, its brass dome glistening like gold.

Who's there? shouted Marvellous. Show yourself, she called out, raising her stick.

And, as if on cue, the curtains of history drew back and the front door opened and there she was. A young woman, as tall and as broad as an oak tree carrying a planter of lavender to lay against the front wall. The young woman stopped and looked up. The tarmac river shimmering with heat between them. She shielded her eyes and tried to distinguish the young man and old woman standing by the water tap. The young man waved at her. She waved back and began to cross the road, excited that life had ventured by. But then she stopped. Aware, suddenly, of who the old woman was. And with the sun at her back, she became a giant dial casting a long steady shadow towards Marvellous and a long-gone time.

Is that you, Peace? said Marvellous.

And Peace nodded and ran towards the old woman who had so carefully, so lovingly, so rightly delivered her into the world.

41

THEY SAT AROUND THE LARGE OAK TABLE WITH ITS VASE OF oxslips and pink sorrel, and its long-gone memories of a long-gone time, and Peace retold the story of her life with Wilfred Gently. She moved from table to stove, from stove to oven, from oven to cupboard and the story went with her, in the laying out of plates and the steeping of the tea. When the loaf was cool enough to cut, she sat down with her guests and handed Drake the knife. Marvellous noticed that the young woman could barely look at him. A faint blush, like a forgotten smear of jam, clung to her cheeks when he thanked her and smiled at her, when he stood up to take the knife. To cut the bread. To offer her the first piece. Butter? he said.

That was my parents' home, wasn't it? said Peace, looking out, pointing to the cottage opposite.

No, said Marvellous, joining her at the window. That was Gladly's home.

Are you sure? said Peace.

Quite sure. She was the first child I delivered. You were my last.

Then where did my mother and father live? asked Peace.

Come, said Marvellous, and she took her arm and the three of them left the bakehouse and strolled up the High Road. It was when they got to the last cottage, the border between man and nature, that Marvellous said, This was their home.

This? said Peace, quietly.

It wasn't always like this, said Marvellous. It took the brunt of the winds, the brunt of people's moods.

I was born *here*?

Yes.

Peace tried the front door, she pushed against the mud-caked windows.

All locked, said Marvellous.

I'd like to go in, said Peace.

Going in is going back, said Marvellous.

I know, said Peace. I know, she said again, a little less sure.

Ouch! said Marvellous, lifting her hand to her hair. What're you doing back there, boy?

Drake held two hairpins in front of her face. Stand back, he said, and he knelt down to the keyhole and inserted the pins. Magic word? he said. Nonsense, said Marvellous, and the lock clicked and the door creaked open under the weight of a tentative hand.

Inside, the cottage was dark and gloomy. Webs draped like curtains and rats scuttled to dark holes in dark corners, and the smell was of damp and decay and the something other that inhabited the space between her broken parents.

It's so sad, said Peace.

It wasn't always so, said Marvellous.

In the far corner of the room, an unexpected shape caught Peace's eye. She turned to Marvellous and said, A piano?

Good times came here once. And song.

There was no money for a piano, said Peace.

There was money once, said Marvellous.

But a piano? said Peace.

He won it.

What?

Cards, I think. I don't remember now, but he got it fairly and squarely.

But who played it? asked Peace.

He did.

My fa— I don't understand, said Peace. He played the piano?

Played beautifully.

Peace went over to the piano. She ran her hands over the battered upright mass. The splintered wood and broken strings looked to her like a bludgeoned body. Pigeons now nested in the cavity of song.

Did he do this? she said.

Grief did. Anger did, said Marvellous. Stopped him taking it out on something living, I suppose.

The sound of rats scratching startled. Peace shuddered and disappeared into the back room.

What happened here? whispered Drake.

Death, said Marvellous. After the boy died – after Simeon I mean – the village believed they were cursed and they became very fearful. They believed the boy should have died in France like the others and not taken his own life back here. And that was enough to start tongues flapping, and flap they did, oh yes. Loudly, and outside this front door. Horrible words, Drake. To a family in grief. People can be very cruel. Frightened people especially, and Marvellous reached for his hand and squeezed it tightly.

What's this? said Peace, coming back into the room, holding up a perfect willow hoop decorated with feathers and shells.

Ah, said Marvellous, bringing the hoop close to her eyes. This, she said, is a rumour-catcher.

A what? said Drake.

A rumour-catcher. She said, My mother taught my father how to make one, and he in turn taught me. As you can see, the hoop is woven with fishing line to form an inner tight web to catch the rumour. Razor-shells, hang down like this – and she demonstrated – to cut the rumour away from the source, and whelk shells hang down too to house the rumour. Lastly, feathers from songbirds surround the catcher, to purify the rumour and to cleanse the air for good.

But how did you know if a rumour had been caught, asked Peace.

Because of the sound, said Marvellous. Rumour has two very distinct sounds. When it flies free the sound is similar to a ship's hull scraping against a harbour wall. But when rumour is caught, the sound is of expiration: like a fearful sigh in the vacant dark whorls of long-abandoned shells. And Marvellous pointed to the whelks.

She knew these sounds well because she'd had a rumour-catcher outside her caravan and it had caught many over the years, most having been carried on the breath of Mrs Hard. She'd launched rumours like royalty launched ships. It had hung not too far from the wind chimes although the songs were very different. The principles of catching rumours were, in fact, similar to the principles of catching dreams, but because rumour was weightier, the catcher had to be positioned closer to the ground. Rumour flew low, dreams flew high and somewhere in between were prayers.

Catching a rumour before it spread was very important, said Marvellous. But some rumours passed even me by and multiplied like germs.

What ones? asked Drake.

The ones about Simeon. That's why I made this for your mother.

Peace took the hoop and lifted it to her ears.

Do you think I'll ever hear rumour? she asked.

I hope you don't, said Marvellous. It's not a good sound, really not a good sound. Not something to wish for, my love.

And they closed the door and locked up the past and silently wandered back down the High Road with a rumour-catcher held under an arm. Drake let the two women walk hand in hand ahead. He stopped at the war memorial and looked at the space where a name should have been.

42

NED BLANEY WAS OUT IN THE BAY RUNNING TWO LINES from the back of his boat. Ever-dependable Ned with his shock of thick curls bleached white by the sun, oh you could recognise him anywhere. Should've been snatched up ages ago, everybody said so. A deep thinker, he was, even before the war. But war had made him quiet; as quiet and as deep as the channel he fished.

He was fishing for himself that day; kicking back, a quiet moment between man and boat. He leant across the seat and adjusted his radio till he found a familiar song. These Foolish Things. Oscar Peterson on piano. He sang along, hummed when he didn't know the words.

He reached down to his feet for the Thermos flask, unscrewed the lid and poured himself a cup of tea. He touched the lines briefly, checked for the flick of life. Nothing. He turned the radio up. A brief thought about war but he let it pass like a floating mass of knotweed.

He raised his cup to the sky even though he didn't believe in Heaven, but he had to put his brother somewhere and the familiar blue cushion above the estuary was as good a place as any.

To Old Times, he said.

43

OLD TIMES RETURNED TO THE CREEK, AND LIFE BECAME busy and expectant, and the valley echoed with the sounds of bridge-building and a young woman's laughter, and Marvellous was suddenly wrenched out of old age like a seed potato wrenched out of the familiar comfort of dark. She had little time to think about Death, pushed aside as it were, by activity, youth and noise. Things were required of her again and this time by people and not by dreams. And Marvellous blossomed, having quite forgotten what an exciting and necessary jolt being needed gave.

But what are you looking for? she said, as Drake disappeared into her shed.

Paint, he called out.

But what kind of paint? she said.

Any kind, said Drake.

But there's lots of different kinds.

Just paint, said Drake.

But there isn't just paint, she muttered.

Drake backed out and looked at her, exasperated. Any paint, Marvellous! Whatever paint you have.

I only have one kind of paint –

– that'll do.

And Marvellous squeezed into the shed and moments later came out with a tin of gloss for boat hulls.

Cobalt blue, she said. Perfect he said, and he ran into the woods without saying anything more.

She was about to settle down for a rare afternoon of quiet when she heard the sound of bicycle wheels clatter over the woodland floor. It was the postman, a man who never came now that everyone she knew was dead.

Letter! he shouted, as he puffed his way down to the riverbank.

I hear you, said Marvellous, walking up to meet him.

The fella addressed it to Miss Marvellous Ways, Gypsy Caravan, Falmouth Wood, Cornwall, said the postman. But this ain't Falmouth Wood, is it? So it's been round the block a few times till it ended up here. But at the bottom it says *United Kingdom*. The last two words he pronounced emphatically and clearly. This 'ere's from *abroad*, he said.

Abroad? said Marvellous.

Aye, said the postman. Feels like a postcard inside, and Marvellous took the envelope from him and offered him a cup of tea and a saffron bun. Next time, he said, declining the offer on account of his full sack.

She undid her oilskin and sat down on the mooring stone.

She wiped her glasses and studied the stamp: *America*. She said the word out loud. She opened the envelope and, sure enough, a postcard was inside. She brought it up close to her eyes: a river at sunset. A wooden bridge and trees growing out of water.

My dear Marvellous, the card began.

I hope this letter reaches you and finds you well. Last weekend I went fishing with my grandfather and I talked about you, about your kindness. I am studying now, business, at Atlanta University. It is not a perfect world, the world I inhabit. But I have a future and not so long ago many men my age didn't. But this time the fight is different.

We were taken by surprise at Omaha Beach. It was chaos. Many boats sank before they could land; often blown up by mines just below the surface. We scrambled from the landing craft and ran into heavy gunfire. We hid behind burned-out tanks and beach defenses and bodies. We were trapped and needed to retreat. To go left or right? That was our choice. In that moment I remembered your words, Marvellous. I went left, as you told me to do. I ran left. Those who went right fell. From the bottom of my heart, I thank you.

Henry

Marvellous held the postcard up to her eyes again and studied his script. She saw gratitude and promise in the flourish of his hand. It had been a long time since she had cried, but she knew she didn't need her tears any more because there was no point in tears outliving eyes, so she let them fall.

And that was how Drake found her an hour later. As he came towards her, she looked up and said, Henry's all right.

I'm glad Henry's all right. But are you all right? he said.

Yes. I think I am, and she reached for his hands and brought them up to her cheek. His cobalt-blue fingertips shone bright under the warmth of a benevolent afternoon sun.

It was late when Peace got back to the bakehouse. She went inside and placed her bags in the cool. She poured herself a glass of water and came back out to watch the spray of colour begin to bruise the evening sky. She felt tired, exhausted in fact, having spent the afternoon away looking for a worthy flour supplier. The millers had been brusque and unhelpful, and she had sifted through bags of flour like a prospector sifting through silt. She knew what was gold and she knew what was fool's gold, and she knew the price of gold and would not pay a penny more. She taught them more than manners that day.

A blackbird sat on the memorial cross. Its song was bright and incessant, last song of the day. The bird revived her, hopping from the horizontal to the vertical. Hop hop. Song song. She went back inside to refill her glass and she was about to prepare for a night of baking when her sight was drawn back outside to the glinting granite cross. It was coated by the last buttery rays of sun, and it was this evening yellow that brought out the vivid blue of his name.

Not S Rundle but his full name, Simeon Rundle, her brother, for all to see. It was neatly scripted in bright blue paint. She touched the S with the edge of her little finger. It was sticky but dry. She leant against the hedgerow surrounded by primroses. She drank her water and watched the sun slip below the valley casting out tears of red and gold and pink and mauve.

She lay awake in the early hours, restless, spooning the curved back of impatience. She opened the window wide, not a sound stirred. She walked down the stairs into the calm familiar smell of her baking. She opened the back door and knelt down. She leant close to the willow hoop, hoping to hear the rumour of love. A light breeze sifted through the fishing twine, and the razor clams and whelk shells clacked. All she could hear was the sound of the sea.

44

DRINKS AT 7. NO NEED TO DRESS UP. MW

That was the note that was pinned to the boathouse door together with a small trumpet of cowslip.

Drake hadn't bothered to heat the bath water, the day had been warm enough as it was. He was in a good mood, a light mood. The troughs were dug out on both banks and the first of the slats added. He dried off quickly and moved the metal tub out of the way by the door.

He ransacked the boathouse for a mirror, but only the glass from a carefully positioned balcony door offered up any kind of reflection. His hair was scraggy, he pushed it away from his forehead. It had been weeks since he had thought about the things that kept his hair in place or made his skin smell nice, but he thought about them then, and searched through his suitcase to see if anything from his old life remained.

He took out a white shirt. It smelt of laundry soap. It felt good on his skin. He did up the top button and loosely knotted a blue woollen tie. He rolled up his sleeves because his cufflinks had long gone. He found a small tube of Brylcreem, the end rolled like toothpaste. He squeezed the pomade on to his fingers and smelt it. Thought it would do. He sat in front of the glass door and ran it through his hair. With a comb he styled it the best he could and wondered why he was bothering about his appearance so much. No need to dress up. That's what she had said. But he was.

Marvellous brushed out her hair and tied it back in a bun. She smoothed her hands over the front and pinched her cheeks as she had always done. She bent down and opened up the cupboard beneath her bed. She took out a clean lavender-smelling fishing smock that had once been red but had now faded to pink. It complimented the tone of her skin well. She slipped it over her head, and in the words of someone-or-other, felt a million dollars.

And then as best she could, she applied lipstick to her wide-smiling lips. At this point she thought a mirror might be useful, but it had last graced the wall back in 1929 – not that she would ever remember the date – and it had been broken up and used in a wind chime. It didn't make sense to have a mirror; she was an ageing woman and a child at the same time: the confluence of two rivers, and everyone knows that confuses the fish.

No need to dress up, that's what she had written.

She reached down to the wireless and turned the volume up as high as it would go. The caravan began to vibrate with song. She rocked side to side in Paper Jack's old boots.

Peace reread the note that had been pinned to her door with a stem of bluebell. She couldn't remember the last time she had ever dressed up and wondered if the requirement to *not* dress up was actually harbouring a secret request *to* dress up.

She stood back from the mirror. She stood in profile and smoothed her bust. She had always had a good bust and Wilfred said she had a better bust than Rita Hayworth. She pulled nervously at the pale yellow cuffs that hung slightly too high above her wrists. Her hands seemed even larger than they normally did, had a strange resemblance to bread paddles. She liked the dress. It was the only dress that had ever suited her and she had bought it for Wilfred's funeral. In his instructions he had forbidden her to wear black but her grief had forbidden her to wear anything jollier than moss green. Moss green matched her eyes, and between her moss-green eyes and her moss-green dress was her wide mouth, now painted orange. She tried to look objectively at her colour palette but she couldn't. She knew she looked like a marrow. But a *beautiful* marrow, Wilfred would have said.

She wished she had unsensible shoes and wished for stockings with seams, and she had never wished for those things before. She combed her fringe and checked that it ran evenly across her brow line. She put on a tailored Harris Tweed jacket, grabbed her handbag and ran out through the bakehouse door.

No need to dress up. The words collided in her mouth like marbles.

She was hot and sweaty by the time the riverbank came into sight. The boathouse door was ajar, and she was aware of how nervous she felt. She waited until her breathing had settled before she called out his name.

Come in, called Drake. It's open.

She entered the quiet space and found him about to drag a tin bath out of the doorway.

Hello, he said. You look hot.

I think I'm overdressed.

Have some water.

She went over to the earthenware flagon and poured out a large glass of cool water.

Delicious, she said. I feel better already.

Of course you do. Tears of a saint, that stuff is. I've drunk it since I got here and I haven't had worms.

My gosh, said Peace. That is holy. 'Spect you'll be walking on it next.

And Drake laughed and she removed her tweed jacket and let the cool breeze from the balcony doors blow across the pale hairs on her arms.

Thank you, she said.

You don't need to thank me. Have another glass.

No. Thank you for Simeon. I wanted to come earlier, but . . . Thank you, that's all, for putting things right for him. For me. And they are right now. So—

And Drake wrapped his arms around her and she leant into his shoulder and smelt washing powder and Brylcreem, and she drank in the Shh that came quiet from his lips.

Here, let me help you, she said, pulling away.

They took an end each and carried the bath out of the door and poured the water on to the honeysuckle and briar rose that framed the wall outside. Drake looked at the sun, looked at his watch. We should head down, he said.

That's interesting, said Peace, pointing to the picture above the hearth.

Is it? I did it. When I was a kid.

Who is it supposed to be?

My father.

You look like him.

I'm not sure that I do. I never knew him, you see. It's just how I imagined him.

And was he kind, your father? In your imagination.

Yes, I suppose he was.

Brave?

I'm not sure about that. I pieced him together from my successes and failures. Bad swimmer but good at running. That kind of thing. I don't think I've ever thought of myself as brave, he said, and he went and picked up his sweater from the bed.

And he's always watched over you? said Peace.

Yes. I suppose he has.

Like God?

Drake laughed. I don't believe, I'm afraid.

Hmm, said Peace, putting her jacket back on. But you believed in a man you never knew and never met watching over you? she said.

Come on, said Drake, smiling, holding the door open for her.

And Peace said nothing more as she walked on ahead towards the waiting boat.

45

THEY SET OUT IN THE CRABBER ON THE DOT OF SEVEN. THE evening was warm, the sky tender, and gulls played tag on the thermals as herons took off smoothly into an iridescent blue westerly sky. Marvellous manned the tiller, looking over now and then to check on Drake whose fear of water had begun to ease over the past weeks. But she knew that it would take nothing more than a small rogue wave to send him reaching for the bowline or gripping hard on to the well-worn seat slats. He ducked down as Peace splashed him with water from her trailing hand. He looked up at Marvellous and smiled.

He looked happy in that moment. And she would remember his smile suspended in that one delectable moment because it was radiant and she knew he had a chance now, to live well.

As they approached Old Cundy's boat, they stood to attention one by one and saluted the good ship *Deliverance* as they passed. The soft evening light bathed them, dripped off them, loosened the awkwardness that had initially threatened to stifle the evening, an ill-at-ease quiet caused by strange clothing in familiar surrounds. The old woman tried to catch a glimpse of her long-gone self in the young woman next to her. She studied that dance of attraction, that funny little jig practised by all creatures – the beautiful, the plain, the slim, the big, the unruly – the same exquisite dance handed down by generations and danced flawlessly by all. To Marvellous it was as clear as day that the girl had feelings for Drake. And there he sat, comfortable like a brother. Smiling at her like a brother, unaware of his attractiveness, still bruised by the blows of the past.

Kids, eh? thought Marvellous, and she began to laugh and it was catching, and the three of them laughed as they passed the sandbar and manoeuvred through the narrow way that kept inquisitives out and large craft at bay.

It was here they encountered a world moving forwards and not forgotten. The air tinkled with the sounds of ropes against masts, as pleasure craft swayed on the dividing currents and flaccid sails flapped like washing on a line. Here, the boat turned left into the Great River where they faced open water and the horizon beyond.

Marvellous watched the two young people sit up in unison and look intently ahead, both unaware that their shift was caused by the infinite pull of that unreachable dream, that shimmering silver line that caused hearts to soar, then sometimes to deflate.

It was more like the sea there, wild and erratic. Fierce winds were known to funnel down through the estuary dismantling the unanchored and the insane. But there was no wind that evening. No clouds pulling at the sky and the only ripples across the water were caused by a casually draped hand stretching out from a primrose cuff, tickling the surface as if it was the cool skin of the man opposite.

The small craft hugged the rocky shoreline where fields and trees fell down to lap at water's edge, where bobbing buoys marked crab pots, and sandy coves enticed the swimmers, the brave and the hardy ones. And always in the distance, the lighthouse keeping watch over the Manacles Rocks, submerged and murmuring beneath the ever-swelling tide, waiting. In 1898 one hundred and six people drowned as those rocks bit deep into the good ship *Mohegan* and feasted well. Nets were required to pull in bodies not pilchards that week.

There! shouted Marvellous, and there it was, the Great Port with its cranes and tugs and sprawl of lights calling the world to its historic hearth. And there were steam funnels spewing black and pleasure craft and fisher craft – red-sailed luggers, and big sailing vessels from Another Time barely hanging on to seaworthiness.

She remembered again the ghost of the *Cutty Sark* with its holds of tea, and magnificent sails billowing and racing with the wind, sailors in the rigging unfurling speed. Saw again packet ships with Jamaica sun hot on their sterns, and Mission Boats helmed by chaplains, God's hand at the tillers, and Big Houses for Important Men who paid thruppence an hour to pilchard-packing girls. And she saw again the fisherman who used to gather along the shores to eye up the morning like a half-dressed woman.

A seagull flew low in front of her, and she followed its path turning left at Henry's castle where lights from fisher cottages guided them in, twinkling in promenade rows along the coast road. Marvellous pulled back on the engine and the crabber veered gently into the harbour.

She moored easily by a set of stone steps that had been laid down three hundred years before. Cheers and laughter greeted them from the hotel in front. Drake gave Marvellous his arm and said, Come on Vivien Leigh, and the old woman skipped up the granite blocks as if her knees were as light as air. Peace waited for Drake to come back and help her, too, but he didn't, and she followed behind with an ache in her chest that she initially thought was the hastily eaten bun that she had devoured on her way down to the creek. But when she felt she was as close to tears as she was to a smile, she realised the affliction was something more momentous than heartburn. It was the rare ingredient that Wilfred Gently had once spoken to her about. She paused briefly at the top of the steps, closed her eyes and let the evening sun lick her from head to toe. She felt like a flower whose petals were finally unfurling in the heat of the unknown. Now I have the chance to become a great baker, she thought.

Peace! shouted Drake, from the doorway.

Peace's heart skipped and so did she. I'm coming! she called, and bounded across the road towards him.

Wondered where you got to, said Drake. I was worried you got lost. Come on in and tell me what you want to drink.

And those were the exact words the young fisherman with blond curls overheard. Ned Blaney had been sitting on a nearby bench overlooking the harbour when Peace had risen like a figurehead into the evening light. He was born knowing the moods of the sea but he was not so good with women – everyone knew that – and he should have spoken to her there and then, whilst she was alone, before the man had come out and called to her. And now here he was, sitting on the bench too shy and too polite to cast for another man's fish. The view of the sea no longer held him. He turned and looked longingly towards the doorway of the Amber Lynn pub.

It was a simple fishers' tavern, nothing fancy, a road-width back from the harbour, and up a short flight of stairs. It was originally named after Henry the Eighth's second wife, but centuries later took on the name of a fishing lugger that had mysteriously disappeared in the famous week-long mists.

A piano still stood to one side with a full ashtray from the night before resting on its lid. At the back was a timid hearth fire, rather heatless. On the floor were sawdust and scraps of discarded seaweed. On the walls, photographs of long-gone men and boats, and some photographs of record hauls of pilchards extending along the harbour front as far as the eye could see. There was a bar with bottles of whisky and rum and barrels of ale, and pewter tankards for the regulars, drinking edges worn smooth by familiar lips. There was a ship's bell, rung solely for last orders. Pipes spewed smoke, the air was hazy and warm and the soft murmur of conversation was about fishing and women, two subjects that old-timers once said were like acorns and dogs, and should never mix.

It was the last pub Marvellous had been to with Paper Jack and she looked about eagerly for old faces to share that bygone time with. But the old faces were now young faces, hidden by low-pulled caps and ragged beards. Old Crisp the barber would have had a field day with this lot, she thought. Every Saturday with his steady hand and brisk blade he had spewed out so many clean-shaven and ansum men that the women were so giddy with choice they had fought over them in the street like gulls fighting over scraps of fish.

They took the table by the window overlooking the river. They clinked glasses and said, Cheers, just as the moon and sun did the same outside. Drake drank steadily from his pint glass, savouring the rich taste. He lit a cigarette and stared out at the geometric pattern of fishing nets drying over the harbour wall. Boats were bobbing on the corrugated water, and he thought they looked beautiful, as the lowering sun cast a rich and golden light against their tilting multi-coloured hulls. He thought Missy would have loved it, and surprised himself by such a declaration. Maybe this was the moving forwards that the old woman had once spoken about. You move on and bring them with you, she had said. We leave nothing behind and they come willingly. Have you come willingly, Missy? Have you?

Penny for 'em, said Peace.

I was thinking of someone, said Drake.

It was the way he paused before he said *someone* that made Peace think it was a woman.

Someone special? she asked, bravely.

Yes, he said. More than she knew.

So, thought Peace, there *was* a wall around his heart and she wondered whether she should hoist up her skirt and scale that wall, but she knew she didn't have the right shoes on for that sort of climb because hers were too sensible for a man like Drake.

Was she your sweetheart? she asked, as casually as she could muster.

Marvellous looked at Drake. Looked back to Peace. Nothing got past her even at the age of nearly ninety.

No, he said. I don't think she was that. I don't know what she was but she kept me going forwards.

She was your horizon, said Marvellous.

Was she? said Drake. Was that what she was?

I think so.

I think that's beautiful, said Peace. I'd like to be someone's horizon one day, she said.

No you wouldn't, said Marvellous. Horizons are unreachable. And untouchable. They *haunt*. Lotta nonsense.

Oh, said Peace, and she lifted her glass and didn't put it down until it was empty. She wiped the froth away from her lip, and said, I don't think I'll ever look at one in quite the same way again, and she got up and walked sensibly towards the bar. I am a baker, I am a baker and my life is bread, she said to herself. The thought consoling the bruise that was inching across her heart.

Peace ordered another round of drinks and when the barman turned his back, she took out a new government-sized loaf of bread from her handbag and placed it on the bar. She stuck an oblong card in the top like a fin: 'Eat Me', on one side, 'Gently with Peace, The Old Bakehouse, St Ophere' on the other. And that's how it started, people's intrigue. How people would eventually get to know where she was.

The tots of rum-hot were doing their job and Marvellous said, You see that young man on the bench outside, the young curly bob over there? That's where Old Cundy used to sit. Fingers held up, like this, between the sea and the sun, calculating the time of day, the walking chronometer that he was. And flying above his head was his own personal seagull, his link between land and sea. And that seagull bore news and messages for him, sometimes even in dreams.

And Marvellous stuffed her pipe with black twist and lit that pipe, and smelt again that pungent ruff-stuff of that long-gone life, and she smelt again the fish on her hands and felt again the tiredness in her muscles as she hauled those pots aboard and worked as uncomplaining as a regular man. And it simply didn't make sense. Who she was then and who she was now. Just. Didn't. Make. Sense.

Did you have your own gull? asked Peace.

No. Too much trouble, a gull. But Cundy told everyone I had my own Bucca, and that I kept it in a bottle.

What's a Bucca? asked Drake.

A sea spirit, said Marvellous. Quite a grumpy one, at that.

Why did he tell them that?

Because women weren't allowed to fish in those days.

What a lot of rot, said Peace.

Of course it was, but Old Times had Old Ways, and Old Times said it was bad luck to mix women and fish. Fishermen weren't even supposed to meet a woman on the way down to the boats, that's why some of the old-timers took the long route across the cliffs, just so they would avoid any contact with the women.

But everyone believed in the Bucca. Everyone knew you needed a Bucca on your side if you wanted to fish well and stay safe because the Bucca ruled the sea. It ruled the wind and the waves too. It was powerful and fickle. It liked silence, so we never whistled or sang out on the water. Unlike sailors, we saved our shanties for shore.

Marvellous paused to drink. Her cheeks glowed rum-red. Where was I? she said.

Old Cundy told the men you had your own Bucca, said Drake.

Ah yes, yes he did. Now why did he do that, you ask? Let's go back-along. Along the coast lived an old Wise Woman called

Keziah. She taught me things my father could never teach me. Things about birthing, things about healing. I was second in command to her. I was very young. I never went hungry, but some days I got close. Until Keziah died and handed her mantel to me, I knew things would be difficult. That's when I decided to make crab pots. I'd seen it done hundreds of times and I borrowed Cundy's stand and collected my own withies and wove pots. I did a good job. Maybe Cundy was sweet on me, I don't know, but he wanted me out in the bay with him. So he helped dress me up as a fisherman, and I took my father's boat and I rowed and baited those pots and went back and pulled up those pots. And I lived and survived. Made a little money too. Put it away for Hard Times.

And then one night, coming into shore, I saw men waiting for me on the beach, torches alight. I knew what was about to happen. They pulled me from the boat, pulled off my cap and smock. Uncovered me. That's when Cundy warned them, warned them not to mess with me. Said the Bucca had come from Keziah. Even the mention of her name sent fear through them.

It took days for them to reach an agreement. In the end they agreed I could fish if I continued to dress and behave as a man. They treated me no differently to a man. Soon they forgot I wasn't a man because the fleet prospered. Pilchards came in close by the tens of thousands, crabs were abundant and oysters seemed to launch themselves into the dredge. But most of all they stayed safe. Rich times, lucky times. And the Bucca watched over them.

So where's the Bucca now? asked Drake.

What's that? said Marvellous, rubbing her ear.

The Bucca. Where is it?

Oh somewhere or other, I expect, said Marvellous, reaching for her stick.

Don't you know?

No.

Isn't that a bit careless?

It's around. Probably in a cupboard somewhere.

Doesn't it need air? Or food?

It's not a pet, she said, sternly, shaking her head, and she got up and headed towards the stairs and the water closet outside. Only when she felt the cooling evening air did she begin to smile because she never had a Bucca in a bottle, just a small sea horse from the day of her birth.

They stood side by side out in the night and waited for Marvellous to say her goodbyes. The moon was a dazzling white sliver, more like a winter moon. Stars cascaded into the watery black, as the lighthouse beams tried to catch them in freefall.

Make a wish, said Peace.

You too, said Drake.

Don't tell me.

I won't.

Eyes closed, they stood. Together yet separate. Smiling into their private unspeaking wish-world.

They said she was the most beautiful woman they had ever seen.

Drake opened his eyes. The young fisherman who had been sitting on the bench all evening was now facing him, talking to him.

Who was? said Drake.

Old Marvellous. They said she was the most beautiful woman they had ever seen. Even waves –

– drew back to look at her, said Drake, finishing the sentence.

Ned Blaney nodded and grinned, and he cast a tender glance towards Peace. By then he knew she swam free. And the joy that carried from her smile was just too much for him and he took off into the night-drenched back streets.

Wait! shouted Peace.

But he didn't wait.

Come back, she cried.

But he didn't come back. Onwards, he strode, listing as he walked, the sudden shifting ballast of a fit-to-burst heart. Up-along the familiar lanes he went until he came to the old cottage where he lived alone, his quiet old cottage called Long Gone, because everyone he had ever known and everyone who had ever lived there, was. He stopped before he turned the key. Looked back towards that infinite shimmering dark. Mast lights near and far winked at him in brotherly assent. It felt like the first time he'd seen a flying fish. He entered his home full of hope and wonder.

Pht pht pht pht.

The sound of the crabber cut through the still air. There was no light at all just different shades of black. Eyes flickered from bank to bank and the occasional gull would dart out of nowhere with a flash of white. Booze-heavy lids hung low by the time the confluence was reached but Marvellous didn't care, she knew the boat would guide them through the narrow and get them home safe. She could fall asleep and did.

Peace watched Drake doze. Earlier in the evening she had looked on him with the eyes of love. Now it was with what? The eyes of a sister? She wasn't sure. She thought instead about the young fisherman who ran off into the night. She thought about his smile, his halo of curls, as she drifted off to the smell of diesel, to the quiet language of boat.

That night an old woman at the end of her life, and three young people at the start of their lives lie in bed listening to the earth turn. It has a melody that only the gentle hear. They each lie thinking about love. Lost love and love to come. The old woman falls asleep first. She falls asleep with moonlit lips upon her lips and the sweet scent of china tea and gorse flower whispering tales from youth-drenched time. The young woman who smells of bread thinks love is like yeast. It needs time to prove. It is complex. She thinks she might get a dog instead. Along the coast in a cottage called Long Gone a young fisherman thinks only of her. He thinks love is like the sea, beautiful and dangerous but something he would like to know. And in the boathouse a young man lights a cigarette. He takes two puffs, one for sorrow two for joy. He thinks about a woman called Missy Hall. For once it is a good memory. The moon falls behind the trees and the lights go out.

46

TWO WEEKS LATER, THE BRIDGE WAS READY TO MANOEUVRE into position. Drake stood on the riverbank wondering how to get the bridge across and had settled on floating it at the highest tide, when he heard the unusual sound of an outboard engine spluttering up the creek. It wasn't the crabber because the sound of the crabber was now as distinct to him as a child's voice. He looked up and watched the high-bowed fishing craft pass through the sandbar, the sun smiling on a wiry thatch of salt-bleached curls.

The young fisherman secured the bowline around the mooring stone and jumped ashore.

Hello again! he said, offering his hand. Ned Blaney, he said.

Drake, said Drake.

What you up to then? asked Ned.

That end needs to be over there, said Drake, pointing to the island. Any ideas?

Ned looked over to the church and squinted. His lips moved, mind calculating the task. He looked at Drake, looked at the boat. Decision made.

Better get an end into the boat, he said and he jumped back down on to the seat slats. Let's give her a go, eh, shall we? and he cast off.

He was stocky and strong, Cornish through and through, and he lined up the bow as Drake slid the bridge towards him. He held the slatted end high above his head, the weight tearing into his arms and shoulders. Drake secured the bridge into the mainland dug-out then slipped down into the water and waded to the island shore. The boat inched towards him and he grabbed the bridge and took half the weight, and together they lowered it slowly into the deep trough. It fitted perfectly. Stable and unmoving. A trusted walkway from island to shore.

They smoked and said little, the comfortable silence of a shared task done well. When Ned finished his cigarette, from his pocket he pulled out the bakehouse card and said, Daft not to get a loaf now I'm here, right?

Drake smiled. He said, Up through the trees and meadow, mate. You can't miss it. Just follow the smell and you'll come to her. Better be quick, though, he said, glancing at his watch. And the young fisher raised his arm and took off into the wood.

Ned Blaney ran faster than he had ever run in his life. He ran up through the trees, across the meadow until he arrived at the bakehouse door, bent double with breathlessness.

He waited unseen until the queue had dispersed and the last loaf sold. As Peace was about to flip the sign from Open to

Closed, he appeared out of nowhere on the threshold, all wind-swept and tongue-tied with a large packet under his arm.

You again! said Peace.

Me again! said Ned.

Sold out, said Peace. Only got half a dozen scones from yesterday.

I'll take 'em, he said.

They're a bit hard, said Peace.

I'll take 'em.

Actually, they're stale.

I'll take 'em, he said, still struggling for breath. Finally he said, I've brought you these, and he handed her the package.

For me?

Yes.

Why?

'Cause I was just passing.

Boat's outside is it?

Ned looked back out through the door. Well, I'll be— he said. Strong tide up 'ere.

Peace laughed. What are they? she said.

Fish.

I can smell that.

Oh. Whiting.

I like whiting.

Hoped you might, he said.

What's your name? said Peace.

Ned.

I'm Peace, said Peace loudly. She was nervous.

Peace, he repeated, softly.

He said, I put in some oysters too. I could shuck them now if you want.

Peace said she did want. And he reached into his smock and pulled out a well-used knife.

Here, he said.

She took the shell from his rough hands. The smell of the sea and the sound of the shore rose from its iridescent heart, and when she tipped the small muscle into her mouth she felt the coolness, the saltiness of a prince's kiss.

Later that evening, Ned Blaney sat in his cottage with its view of the sea and the falling sun, and ate a plate of mackerel and potatoes. Midway through, though, he stopped eating and anyone watching might have thought he had swallowed a bone, but he hadn't. He sat quite still and brought his fingers up to his lips, brought his eyes down to his glistening fingertips. He got up and went to the kitchen and ran his hands under the tap. He watched intently as the soap lathered, felt something release as his hand moved across his other hand. He went to his desk, his movement and breath slow. He sat down and picked up a pen. He looked at the photograph of him and his brother just after they'd joined up, and words that had so long evaded his mouth now gathered at the nib of his pen, and he wrote down everything he felt and everything he could see.

He wrote to Peace once a week between their courting, and what he couldn't get down on paper that first week he continued into the second week, then the third. He wrote sitting on a harbour bench, he wrote at the tiller of his boat. Peace got to know her fisherman through his letters. And when they met up she made him read them out loud, so that the words that had gathered at the nib of his pen found their rightful place upon his tongue.

47

FISH AGAIN TONIGHT! SHOUTED PEACE AS SHE GALLOPED through the woods and stopped by the bridge. Drake looked up from his fishing.

What's it this time? he said.

A large pollack.

Getting serious.

Oh Drake, said Peace, blushing.

Come and sit down with me, he said, and she did as he asked, feet dangling over the river, looking downstream towards the gateway to another life.

So how are you?

I'm OK.

How long now?

I'm not sure.

Really?

Six weeks and three days.

Drake smiled. Do you like him?

He likes me.

That's not what I asked.

He brings me fish instead of flowers.

You'll never go hungry.

I like flowers.

He laughed. Grow some, he said.

What's the matter? he asked.

I just have to make sure.

I know you do.

I'm that kind of person, Drake.

He put his arm around her. I know you are, he said.

Here, she said, and pulled a small bun out of her pocket. It was still warm.

What's this?

You tell me, she said.

He bit into the vanilla icing and smiled. She was sure, he thought.

Delicious, he said.

The late sun was as sweet and as orange as the bun. Marvellous awoke to the enthusiastic calling of her name. She stumbled from her caravan with the haze of an afternoon nap clinging to her like resin.

Look Marvellous! Look at this, said Peace.

Marvellous shuffled carefully on to the bridge and looked down into the river.

Starfish!

They came slowly, one, three, six at a time, drawn in by the spring tide, and they were a starry gathering down there in the shade of the bridge.

Jack loved starfish, said Marvellous.

He did? said Drake.

Oh yes. He used to tell the village children that they were once stars from a night sky that had fallen to earth after an argument with a comet. He said they'd had a disagreement as bright things tend to do, and the comet had lashed out with its tail and had knocked them off their spot. The stars began to plummet and they reached out to grab on to something and out of that reaching was born their five arms. They cried out in freefall and the cries were heard by the earth and the earth spun a little faster so the stars would fall into the sea and not crash on to land because everyone agreed that such a fall from grace was punishment enough. And sometimes, you can hear the starfish lament because they are continually homesick and some nights you can hear them sigh as they lay on the shore looking up at the sky and all that might have been. That's why they help us get back home. They are filled with empathy for the lost.

They all three looked down into the watery universe as the orange stars twisted and danced on the gentle current.

Who are they going to take back home? said Peace.

Me probably, said Marvellous, and she dipped her stick into the water and watched an orange arm reach out to hold. Definitely me, she whispered.

How did you know he was the one? said Peace.

What's that? said Marvellous, leaning close.

Jack. How did you know?

Because life without him would have been so wrong.

What was he like? said Peace.

Ordinary, really. But he had a stowaway poet that lived in

his soul and that poet made him restless. But that poet also made him see the world like no one else. He was too good for the life he was dealt.

And what life was that? asked Drake.

The life of a miner. He wanted so much more. Deserved so much more. But what he wanted and what he was destined for were two very different things. He told me that the first morning he went to the mine, it was as if it was his last morning, and everything beautiful had to be etched on to his memory before the dark amnesia swallowed him whole.

He said he watched the rising sun burnish across the moorland, the gorse ablaze, more yellow than yellow, amidst the claret-dark sweep of heath. He had noticed colour before, but that morning it was different because he knew he would not resurface until his hands were the hands of an old man. His feet were already sore. He was wearing the same boots his father had died in.

He said he stopped and watched a sailing ship blow across that shimmering distant line and he gave that ship his heart for safe-keeping. He felt the moment it climbed from his chest and watched it fly towards the billowing sails whose cargo was tin and kaolin and other men's dreams.

Two hundred and fifty fathoms below sea level they went looking for tin. Him and his brother, Jimmy, worked the deepest lodes that stretched out far far under the sea. They could hear the groundswell overhead as waves pummelled down on waves, and now and again they would stop and listen as pillars of pitch pine creaked like masts in the man-made gloom.

They worked in the scorching heat. Boots full of sweat and torsos bare, their white skin ghoulish in the candlelight. Jack told jokes but Jimmy didn't laugh. He'd woken up with the bad luck shadow across his chest and he was looking out for Death instead. His fear was contagious and began to travel through the tunnels. Gradually the *tap tap tap* of hammers grew still, till only the *boom shh boom shh* of waves could be heard overhead.

At first, no one knew who started it. That's what they said later. Some said Sammy Dray, others Tommy Ruff, but those boys weren't singers, and this here voice came out of the gloom, a sweet voice they all said, belonging to no one they knew. But they did know him, of course, for the voice came from Jack. He sang:

> Amazing love! How can it be
> That Thou, my God, shouldst die for me.

Then Jimmy began to sing too, and gradually voices echoed along the shafts until there was the sound of eighty voices, a hundred voices and the sound of waves, and the earth holding itself tight in those tunnels, and those who were above ground swore they could hear that hymn coming from below grass, and the sheer beauty near enough stopped those engine houses. And those voices rose until the twelve miles of working tunnel were ablaze with song, as if that alone was support enough to keep back the weakening stope. And there were men who cried in that space touched by something divine. And as the last voice fell silent, so rose a crescendo of falling waves above just like cymbals. And in that darkness, came the light. And for a moment all fear abated in the hushed stillness of answered grace.

Those were the days when legends were born and names given, said old Marvellous. Singer Jack, that's what they called him then. Singer Jack. Because those were the days when he still had a song.

48

THE POLLACK HAD BEEN AS TASTY AS NED BLANEY SAID IT would be, and Peace had baked it and served it with piles of saffron mash and spring greens. They had feasted well and their stomachs knew it. Drake sat outside against the bakehouse wall and watched the young woman with an old soul and the old woman with a young soul rock on their chairs in swatches of light. The slow creak of wood, the forwards-backwards motion of time, acted like a metronome to the gentle fall of sundown, and the dark blue stain that spread across the sky brought out the scent of lavender and violets, brought out the bats and the familiar haze of the moon too.

A man will go there one day, said Drake, looking up.

Why? said Marvellous.

Why? To explore, of course.

Men need to explore in here first, and she pointed to his

chest. The moon has done fine without us, she said, and she pulled out her bottle of sloe gin, magically refilled from the night before. Some things are best left untouched, she said. Tides rise and tides fall. That is perfection enough.

I've upset you, said Drake.

No you haven't, she said.

You can't stop progress.

So they say, she said.

Wouldn't you like to go, though?

To the moon? she said, and she took a swig of gin. I've been, she said, and as Drake was about to speak she raised her finger and silenced him.

They sat quiet. The satisfying rumble of digestion encroached on the silence and the *flflfl* of an overhead wing carried far across the valley.

The thing is, said Marvellous, it's progress I find upsetting because progress finds war. And by the time I got to be old, the things that were once of value have diminished in worth, and it's hard to keep up when you're old. Not keeping up is upsetting. Let the moon be, and she raised her bottle to the white orb.

What were you like when you were young? said Peace.

I had little care.

Little *hair*? said Drake.

Care. Don't know what's got into you tonight, she mumbled.

I bet you were beautiful, said Peace.

No. I was never that. But men used to say there was something about me. Maybe they were referring to something sexual in my nature.

Drake looked away.

I see you, whispered Marvellous.

Are there no photographs of you? said Peace.

No, none. But I think I would have liked one as a child. I could have held it up next to my face, like this, and you could have told me if I was still here, somewhere in these features.

What colour was your hair?

Dark brown. Like my mother's.

Were you tall?

Average.

What was your best feature, do you think?

My hope, said Marvellous.

Peace laughed. Who was your first kiss?

A lighthouse keeper with no name, said Drake.

How old were you?

Seventeen, she said.

Seventeen, sighed Peace. And who came next?

Jimmy came next, said Drake, then Jack.

Three loves, said Peace.

I think I had room for one more, said Marvellous.

Tell me the story of Jack, Marvellous. Tell me more about Jack.

And Marvellous said, You can't have the story of Jack without Jimmy.

So tell us about Jimmy, said Drake, and after much cajoling, eventually she agreed. She asked only for a moment so that the cataract veil between Time-Past and Time-Now could shift.

She sat back and closed her eyes. It was a sweet sensation, like a hand in her hand, taking her down a long disused corridor with locked doors on either side. It was dusty and smelt of must. She tried each door but not one opened and it was only when she faced the last door, the battered blue door on the right, that she turned the key and the lock gave way slowly. And behind that door, she saw herself as a young woman, and the sight near took her breath away.

Is that you? said Marvellous.

Is that me? said the young woman.

Marvellous opened her eyes suddenly. She asked Drake to light her pipe and to bring her a glass for the deep ruby liquid that came out at night. When all was still, she wiped her eyes and the telling began.

I am twenty-four, I think, said Marvellous. Quite young anyway. I have travelled west to the End of the Land as my father did before me to carry out my calling, and have anchored the wagon behind a windbreak of high dense gorse bushes. I am dreaming as young women do, most probably of love. It is June. Midsummer's Day, and the air is sticky and sweet. I drop an egg white into a glass of water and under the hot eye of a midsummer sun I leave it there to think. The viscous fluid plumes and funnels and dances, and when it settles, I know it will reveal the image of my true love's face whose arms will carry me for ever upon this earth. I wait. Hours later, a face forms. To this day I will never forget the shape of that face.

To Marvellous, the face was beautiful. She felt excited and impatient, so she kept herself busy by collecting skeins of furze for the stove – great armfuls of the things – and she waited. She went and filled saucepans from the stream and she waited. The sun cooled and the mists rolled in at three. Jimmy rolled in shortly after. She had smelt him coming, you see, because he was the smell of the land.

He knocked with the lightest touch and greeted her with the sweetest smile and offered her the warmest coin that he had clutched an hour-long in his palm. The face was a good enough match.

He was looking for a potion, he said shyly. A potion to make a girl notice him, a particular bal maiden who worked at Levant mine. You don't need a potion, she said, you just need to find the right girl, and he laughed and she gave him back his coin and told him to go away and think about what she'd said.

He came back the following day after shift and she offered him a glass of rum that brought sweetness to his words and redness to his cheeks. She asked if he still wanted the potion and he said he wasn't sure but would return the next day. He did that for another three days. Came after shift to drink her rum, and the more he came the less his words became. What have you been putting in my rum? he asked suspiciously. Hopes, she said, and he took her hand and kissed it.

She watched him go across the fields. He had a swagger. He carried his status between his legs and she'd never met anyone like him. She probably should have kept away, but that's nature for you. Most women want the King.

(Peace laughed and looked at Drake. Hush, said Marvellous, and the story continued.)

Jimmy asked if she'd like to join him for a walk that coming Sunday. She didn't hesitate. Eyes said yes before mouth could speak.

The sun was high, so warm. Linnets and yellowhammers sang across the day. The grasses were hot and steamy and pungent as they clambered over the dense bracken to a cliff path below. That's when he told her he was a legend around those parts. People called him Fire-Out Jimmy on account of a fire he had put out in a bar room. She told him she hadn't heard of him and he better not put her fire out. She had a mouth on her in those days. He said an oil lamp had ignited a woman's skirt and he had ripped that skirt off her, and had jumped all over that skirt and stamped his feet until the fire went out. And that jump and foot stamping became known as Jimmy's dance, and on Sunday mornings when they all drank, they shouted, Dance Jimmy dance, and Jimmy would, until the hobnails glowed red and flew out of his sole.

She wasn't used to wearing a skirt, her father's trousers were her familiar, but she wore one that day and her boots caught on the hem and it became ragged before they had even touched sand. She must have looked so awkward and unruly, but Jimmy said nothing; just held her hand every step of the steep pathway and his hand was clammy because nature was tumid, pulsing hot.

Over here! Jimmy shouted. A cave at the bottom of the cliffs, a great maw, potted by tidal pools and they struggled over the rocks with the ever-present counting-down at their careful heels. Inside, the slow drip of moisture fell on their heads, a clammy cold caressed their cheeks and always the counting-down, the sweet counting-down in the dank silence, to the time, of course, when they would eventually kiss. It was inevitable; he was bursting and she was eager. He caught her unaware. She was securing a lock of hair that had fallen loose. Leave it, he said. She left it and their lips joined. She felt her feet fall away. Felt the soft damp sand at her back, felt the hard warmth at her front.

He came every day after shift to her wagon and they made it rock and she became known as Jimmy's Girl: a label as good as a ring. She was so happy that she hummed and he felt so lucky that he shone, and his sheen kept that bad luck shadow at bay. But while Marvellous saw him as her love, Fire-Out Jimmy,

Legend of the Moor, began to see her as his lucky and indispensable charm. Luck was important to Jimmy because he believed in it, both the good and the bad, and he knew you couldn't have one without the other because luck was life and life was luck. He reckoned he could hear the sands shift and watch the landscape darken as the bad stuff rolled in like swollen clouds.

One afternoon as summer was coming to its overripe end, Marvellous heard a knock at the door. She rushed to open it, blouse undone, and when she did she froze. For there, with a low sun at his back, was a familiar dark silhouette. The hazy shape of a face in the afternoon balm was Jimmy's face, but not Jimmy's face. It was a younger, softer, more *perfect* face with a huge smile. She staggered back and barely caught his words: *Jack. Jimmy's brother. Nice to meet you*, because those words were faint and all she was aware of was that her heart had skipped a beat and in that gap had slid Doubt – staring up at her, drumming its fingers, waiting for her. She tried to shove Doubt aside but Doubt laughed because you can't shove Doubt. It gives way a little because that's what Doubt does. But it waits. Waits like a germ for the perfect conditions. Then it spreads. Then it suffocates.

I found this on the beach, said Jack, and I thought you might like it, and he handed her a dried-out starfish. It was orange and beautiful and oh she so wanted to keep it, but she gave it back to him and said, Give it to me when it matters, and she went to the stove to make tea. She said little after that. Snatched glances, that's all, to the rare contours of his face.

He told her things he'd never told anyone and she kept silent. He told her he wanted to run away and explore the world. He told her he wanted to kiss the horizon and find love under a different sun. And he sang a song of his own, and his voice was so sweet that her veins filled with longing and jealousy, that heady little cocktail. She turned away in silence and rinsed a pan of rock samphire. One day in the distant future he would tell her how rude she was that day.

Autumn fell abruptly with the leaves. Her and Jimmy took a cottage on the moor, made a home. Her stomach stayed flat so they never married. He was the King, but she was never the Queen and he began to disappear at night, come home smelling of booze and other women's cunny and with those smells and words of remorse on his lips, he would take her out of sleep, have her too, tell her never to leave him.

At night she listened out for footsteps on the roadway. She would take the lantern to the door and often see Jack alone, looking at the cottage, covering for his brother, telling her he was somewhere where he wasn't. But mostly she would look out and there'd be no one there because the footsteps were the sound of Doubt coming to her door.

And once – silly her! – she invited Doubt in and they sat on the bed and she asked Doubt why he was here, and Doubt said, You know why. And she said, But Jimmy's the one for me, and Doubt howled like a wolf and said, Then why invite me in? You and me could be friends you know, under different circumstances, and Doubt lit a big fat pipe and lay back on the bed and rubbed his stomach seductively. That's when Marvellous told him to go. Didn't want Doubt's smell to linger, certainly not for when Jimmy got back that night.

Winter trapped the moorland, and daylight battled to find space between the nights. The cottage was always cold.

Marvellous asked for little and gave little in return. She became ill and rattled like a bag of bones. Her mother no longer swam to her at night because her dreamscape had become a dry riverbed where everything had died. She couldn't even hear the sound of water when she stood up to her knees in the sea. And she no longer swam except in Jack's eyes, where she saw everything she used to be and everything she could be, and some days that was too painful so she no longer looked him eye to eye.

She was too tired to think about life beyond because her courage had crept away and her flame had gone out. Oh Fire-Out Jimmy, so true to your name! And then one day when Jimmy was out, Jack walked through the door. He sat at her table all stern and white and tense, and looked more like an egret than a man, and with barely audible breath he whispered three halting words and everything changed. As if winter had suddenly turned into spring. Then Jack reached out for her hand and said three more words:

It was me, he said.

Three more again: In the glass.

And Marvellous said, I know, and she held his face and kissed him hard, and Doubt never came back after that.

49

JACK BEGAN TO VISIT OFTEN. BEGAN TO SMILE AGAIN because his dream-horizon was suddenly within reach. He began to sing again too, most noticeably in Marvellous' presence, and her expectation and hopes grew. People began to remark about their ease and joy, and rumour quickly took flight. Birds looked up and ruffled their feathers thinking it was the wind until they felt a heavy whack upon the backs of their heads. What was that? said one thrush to another. No idea. Never saw that coming.

Never saw that coming, thought Jimmy as he lit his pipe and watched his brother sing a song to his girl. Suddenly, he felt the sands move and the sky darken. He gripped the table hard as the shifty little bad-luck shadow crept towards him, calling to him, whispering his name.

Marry me! he shouted out to Marvellous suddenly. The shadow stopped its approach.

Marvellous looked up. What's that?

What's that? whispered the shadow.

Marry me!

The shadow hesitated.

Marvellous couldn't answer.

The cottage held its breath and the fire crackled and the old clock ticked, tocked.

Marry you? Her voice was as dry as a kiln.

Don't you want to? You got some better idea? he said, looking over to Jack.

'Course she'll marry you, said Jack, and he got up and put his arms around his brother and thumped his back hard, whispered good words because he daren't look over towards his love because their life together was over.

And that night, in a haze of rum-hot, the three of them made plans. America! South Africa! Australia! The world was theirs. They could go anywhere. Tin prices here were down and the world wanted Cornish miners, would pay for their miners. It was a way out and Marvellous drowned her sorrow like a litter runt, and they toasted and they drank To new life! To *our* new life in Australia! And Jimmy wept, for that shadow had shifted and it was racing over to some other poor unlucky sod. And by God he was grateful. That murky bitter shadow had gone for a time . . .

But of course, it hadn't gone, had it? For nobody had bothered to look in the corner of that smoky little room, they were too boozed to care. But it was there.

The next morning fear rose with the sun. A fine sheen, like a fever, had crept upon Jimmy in the night. It was a fear that stole words. He dressed in silence, ate little in silence. He gathered his matches, his pasty, his soon-to-be wife in silence, and ducked out of the door and made his way to the mine.

The sky was low and racing clouds dark and hungry ate all colour from the moorland. The day fought hard to lighten but would lose the battle by ten. They sat upon a stone hedge and breathed the crisp air as they waited for Jack to appear. Marvellous noticed that Jimmy was shaking. She placed a sprig of gorse in his handkerchief and he was grateful. From her hands everything became a blessed charm. The weather worsened and so did Jimmy's mood as Jack failed to appear. He strode silently towards the stacks and engine houses. Only when Jimmy was far out of sight did Marvellous' pain bend her double, did her tears finally fall. She howled and punched her face and by the time she got to her cottage she was bloody and spent. She dragged herself in and fell upon the frigid flagstones, as merciless to her as a coffin. She lay on those stones for a full hour and it was only the scurrying of a busy mouse that kept her will alive.

She staggered up and went to the stove and the warmth soothed her and heaving sobs tore again at her sight. That's why she thought she was dreaming at first. Hoping or dreaming, it was all a blur. But when she wiped her eyes, there it was on the table: clear and perfect and orange. Come to take her home.

She picked up the starfish and ran round to the back. Both her dray horse and caravan were gone. But then she saw them: a distant speck up by the tor. Not moving, just watching. Like a beacon.

She tried to run but it was tough going. Pools had formed after the rains and bog was hiding below the scraggy coarse grass and she stumbled twice as her skirt soaked up the mud. The rain lashed down and it bit hard but she felt none of it because soon his lips were on hers and he said, Let's go. And she would always remember a sunray stealing out from the dark cloudscape and she would always remember her dray and caravan tucked away behind the gorse and she would always remember he had thought of everything that morning, that beautiful beautiful morning when they were about to run towards their horizon.

He had thought of everything. Almost everything. Almost.

Because as they walked hand in hand towards the wagon they both suddenly fell to the ground, as if their legs had been sliced from beneath them. They felt the earth upon their backs, the breath forced from their lungs. They knew, you see. What Jimmy felt, they felt.

Jack wouldn't leave his brother's body, not there in that tomb. And he ran back to the mine and fought with them all and he went back to look for him, even as the earth continued to move and threaten, even as the dust hung as thick as smoke. He searched for him, until in the furthermost reach he found him. He moved the stones off him, lifted him in his arms and carried him through the darkness, the inch nub of a candle urging him on. He carried that body as if it was a jacket thrown over his shoulder, and secured him to the stretcher and followed him to surface break. And as the warmth of a sunburst brushed his ear, Jack swore he heard the faint sound of his brother's voice before it ventured back, for one last time, into his broken body. And he would never tell anyone what he heard that day. Because it haunted him, saddened him, and placed an unbreakable cursed chain around his heart.

50

MARVELLOUS LAID JIMMY OUT HERSELF. UPSTAIRS IN THE cottage, in the front room. She washed and dressed him in a winding sheet and placed two small rounds of slate upon his eyes instead of pennies. She placed a chain of gorse flowers around his neck. She opened the windows and doors and sat with him for days and nights. She watched his mother and sister and the preacher come and go like a sad black tide. She welcomed women she didn't know. Those women wept and she comforted those women because they had shared the man, so they shared the grief.

The last afternoon, Marvellous signalled for the room to still. There was a sudden whoosh of wind. She closed the windows and doors. Mirrors were covered. Prayers said.

Jimmy had gone.

The preacher carried a lame girl to the bedside. Such were

the curative powers of a life just ended, or so rumour had it. The preacher lifted Jimmy's hand and placed it on the girl's withered leg. Marvellous had already left the room. As rumour came in, so she went swiftly out.

The coffin bearers put on black gloves. Jack carried the coffin with three others. They walked slowly the three miles to the church, and the rain fell. And the women wept and the men stayed silent and a young boy played the fiddle and found it hard to keep to mournful tunes because he had joy in his soul and preferred weddings because he wanted to dance, wanted to sing. Marvellous couldn't take her eyes off Jack's back. The road ahead disappeared into a blazing horizon of moor hills and sea beyond, and she wanted to know if he was thinking the same as she was, as she looked at that never-ending line of possibility that was suddenly theirs.

Only afterwards, in the cottage, after the tea and saffron cake and music had played and the stories were consumed, when everyone had gone, did Marvellous get her answer. They sat opposite, a fire in between. The unsaid as thick and as heavy as peat smoke.

She got up and sat at his feet and rested her head on his knee. They were a two. They had existed on snatched time and now Time was theirs and they felt awkward. She didn't look at him as she unbuttoned his fly and he didn't stop her. The fire crackled, and they felt hot, but nothing grew under the beat of her hand. Eventually he took her hand in his and said, I'm leaving.

She said, I know. She said, I could come too. She said, We could find love under another sun. Isn't that what you always wanted? We are free to love now.

He said nothing.

She said I want what you want. Always have. You are my life.

He said nothing. Because had he opened his mouth he would have cried and told her the curse that Jimmy had laid on them before he died. And so he said nothing.

The fire began to smoke as sap oozed like tears. That's how she knew.

She said: Best not hang about, eh? And she got up and went to the door.

She said: Look after yourself Jack.

He said: I'll come back.

When?

Soon.

How soon?

When things have been forgotten.

He said, I love—

Don't you dare, she said. Don't you ever insult me by leaving those words at my door. Stay or take them with you.

He took them with him.

He flicked the catch, and there was a gust of wind as he left. The room fell still, became airless and the mirror darkened by itself. As if he, too, had suddenly died.

She waited for him to come back. Waited by the window. Two weeks passed, then three then six and the rains came and the mists came and dirty nights became long lonely ones. She went out into the squally dark and called his name but the wind brought it straight back to her.

On the last night she walked to the End of the Land where nothing existed except melancholy and ruins and ruined memories and the wind moaned. Or maybe she did, she couldn't be sure. She shouted his name again but this time the wind was behind her and carried his name beyond the cliff face itself, past Gannet Rock, out across the shimmering black bay that stretched a lifetime away, and she felt sad but glad too. And his name flew and danced like a gull towards the horizon towards the flickering lights of a ship slowly moving from left to right. His name made safe landing on the deck and slipped down into the cuddy where it purred in the tunnels of his sleeping ears. Marvellous raised her arm and shouted, Be safe, my love!

The lights flickered.

Be safe.

She turned and climbed aboard her wagon. The reins felt soft and familiar in her hands. She fell asleep and let the dray horse take over.

Days later she was back in the familiar landscape of her home.

Look who's come back, said Mrs Hard, chewing on her words as if they were a bridle.

Marvellous said nothing. Instead she stripped naked in front of Mrs Hard and waded into the river, and that had the same whiff of provocation for Mrs Hard as if the young woman had crouched next to her and shat.

She had grief in her veins and it flowed heavy and her heart pumped dull and it unbalanced her. Coming home, she realised all she had given up for love. That night, Marvellous went over to the church and lit her first candle. Lit one the following night too. And the night after that. And that was when she decided to light a candle every night because it was her light and no one else's, and it was there to remind her what some men can do to women. She would never let that flame go out again.

Didn't he ever come back to you? asked Peace.

Once in a while.

Not for good?

Eventually for good.

When?

Sometime after the First War. That was our time. Everything has its time. That was ours.

Drake refilled her glass with the sloe.

Why didn't he get to you before Jimmy?

I asked him that myself eventually, said Marvellous quietly.

What did he say?

Hush now, said Marvellous.

It was the unmistakable sound of rumour that Marvellous heard first that fateful long-gone morning. She knelt down and lifted the rumour-catcher to her ear. The words spilt hot and her heart went cold.

Rumour said: *Morning my lovely! Today is the 14th of April 1921 and here's what I know: Jack's dressed himself in a coat of newspaper! He adds stories along the way! They call him Paper Jack now and he'll tell you the news before it happens! His lungs are fucked! He's just crossed the Tamar. Rumour (me) says he's coming back to die . . . Over and out, baby.*

Not long after, Jack came back. She heard him before she saw him. Heard his rasping cough fall like hailstones upon the woodland peace.

She walked up through the trees to meet him. Celandines and foxgloves coloured the green floor, and nature was renewing, celebrating, shouting from every bud and every petal and every beak of returning bird. And amidst this beauty, limped Paper Jack: a face of beard and eyes of blue. He had made a new coat and in the sunlight it glistened white and rustled loudly.

You again! said Marvellous.

Me again! said Jack.

What's with the coat? she asked.

Lost everything. Even the shirt off my back.

You look like a ghost, she said.

Of my former self, he said, and laughed. She didn't.

Trouble in Ireland, he said, pointing to his right sleeve. Civil war. War is not civil.

Stop it, Jack.

And look what's happened in London. *Daily News* on my left sleeve. Very current, oh yay oh yay oh—

Stop it, she whispered.

I tried to outrun it, Marvellous, believe me. I ran and ran until I had this blinding insight.

And what was that, Jack?

That my peace is with you.

A soft breeze lifted the canopy of leaves.

Always with you. So here I am.

And she said, It's been twenty years, Jack!

And he said, Was it really that long?

She said, I'm old now.

And he was quiet.

And she said, *Old*, and the valley moaned.

He said, Where has all the time—

It's gone, she said. That's all you need to know.

And he was about to answer but the coughing ate his words and knocked him double. He spat blood on to the floor. He wiped his mouth, looked up and smiled the sweetest smile.

When I die, cut open my lungs and you'll be a rich woman. Full of copper and tin and gold dust they are. No one can say I didn't provide, oh yay oh yay.

Marvellous turned to walk away.

Wait! he shouted. I'm sorry. Please wait, and he held out his hand. We can be young again, if we think hard.

Marvellous stopped.

Don't cry, Marve. This is our time now. Don't say I'm too late. I can't be too late. Am I too late? And from his pocket he pulled out a small chaffinch that lay still in his palm.

I thought if I could get it to you in time, it might be all right. It's a sweet little thing, don't you think? I fed it and breathed into its mouth. I tried to give it my song, but my song's long gone because I left my song underground. Bring the bird back from the dead, Marvellous. Bring me back from the dead.

She went towards him and took the bird in both her hands. She breathed her warmest breath over it. The feathers stirred, the bird didn't. With the side of her little finger she felt against its chest. She unpinned her hair and wrapped the bird up in the thickest part, before re-pinning it high. She covered her hair carefully with a scarf.

Come, she said, and led Paper Jack silently down to the boathouse and river.

She burned that suit of headlines. Watched the doomed stories of '21 leave in a spiral of smoke, as if all it took was a slight breeze to blow away the imprint of history to another shore.

She bathed him at high water, scrubbed years off him and covered him with the scent of violet. She dried him, dressed him in clean warm clothes. She cut his nails, cut his hair and shaved him, and where his beard had been his skin was soft and white and of another time.

She warmed rum and she added lemon and cloves and he lay down and slept soundly before the sun had reached its highest point. She watched him sleep: her half-man of bones and memory, a nothing weight with broken lungs. She opened the doors to the balcony and listened to the soft lap of the river below, and as she did, she caught her reflection in the glass, and she didn't recognise herself at first and she gasped and she had to fight hard to keep those voices at bay, because those voices were critical and so eager to turn a good day bad.

Why didn't you get to me first? asked Marvellous, as she lay naked in Paper Jack's arms. Why didn't you just get to me before Jimmy?

I was looking at the horizon, said Jack.

That was it? That was why?

Yes, and he cried for Lost Time, and Lost Time felt so flattered by his tears that it gave him more time in return.

Just under a year, that's what they were given in the end, but their joy made the year feel like two. It was happiness that dried Paper Jack's lungs enough to become a songbird again and when he sang he never coughed, and when they visited the Amber Lynn pub further along the Great River, there was a piano and a banjo player and Jack set his voice between those two instruments and they became a trio and became known as The Odd Quartet.

At night in the boathouse, Jack lay wide awake in the darkness, not wanting to miss a moment more. He never slept, never took his eyes off Marvellous. Questioned constantly why he had ever left at all. Why had he put a dead man's heart before his own? He no longer sought the horizon because that unreachable lure had been swallowed by the dense overhang of gorging tree cover, and that shimmering line of promise was now embodied by his woman, for only she promised infinite happiness and unknown adventure, and night after night he wrapped himself up in her chrysalis protection, aware that like a butterfly he would soon be required to fly away, colours blazing.

His lungs rattled and he struggled for breath and she held him as he gasped, and she calmed him, forced his chest to expand, to constrict. In the stillness of struggle he said, Marry me. In the stillness of surrender she said, Yes.

There were no rings to exchange, no vows, no I do's, because they always had. Marvellous rowed along the creek, dropped anchor by the sandbar. They pronounced each other married, witnessed by an owl and two dozen starfish vibrantly orange in their wedding best. And sea horses galloped across the silver-tipped waves and nightingales sang from the branches above, and Marvellous stood up, stood tall and commanded the moon to fall, and that moon dropped mysteriously low. And they stood on tiptoe showered by its white watery grace and they stretched as much as they could until they were the first couple to touch the surface of the moon, the first couple to bury their promises beneath the surface of the moon.

They spent their wedding night lying naked along salty seat slats, drinking moonshine in the moon shine. She climbed on top of him and ignored the gnawing pain of age in her knees, in her hips. She noticed that tens of thousands of discarded fish scales had stuck to her legs and feet and buttocks and they glistened in the lit night. She had never felt happier.

What will you do? asked Paper Jack, as he combed out her hair with the last of his strength.

This and that.

Don't be alone.

Oh I shall be.

You'll need someone to comb your hair.

I'll cut it off before I get someone to do that.

You've always been stubborn.

Good job too.

But where will you go?

I'll not go far.

Will you stay here?

Yes I'll stay here.

Like this?

Like this.

Sitting by the river?

Sitting by the river.

Listening to music.

That has your song.

I'll try and come back.

That would be nice.

I want to come back.

Well, you know where I'll be.

And you'll be OK?

Sure I'll be OK.

He stopped combing her hair. The last of his breaths came in groups of twos, groups of threes like shallow waves, and the rattling in his lungs ceased. Marvellous wouldn't turn round. I'll be OK, she sang quietly. I'll be OK my beautiful boy. My beautiful beautiful midsummer boy.

She paused momentarily to see if Death was still around, because she wanted to talk to Death. She felt the cool liquid slide down her spine.

She said, We've met many times before, and you passed me by – wouldn't even look at me, maybe I wasn't your type. But please don't pass me by now. Take me. Let's barter a life for a life. Don't take that child I know you want to take, or that

286

fisherman about to be trapped in the trawler winch. Or the bride with the burning fever. I know you want to take one of them because they'll be missed, and they'll be mourned, and the sound of grief is the sound of your song. I know you and I know what you're like. But what I'm saying is, don't. Do something different. Take me instead. It's a good offer.

But Death said, My my, what a lot of fiddle-faddle, and he laughed and left through the front door (instead of the back) and when he was gone, warmth and sunlight shone in and that's when she knew Death had gone.

For two days Marvellous lay next to Jack's body. The sun rose, the day warmed and the birds sang. The tides flowed, the fish returned and the sun set. The moon glowed. The stars came out. The robins sang. The saints murmured. Onwards time, impossible to stop, but she tried, she tried.

It was on the third night that her mother swam across the dreamscape wrapped in mist, and Marvellous smelt her mother and her mother became a buoy and wrapped herself around Marvellous' neck and stopped her from sinking, made her float away from the cold white body next to her. And that was sign enough. Marvellous knew then what she had to do.

The next day, the boat was ready, the sea calm. She lifted Paper Jack from the bed and carried him down to the riverbank. The water was alive with thousands of orange stars, caught in the tide, waiting to take him home. It was strange because there were people there to see them off, people she hadn't spoken to in months. And as she walked down towards the mooring stone, the people dressed in black took him from her. The ones who weren't carrying spades.

But I'm taking him back to the sea with me. To be with my mother and father, Marvellous said.

No one listened.

Please don't bury him. He never wanted to go back underground. Please don't put him underground.

No one listened.

Someone held her arms. It should have been gentle, but their words were harsh. She remembered very little after that. Just dirt in her hands and prayers on their lips. And then he was gone, and there was a mound where nothing ever grew.

She went back and scrubbed that boathouse. She took soap and a stiff-bristled hearth brush and walked down to the river. She sat down on the mooring stone and looked over at the church. It was casting deep shadows across the shallows. She undressed, climbed down into the water and wet the soap. She scrubbed her face and her body until both were raw. She stayed in the water until the tide rose and engulfed her, until the burning of the salt near killed her. It took effort to climb out. Her skin was tight, much too small, and every movement broke the seams; it wept, she wept.

Once out, she unpinned her hair, carefully reached up for the chaffinch and held it in her palm. It looked at her, ruffled its wings, and flew to a flowering blackthorn bush. She didn't re-clothe for a month, but became a bird instead. She lived naked in the woods, took what weather was offered and flew with Paper Jack's soul, and for that month she drank in the last song of his love until the moment she awoke back in her bed and the feathers that had graced her heart lay on the floor, plucked and scattered by a cruel hand, one that reached for a stethoscope as it casually informed her that Life Had To Go On.

And it did go on. And she went on. And the tides rose. The tides fell. And her moods rose, her moods fell. And she forgot lots of things. But most importantly she forgot to die.

A dark starlit night caressed the end of her story. Old Marvellous said little afterwards, for she still inhabited Time Past. She stood and watched her young self walk confidently down the road until she disappeared round the shadowed curve, for ever. The old woman waved.

Drake held her hand and led her across a field of dew, a line of torchlight marking their way. She gripped his hand the way a child would. And at the border between grass and woodland, Marvellous sank to the ground, exhausted. In the time it took for her to drop, soft snores had already escaped from her mouth.

Drake lifted her easily, and the movement of his carrying must have felt like the play of waves because she drifted, she drifted.

She slept peacefully, unburdened, memories now in order. Drake sat with her, placed his hand upon her brow. In the flicker of candlelight, he looked above the bed and saw there were no longer any notes pinned to the quilted roof. No notes from her to her for nothing needed to be remembered, any more. He blew out the candle, kissed her forehead and walked out into fresh Cornish air.

The saints were loud and he heard them on the back of nightfall, riding east to an early rise. Some were chanting sacred songs, others were chattering, outdoing one another in feats of sainthood and happy sinning, simple men the world over.

He felt something stir deep within him. He began to cry. He had often been fearful, the feeling gnawing at the pit of his guts, but he knew it was his mother's fear, an unsurprising fear born of the disappointment and inconstancy of life. She had been dealt a losing hand and no one had ever taught her when to call when to raise and when to fold. She had been young as he was young. She had only ever wanted what he now knew he wanted. Like the toss of a coin, heads suddenly became tails and fear became excitement. He closed his eyes and leapt. Felt he was riding with the saints towards a new dawn.

51

MIDSUMMER'S DAY AND THE RAIN FELL HARD AND BUSINESS was slow. Peace hadn't slept all day or night and she closed the shop early and went into her back yard. She had cleared the weeds and chaos and had created order, just as her mother had predicted. Vegetable beds had been planted and raspberry canes salvaged, all because she was a Doer.

But as the rain fell, she felt more like a quitter, because the week before she had taken the unusual step of refusing to see Ned Blaney any more until she knew. Knew what? he had asked. She couldn't say, If you're The One.

The branches of the apple trees were sodden, hung low like her shoulders. She had tried not to put this torment into her baking, but the loaves and buns were dull and heavy and she suddenly realised that it wasn't fear or regret that she was kneading into her dough, but the fear *of* regret.

She searched a good hour before she found an egg because the chickens were poor layers – she knew she shouldn't have given them names. Eventually, she found a warm brown one nestled in a pile of grass clippings. She gathered it gently in her hand and lifted that hand skywards and whispered, Please show me his face.

She was drenched by the time she reached the boathouse. She entered pale-faced and clench-fisted, and Drake wrapped a blanket around her shoulders and led her to the waiting fire.

What's the matter? he said.

I have to know.

Know what?

And she held out the freshly laid egg, and said, If Ned's The One.

Hush, said Marvellous, rolling up her sleeves. She took off her glasses and handed them to Drake to wipe. She said again, Are you sure, Peace? and Peace said, I'm quite sure.

Marvellous put her glasses back on and poured out a glass of water from the flagon. She handed the egg to Peace.

Ready?

Peace nodded.

Then continue.

Peace broke the egg and separated the yolk. She dropped the white into the glass of water where it instantly plumed and danced.

Now look away! said Marvellous. Or you'll only see what you want to see.

Peace looked away admonished by such wise counsel, and Marvellous gently covered the glass with a cloth.

Now let's leave the magic to begin.

They went to her caravan and sat nervously in the cramped space. They drank tea, they dozed to the tap of falling rain. They listened to the Shipping Forecast. Drake looked over to the bookcase, his eyes drawn again to *The Book of Truths*. Marvellous watched him before she fell asleep.

What if it's a face I don't recognise? said Peace, quietly.

Then you have an adventure in front of you, and Drake reached for her hand.

Wouldn't you like to know if there was someone for you?

Drake thought for a moment. Not sure that I would really. I have you and I have her. That's enough.

For now, said Peace. Enough for now.

Three hours later the rain stopped and the sun crept out, and as if on cue, Marvellous awoke and said, It's done. Let's go.

They bustled back to the boathouse, a mix of nerves and expectation.

Here, said Marvellous and she handed Peace the glass, the hidden answer to her future. Marvellous said, Go on, nothing to fear, and Peace gently pulled the cloth away and raised the glass to the light. She gasped. For there was her answer. As clear as day. And had Ned Blaney been sitting next to her, his heart would have skipped because looking into the glass would have been like looking into a mirror.

52

THE DOG DAYS OF SUMMER ARRIVED, AND THE SUN ROSE
hot and the dawn wind blistered across corrugated sands,
slowing nature and slowing tasks.

Peace kneaded her bread with extra care and extra flour
with a bowl of cooling water for her sweating hands. Out in the
bay, Ned Blaney, distracted and in love, pulled in crab pots he
had forgotten to bait.

In the boathouse, Drake slept in late. He threw off the sheets
and lay still, hoping to feel a stream of cool air blowing in
through the balcony doors, but summer's breath was hot and
clammy. He got up and pissed in the bucket near his bed. He
pulled on a shirt and a pair of trousers and rinsed his face with
tepid water from the basin. He went over to the hearth and
stood in front of the scraggy collage of a man who had travelled
the streets and battlefields with him. He had kept him safe, and

had been a good enough man, this imaginary father. He had done his job and had brought him here, to a shack by a shore that had become a home.

It's my birthday today, Dad and I'm twenty-eight years old. said Drake. All is well.

He opened the door and the smell of summer kissed him. Mists of drunken insects buzzed quietly around honeysuckle trailers. Fractured light crept through the bosky wood and fell lazily upon the ferns releasing their pungent sweat. He picked up his fishing rod and walked barefoot into the sunlight.

He sat on the bridge, unhooked the spinner and cast out. He felt at peace. Sunlight caught the brown scum of fermenting weed, the scent as ponderous and heavy as female musk. He slapped dead a horsefly, full of his blood. He watched as shrimps pinked in the search for shade. The summer was so sweet it hummed. Marvellous sat in her deckchair, not commenting, not moving.

By twelve the creek was dizzy with union. And as Drake fished and Marvellous dozed and Peace baked, something else crept up on the back of the rising mercury: the sound of bicycle wheels.

Peace had just taken Drake's birthday cake out of the oven and had placed it on the window-ledge to cool when the postman's wide smiling face loomed at the window waving a letter. He delivered one to her every week now, a blue envelope that smelt of fish and cologne and had silver scales caught in the triangular opening.

Thank you, Sam, said Peace, and she put the letter into her apron pocket.

One for the creek next, said Sam.

Want me to take it?

No, that's all right, m'duck. I quite like free-wheelin' on hard ground. It's for Mr Francis Drake this time.

Drake was still on the bridge when the sound of the free-wheelin' postman clattered through the trees. He put down his rod and looked up, saw the excited approach of a letter waved high in the air.

You and your fancy friends, down 'ere! the postman shouted. Another letter from abroad!

Abroad? said Drake.

Abroad? said Marvellous, heavy with doze.

To a Mr Francis Drake, care of Dr Arnold, Monk's Rise, Chapel Street, Truro, Cornwall, *United Kingdom*. Redirected to here. There you go, boy, and the postman handed over the letter.

Drake watched the postman clamber up through the wood. He looked back down at the letter, at the Australian stamps, felt the clean line of a postcard inside. He went and sat next to Marvellous. Felt her hand lightly on his back. He opened the envelope and took out the postcard. It was a black-and-white picture of a bridge and a river at night. At the bottom was printed: Murray views. Harbour bridge. Floodlit. Sydney N.S.W.

He turned it over and read:

Freddy, I saw the mermaid.

x

53

HE RETREATED SO FAR INTO HIMSELF HE COULDN'T SEE out. The women became shadows, faint and mute, and he shunned their company, shunned their food, smashed plates and bowls and walked barefoot on the shards of his rage and it was a relief to finally bleed.

His world was upside down. Day became night and he took to his bed when the sun sweated but wandered out to the call of owls, and the women knew he was out because they heard him howl like a dog.

It'll blow through, said Marvellous, like a storm. And it did blow through but left little in its aftermath. A red-eyed mass, that's all. Not moving, not caring. But hurting.

He woke to the sound of another person moving through the boathouse. He opened his eyes and saw the halo of spindrift curls above him. Felt himself being lifted, carried out into the briny warm light.

He lay across seat slats, followed the drift of clouds buoyant in the blue, and the gulls above him hovered, swooped in play. The engine reverberating through his spine and ribs and lungs, shaking out the pain, making him breathe again. Deeply now, deep slow breaths. The sun came out. Disappeared. Warm and then not. He closed his eyes. The boat veered left, he felt it slow down. Felt it stop. Arms under his arms. Up now. Words gently spoken.

Up the hill. Breathing deeply again. A cottage built at the end of granite steps. He followed him in. Wildflowers in a vase on the table. A photograph too. Brothers with the same unruly mop of bleached hair before it was cut regulation style.

He sat on the bed next to a towel and soap. Say something. Anything. But he couldn't. The door closed and he rammed the heel of his hand into his mouth to muffle the only sound that wanted to come out.

He slept through the night and woke to sunlight and a new day. He felt hungry. On the chair next to the bed was a plate of cold mackerel and potatoes. He ate slowly. Gratefully.

He pulled back the curtains and light fell into the room. He went over to the dresser. Inside he found the life of a brother packed neatly away.

He heard the front door close. He stood at the window with its view of the sea and saw Ned Blaney walking down the steps, a Thermos in hand. He lost him behind rows of fisher cottages but caught sight of him again by the harbour climbing down into his boat.

A speck now, no bigger than the top joint of his little finger. He watched him anchor by a buoy. Watched him haul crab pots. Methodically. Slowly. Alone. Watched him.

He joined him the next morning. He surprised him at the door and knew that he had, but he was glad of the company, he said so twice. Together they walked down the cool sunless steps towards a sea pressed flat by a low grey sky. They said little. Didn't have to.

They stacked the crab pots on to the bow of the boat, sat away from the dustbin full of stinking, rotting bait. They lit cigarettes as the boat carved easily across the glinting surface, skimming like a slate stone. He had his sea legs now and baited the pots standing up. Fish oil marked the surface where the pots were sunk and gulls fed frenziedly on the floating scraps. He leant over the gunwale to wash his hands and saw himself reflected in the mirrored surface.

Ned called for Drake to take the tiller. He clambered across and the tiller felt good in his hand. Ned reached down to his feet and picked up the Thermos. He unscrewed the lid and the liquid didn't steam and when Drake took the cup he knew it was Scotch.

There was no grand gesture, no loud pronouncement or toast. It was a quiet acknowledgment barely heard. To life, was all Ned said.

Ned signalled portside and Drake turned the boat towards open water, and the engine purred and the warm southerly breeze clung to him. He looked at the gunmetal sea and sky, a matrimony of sorts, and he set his sights on the bright silver line that shimmered in between.

He knew she was out there somewhere. Living. And to know that was everything.

V

54

AUTUMN FELL ONCE AGAIN, AND THE AIR WAS RICH WITH
leaf mulch and saltmud. Marvellous stood outside her caravan.
The breeze stirred and lifted her hair, she looked up to the sky.
Night was closing in on her, the moon impatient for the fall of
sun. She looked at the bunch of hanging keys and tenderly
prised away the smallest one. She held it up by its ragged aquamarine braid and brought it close to her eyes: it was the key to
understanding. She smiled, remembering why she had ever
called it that, and she put it in her pocket and climbed back up
the steps.

Inside was warm. She closed the curtains for the last time.
She thought she was prepared but the simple act choked her,
the drawing time on her life. She opened them quickly to relieve
the unexpected panic that she felt. How beautiful to see again
the familiar outline of her world on earth!

She noted the falling sun and the burnished treetops ablaze, and the emptying nests, and the shells placed in the chimes clacking in the wind, once silent by the shore. She noted the useful things of her life: smooth stones resting by the stove, ready to be heated and placed in her pockets, in her palms, and the clothes that had draped her – nothing fancy – for warmth or to spare nakedness, vanity long gone. She ran her hand across the sheets that would cradle the last of her nights. I have waited for this moment and yet I am unsure what to do. She picked up a pen and attempted to write, but there was nothing to write, for everything to say was really what was to come.

She took off her clothes and hung them carefully on a hook. She heard Drake singing in the boathouse below. Marvellous felt scared, but she wouldn't disturb him, not tonight, not her last night on earth.

Was that the door? A shaft of light ran across the threshold and fell across her bed. The air became hot.

You again!

Me again! Said I'd come back.

I didn't believe you.

Budge up, Marve, said Jack, as he sat next to her on the bed.

You look well.

I'm young again.

Well don't look at me, said Marvellous. I'm not who you left.

He leant over and touched her cheek. His eyes never left hers. He began to undress. His skin was white and youthful. Measles scars dotted the top of his buttocks and Marvellous lightly placed a finger on the furthest left. Jack leant in to kiss her.

Wait, said Marvellous, and she turned her back and opened

a small drawer next to the bed. The clutter slowed her search, but finally she found what she needed. She nervously coloured her lips with rouge.

What do you think?

You're beautiful, he said, and he kissed her over and over until his own lips glistened red, and he whispered beautiful, so beautiful till she almost believed him.

Marvellous pulled back the covers and patted the sheet.

Better get in, she said.

55

DRAKE STOOD ON THE SHORE BY THE SANDBAR LOOKING over at *Deliverance*. The late afternoon air enveloped him, and he felt the passing sands of time hot between his fingers. Something was different. He could sense now, changes of nature, of time and tide, both potent and slight. Something important was in the air.

He raced through the trees and called out for her, his hand tight around his heart so that nothing should spill. The whispered sound of words like prayers rolled across the landscape, coming towards him as they did that first night and every bright night thereafter, a comfort now, nothing to fear, silly old words, clutter of his mind. There was no plume of smoke at the caravan and when he entered it felt cool.

The bed was made and she had laid out her life upon the sheets: a gorse flower, a starfish, a penny and a lipstick. A postcard from America and a small shell box that once hung around her mother's breast. Her house was in order.

Bottles were lined up on the floor, messages answered, his answered ten times ten and more. Sloe gin, brown packets of herbs to heal, all laid out, he knew for him. Her yellow oilskin hung on the back of the door. And there on the ledge above the bookcase, her book – *The Marvellous Book of Truths* – caught in a perfect shaft of sunlight for him to see. From the lock, a tiny key hanging on a ragged aquamarine braid. There was nothing, no one to stop him this time.

He sat on the bed and rested the book upon his knees. He unlocked it, opened it, and scanned the pages until a lightness, an effervescence almost, entered his chest. For there was nothing within those crumbling leaves except dust and a dead fly. He flicked the pages, front to back, front to back again and laughed. Nothing. No truths at all. He stood up and went to place the book back on the ledge when all of a sudden, a curled edge dropped below the page line. His heart thumped. How could he have missed it? He pulled it out. Two words on the back of the photograph: *Your father.*

He didn't turn it over straight away because he sensed the truth before he saw it. By the strange beat of his heart, he sensed who would stare back at him. And when he finally turned the photograph, there he was: with the same eyes, nose, beard and mouth that he had cut out from his mother's magazines, when life without a father muddled his small world. It had always been him: the man who had encircled his life like a moat. It had always been him.

Marvellous was saying goodbye to everything. It took time because she knew every corner of the wood and river and she didn't want to miss anything, for that would be rude. She had started down by the willow saplings. She gave thanks for her life, for every flower and tree and shrub that had held an imprint of her time, her youth, her middle age, her longing, her body, her sorrow, her laughter, her plans, her tiredness, her fate. This was the scene of her theatre. One last bow for the lady on the rock. The leaves rustled, some fell, and a flock of gulls soared in formation towards a hazy, milky west.

She sits down upon the mooring stone for the final time. Her breath is scant. Things – time – are running out. The pinking light coats a seagull in flight. Time is standing still. Marvellous knows this moment is everything because it is her last moment, the lush-textured moment, and she knows this moment is love.

Drake sees her. And the clenched fist that resided in his chest opens and reveals a life, and in the middle of life, sits her, Marvellous Ways. And he has known her his life long and beyond, and now he knows why.

He waves to her, she waves to him. The seagull stalls mid-flight, frozen in a lick of aspic. He reaches for her hand. She feels cold. Her breathing is shallow.

What's happening? he asks tenderly.

Come, says the old woman.

She takes his hand and it becomes his mother's hand and the riverbank becomes the cobbles of London, of Fleet Lane where she leads him towards his childhood pub and the smell of beer that was as good as a meal when he awoke starving at night. And they cross creek bridge and he feels he is walking up the stairs to that cold room, the room that is home, where he asks his mother questions until all colour has drained from her face.

What colour were his eyes, Ma? What colour were my father's eyes?

The colour of longing.

What colour's that, Ma?

The colour of the sea.

He stops at the midpoint of the bridge that gives him a view down the river towards the strapping pines and the sandbar. The tide is racing in, wavelets crested by spume and glistening fish backs. He knows time is running out.

Come, says Marvellous.

On the other bank she reaches now and then for tufts of grass either side, and as she passes the Dearly Forgotten, the sun quite rapidly loses its warmth. She stops and looks up, looks into the piercing orb, and she doesn't blink. She looks into it and sees beyond it. Almost there, she whispers, and she takes his hand and leads him over to a gravestone he has never noticed before: a stone of simplicity, of pink granite, of two words:

Jack Francis

Here he is, says Marvellous. Your father.

The murmur of words becomes loud, Drake looks around. He kneels upon the moist grass and leans his cheek upon his father's grave. Marvellous places her hand upon his back.

Listen, she says.

I can hear, he whispers.

It's your story. It's only ever been your story.

He turns to her and reaches for her, but she is already moving away. She walks towards the rippling waves in the soft evening light, and she can feel her clothes fall away, can feel her skin fall away and this time it is different. They are all waiting for her and she sees them, there on the crest, and she is running now for there is no more old, and she dives, and breathes her first breath, and her body floods. And she is home.

Acknowledgements

I would like to thank the following people for their support, generosity and kindness during the writing of this book:

My family, especially my mum, for being so inspiring, and my nephew and niece, Tom and Kate Winman, for being such enthusiastic early listeners.

Everyone at Tinder Press for their energy and commitment, most notably my editor Leah Woodburn for her guidance and for encouraging me to write the story I wanted to write, and Vicky Palmer for her marketing magnificence.

My friends, here and abroad, for everything we have shared and continue to share. Sharon Hayman for your wisdom and encouragement and for all that you are. Patricia Flanagan, David Lumsden, Sarah Thomson, Simon Page-Ritchie, Melinda McDougall, David Micklem, Andrew McCaldon, Vin Mahtani and Maura Brickell, for that perfectly timed phone-call or dinner or drink or walk, or for making me laugh when I often felt like doing the opposite. Selina Guinness for knowing the right thing to say. Thank you to The Gentle Author and the community that has grown around Spitalfields Life blog – you are a constant reminder of why we do what we do. Thank you to St. JOHN Bar and Restaurant, Smithfield, for always being there.

Thank you Nelle Andrew for looking after me so meticulously over that summer, and everyone at PFD for your unwavering support. Thank you to Samia Spice, Paddy Ashdown and Tim Fraser for your help with the last minute panic. My sincere thanks to Tim Binding for taking the time to help me see the story clearly. Thank you Graham and Sheena Pengelly for the starfish, Maureen for afternoons of tea and putting the world to rights, and Old Stan for evenings of whisky and tales.

Research is not something that comes easily to me and I find it sleep inducing at the best of times, frustrating at the worst, and a hindrance, always, to my childlike impulse to spontaneously tell a story. However, the following people, institutions and organisations have made this process enriching – even enjoyable, dare I say it – and I thank you all: The British Library, London Metropolitan Archives, Brian Polley at the London Transport Museum, National Railway Museum and First Great Western, Dover Ferry Photos, Angela Broome at the Royal Cornwall Museum, the Cornwall Record Office, Alison Courtney.

And finally . . .

Robert Caskie. My dear friend and agent. You have endured so many versions of this book and maintained a smile throughout that thanks hardly seem enough. But I am forever grateful for the way you have guided me through this process with such humour, loyalty and belief. In the words of Tina Turner, you're 'Simply the Best'.

Patricia Niven. I have you to thank for everything.

A Year of Marvellous Ways

Bonus Material

To Be a Reader

Q & A with Sarah Winman

Reading Group Questions

To Be a Reader

To be a reader, for me, is about entering a world of unimagined possibility; to have the willingness to suspend disbelief and to journey trustingly across the terrain of another's imagination.

To be a reader is to feel a little less lonely. To be a reader is to be challenged. To feel anger, to feel outrage and injustice. But always to feel, always to think. To be a reader is not a passive state, it is active, always responding.

To be a reader is to have the opportunity to question ourselves at the deepest level of humanity – what would we have done in this situation? What would we have said? To be a reader is to feel empathy and compassion and grief. To be awed and to laugh. To fall in love, with characters, locations, the author. To be a reader is to learn and be informed, and to rouse the dreamy inner life to action.

To be a reader is to take time out from the group. To not fear missing out; to turn off the TV, Youtube, the internet. It is to slow down and engage; to be of the present. To be a reader is to find answers. It gives us something to talk about when we're unsure what to say.

To be a reader is to have the chance to collect stories like friends, and hold them dearly for a lifetime. It is to feel the joy of connection.

To be a reader is a cool thing to be.

To be a reader is wealth.

Q & A with Sarah Winman

Both of your novels are set in Cornwall; do you often write and research there? Were you envisaging a specific place in *A Year Of Marvellous Ways* and if so, why did you chose it?

I do escape to Cornwall whenever I need peace or I need to focus my writing. I am very fortunate that my mum still maintains my grandparent's home in Looe – Looe being the Cornish setting for *When God Was A Rabbit*.

The inspiration for *Marvellous* came from a beautiful tidal creek off the Carrick Roads in Falmouth called St Just-in-Roseland. Nine years ago, when I first went there, I saw this small boathouse opposite a church and wondered who would live there. Four years ago, I asked myself the same question. But this time I gave myself an answer: a man who was afraid of water and who didn't believe in God.

Although St Just was the inspiration, I have fictionalised the creek and the surrounding areas to give myself more freedom in the storytelling. I researched a lot in Cornwall, at The Cornwall Records Office and Royal Cornwall Museum, as well as spending much time in the creek itself. These Cornish books were of particular importance too: A.L Rowse, *A Cornish Childhood*; Fred Majdalany, *The Red Rocks of Eddystone*; J Henry Harris, *Our Cove*; and Claude Berry, *County Cornwall*.

Where has your interest in using Cornwall as a backdrop stemmed from?

My grandparents moved to Cornwall when I was four. It is the county I am most familiar with, the county I have a genuine and longstanding connection with. This is where I turn to when I wish to write about nature. Such familiarity gives me the joy and freedom to write knowingly about the land – about the texture of light, or about the sea, or about the seasons. The fact that Cornwall and I met in childhood is significant, since it allows me to coat my memories with the golden light of nostalgia!

Missy is an important character who in many way softens as the novel progresses. She is also, arguably, the launchpad for much of the plot; would you agree?

That's a very interesting question, and my answer might change as the weeks and months go by. But, for now, I still think the letter from the soldier was the launch pad for the plot. The bottom line, being, that Drake had to get to Cornwall.

However, I love Missy. Missy is the character who introduces the idea of a mermaid – the idea of how life can change; she is the ever-hopeful Missy who won't let circumstance restrict her. Missy is a survivor. In 50 years time she will be Marvellous. Missy was Drake's horizon as Marvellous was Paper Jack's. Both women instinctively knew they deserved better from the men who professed their love.

Within the novel, post-war London is recuperating and so is Drake; how would you describe the change in him as the novel progresses?

When Drake arrives in Cornwall he is a broken man – by war, by love – and he sees no point in continuing. But it is nature (and Marvellous, of course) that gives him answers, and begins to heal him. Nature is frightening to him at the start. Then it ignites his curiosity. By the end it provides peace and constancy, beauty and meaning. Nature fades, dies, and regenerates. And so every character in the book is healed by the creek in some way. It is a blessed land, but not in the religious sense that the priests declared. It is a haven after the destructiveness of war; after the inconstancy of love.

From the outset the character of Marvellous is absolutely enchanting. Have you drawn on anybody from real life?

No, not really. She is an amalgam of many people – relatives and old friends, of course, both men and women. But what I knew I needed to do right from the start was to describe her physically to the reader. Like setting down a photograph on the table. Her physicality for me was the key to the enchantment, as you call it. I have an old friend who is very small, who wears glasses, uses a stick and is out and about everywhere in her red mac. She is noticed and brings a smile to everyone. That seemed a good place to start. People are open when they face her, and this openness – receptiveness – is the key to Marvellous' storytelling.

The diversity of the Cornish countryside is echoed in all the characters; was this deliberate?

It was deliberate because the countryside was there to heal each character in whatever way that needed to happen, and therefore, the countryside becomes its own character. Its interaction with each character is unique.

It seems unusual for a novel not to have a character that is disliked by the reader; did you choose to use the war as that 'character'?

No, not consciously, but I like this suggestion. The likeability of the characters didn't seem that important to me, even though I don't find Drake particularly likeable at the beginning. What was important to me, however, was how fractured each character was. It was this wound that would be the key to each person's journey: the redemptive need to put things right.

The relationship between Francis and Marvellous comes across, quite beautifully, as being mutually dependent. Where did the idea for this as a key part of the plot come from?

I think we are all mutually dependent. An old friend of mine once said, youth keeps youth alive, and I think that's true. So in the way that Marvellous can hand on her experience and wisdom – the natural consequence of having lived a long life – so Drake can ignite her memories of youth. She needs him to bear witness to the life she has led. He needs her to love him and to bring forgiveness into his life. She needs him to give her an ending. He needs her to provide a future.

Throughout society, young men and grandmothers have

been shown to have enriching and respectful relationships, so I always knew the many possibilities of bringing these two people together.

What is your next project?

I have the opportunity to go back and reacquaint with the first book that I ever wrote, a book that wasn't published at the time. It is a small story; one, primarily, about secret love. There is no magic realism, no breadth of nature, just people doing their very best and dealing with the consequences of decisions and circumstance. I think it will be interesting to go back to it after all this time.

Reading Group Questions

1. How did the use of unconvential punctuation influence your reading experience? Did you feel this impacted upon the tone of the novel?

2. Traditional family structures are conspicuously absent in *A Year of Marvellous Ways*; what effect did you feel this had upon the relationships in the novel?

3. The novel is in many ways an exploration of the grieving process. Discuss how you identified with the characters' various methods of recovery.

4. There is a blurred line in the novel between magic and reality; did you imagine *Marvellous Ways* to be set in the world we inhabit?

5. *A Year Of Marvellous Ways* is a novel of contrasts; between masculinity and femininity; old and young; love and hate. How did you feel these oppositions drove the plot?

6. How would you say the characters of Marvellous and Drake influence each other throughout the course of the narrative?

7. What is the novel's attitude to death? How did you identify with this?

8. How are war and sexuality juxtaposed in the novel?

9. Memory is a central theme in *A Year of Marvellous Ways*. Did you feel it was presented as reliable?

10. How does food play its part in the novel, especially in connection with romantic love?

SARAH WINMAN

When God Was a Rabbit

This is a book about a brother and a sister.

It's a book about childhood and growing up,
friendships and families, triumph and tragedy
and everything in between.

More than anything, it's a book about love
in all its forms.

'Captivating . . . rendered with an appealing frank-
ness, precision and emotional acuity' *Observer*

'Beguiling . . . you can't quite get the voice out of your
head' *Daily Mail*

'Mesmerising' *Good Housekeeping*

'Sharply funny, whimsical and innovative' *Guardian*

978 0 7553 7930 9

TINDER
PRESS

You are invited to join us behind the scenes at Tinder Press

TINDER PRESS

To meet our authors, browse our books
and discover exclusive content on our
blog visit us at

www.tinderpress.co.uk

For the latest news and views from the team
Follow us on Twitter

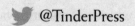 @TinderPress